03. 05. 01

D0271750

SHIFTS

Adam Thorpe

Jonathan Cape
London

Published by Jonathan Cape 2000

2 4 6 8 10 9 7 5 3 1

Copyright © Adam Thorpe 2000

Adam Thorpe has asserted his right under the
Copyright, Designs and Patents Act 1988 to be identified
as the author of this work

First published in Great Britain in 2000 by Jonathan Cape
Random House, 20 Vauxhall Bridge Road, London SW1V 2SA

Random House Australia (Pty) Limited
20 Alfred Street, Milsons Point, Sydney,
New South Wales 2061, Australia

Random House New Zealand Limited
18 Poland Road, Glenfield,
Auckland 10, New Zealand

Random House South Africa (Pty) Limited
Endulini, 5A Jubilee Road, Parktown 2193, South Africa

The Random House Group Limited Reg. No. 954009

A CIP catalogue record for this book
is available from the British Library

ISBN 0 224 05281 0

Papers used by Random House are natural,
recyclable products made from wood grown in sustainable forests;
the manufacturing processes conform to the environmental
regulations of the country of origin

Typeset by Deltatype Ltd, Birkenhead, Merseyside
Printed and bound in Great Britain by
Biddles Ltd, Guildford & King's Lynn

In memory of Tim Bourner, player and traveller

CONTENTS

19 February. When I wanted to get out of bed this morning I simply folded up. This has a very simple cause, I am completely overworked. Not by the office but my other work. The office has an innocent share in it only to the extent that, if I did not have to go there, I could live calmly for my own work and should not have to waste these six hours a day which have tormented me to a degree that you cannot imagine, especially on Friday and Saturday, because I was full of my own things.

Franz Kafka, *The Diaries 1910–1913*
translated from the German by Joseph Kresh

BINS

Well. It was the days before wheelies, compulsory black liners, automatic bin-hoists, all that soft rubbish, when I was still on the rounds, out in the fresh. I miss that sometimes, stuck in here. View of that nice brick wall there. I miss the rounds, the little adventures, the bloody exhaustion of it. The cup of morning tea at Mrs Talbot's on a Tuesday and the mug in the afternoon at Miss Rainer's, Thursday. Those two didn't change much, though they must have been plying us for at least fifteen years, week in, week out. Wet the whistle. Much appreciated when it was a mite on the chilly side, the weather.

A bit of history, then. When I first started out, a little younger than I am now, as it were, the cart had a *curved* body, didn't it? Two doors in the side, one at the rear. You had to yank those side doors up, they slid up into the body, proper engineering if kept well greased. When the front was full of rubbish, you'd pull down that first door and use the second one. The rear end was only opened for tipping, on the waste tip. All very practical. We'd keep the side doors open for the early part of the day and you'd smell us coming a mile off. You got used to it. Close your eyes and think of England. That was a very long time ago. Hard job in those days, took a bit of getting used to, running about with them metal bins, ashcans, you name it. No mod cons. Though there was much less rubbish about. I think it's supermarkets.

Interesting incidents.

Well.

No horses, no! Oh no. I'm not that antique! When I say 'cart', I mean dustcart. Lorry. Big Bedford chassis, always a big Bedford chassis. Refuse wagon, was the *official* term. They've dropped the wagon bit, now. It's refuse 'vehicle', now. I don't care what they bloody call it, frankly. I'll stick to cart. Much larger these days, of course. More capacity.

We'd always ride on the footstands of course, at the back, big footstands on the older type of cart, not the one with the side doors, that went out with short back and sides and decent behaviour, worse luck. We'd hang on for grim life when Phil took those curvy lanes the way he did. Now I spend my time ticking off the youngsters for doing the same, it's against regs. They haven't got proper footstands now, have they, just a poxy tailboard. It's the bloody insurance, you see. I bet they'd take fingerprints off the back to prove some poor bloke who'd lost them for good's ineligible. When Jim Wallet lost his fingers jumping up onto a footstand out of the way of that dog and grabbing the rear, like so, just as what we'd call the mash-blade came down, scooping the rubbish, it was only the broken dog-chain that shut them up. We could have sued the dog's owners, I suppose.

That was at Highfield Farm, I forget their names. Horrible dogs they always had. We'd always creep in and out as fast as we could, even before Jim's mishap. Never seen so much blood. Spattered all over the wagon, red on yellow, our livery was yellow in those days, District Council white horse on the cab, very smart, nice big Bedford chassis, could carry all the rubbish those politicians speak in a year without groaning. Jim screaming his head off, dogs barking. Scared the loose one off, though, his din. If only Phil had slammed off the hydraulics the instant he heard the screams, we might have recovered the fingers, I suppose. But there wasn't any point shifting through the muck once it had been mashed the other side of the blade.

The things they can do these days, or even twenty years ago, Jim might have had them stitched back on again and not spent the time since at home, twiddling his thumbs. As it were. Pat says he does get right under her feet.

Healthy job, really, if you didn't mind the back tweaking a bit now and again. All they do nowadays is prat about, twiddling with knobs, watching the cart do all the work. It'll be robots soon. All computerised. Don't want to get our hands dirty, do we? We've even had them complaining about the odd ashcan here and there. Glass. We used to pick up broken slabs of glass and chuck them in, we had proper leather gloves — but now you'll get some wet-eared youngster coming in here and telling me how he went and nicked himself on a shard left out next to the bin, moaning about it as if I can visit every domestic residence and tell them personally not to deposit their broken mirrors and windows for our boys to slice themselves on, and what am I supposed to do? Give him a free plaster out of that First Aid box? Unions breathing down my neck. Rules and regs. Higher management imposing this and that. More juice for less orange. Squeezing so as I can hardly breathe. No wonder I smoke too much. They'll only allow folk to chuck out their tissues soon, at this rate. Cotton wool.

Mind you, that was my worst. Swabs. Outside the hospital. Or a normal domestic house. You were never quite sure what they had been used for, were you? You know what I mean, those little balls of cotton wool. Stained. Never quite sure. And people would always be placing them on the top, ready to roll off onto your face. We don't know why people do certain things, do we? It doesn't come into it now, of course. It's all concealed in compulsory liners, now. The youngsters don't even pick the bins up, now. We could have girls doing it, now. The job wouldn't even chip their nail-varnish, the way it's all gone now.

Ear cleaners. What do you call them then? What you

poke about in your ear with: No, neither can I. Escaped me. Can't be age in your case. Whatever, I didn't like the used ones of them, neither. You'd think folk did nothing else all day, the number that used to drop out at your feet.

Healthy, though, in the old days. You had to run like the wind. Run with a full ashcan on your back, if Phil was a little ahead of himself on the accelerator. All in our own interest: you could be back before half the afternoon was out, if you kept the pace up. No wheels on anything but the dustcart. We'd take refrigerators for a small tip. Only notes, mind. Clipped above the dash. By the end of the day it could be quite a decent wad, shared out fair as fair. Had a flutter with it now and again, on the horses, if Bob Thomson were there. Him and his *Sporting Life*. Never declared it, anyway, like we were supposed to. Ill-gotten gains. We weren't supposed to take heavy stuff like refrigerators, you see, but that cart could mash anything up. Not just refrigerators. All kinds of junk. Clapped-out stoves, old carpets, carburettors, chairs, kids' bikes. Even a splintered wardrobe once. Looked as if somebody had taken an axe to it. Perhaps they had. You don't know what goes on behind those closed doors. All you see is their rubbish.

Not always rubbish. I'm not ashamed to say that this coat was left out on a bin, nicely wrapped in plastic, laid there for the benefit of us. Perfectly good quality, almost new. Some widow, I suspect, wanting her husband's remains to go to a decent home. We even got pictures laid on the lids sometimes, in their original frames. Nothing very fancy, of course, but something you could hang in the toilet without blushing. Daft, what certain people do. Mind you, this was before the days of the car boot sale, where folk get rid of rubbish you'd be ashamed to see sticking out of a bin. In those days rubbish was rubbish. And I don't suppose people give things away as they used to. It's everyone for themselves, these days. Nobody can bear to see anyone else gain at their expense, can they? Charity stays at home, these days, behind those four walls. Curtains drawn.

Not that it was charity, as such. It was more gratitude. That's how we saw it. A nice big thank you for clearing up their mess, hiding it away where it won't ever come back. The worst was always the big houses. There was never a thank you left out there. It was the little old ladies on the estates, the council estates in the days when they *were* all council, who left out most. Those who have least to give, give most. They even tipped us, some of them, for taking broken china, all packed up in newspaper ever so. I'd say: 'Whose wedding is it, then? I hope it's mine!' I liked to rib those little old ladies, they'd always appreciate it. Lonely lives they led, stuck in their rooms. We were a distraction, I suppose. It's only Christian, to want to cheer folk up a bit, buck them up a bit on a wet morning, like this one. November's the bad one, isn't it? Bloody Christmas to get through.

Interesting incidents. Well.

The big houses were the worst every time. Massive detour just to get up their drive and find the bloody bins, the cart practically stuck in the gravel, and they were always full of rich food. That was the worst of it. You could smell the wealth dripping off of them. A real stench, it was. And they'd always sneak in some garden refuse. Bloody grounds the size of ten football pitches and they'd always sneak in a lump of wet leaves or some grass cuttings. I think they did it deliberate, because they liked to show who's boss. Rules didn't apply to them. Never do, do they? Most of them wealthy ones don't even pay their taxes, do they? They get us free. Their rubbish collected free. We're paying for the privilege of emptying their rubbish. Marvellous, isn't it?

The best run was around the caravan site, mostly gypsy, hundreds of caravans probably, all in their own little plot, nicely arranged and managed. Never any trouble, and hardly anything in the bins. Waste not, want not. Maybe they weren't proper gypsies, but anyone who tells me that gypsies make a mess should lug about what some of them big houses chuck out and then make a comparison. And that gravel was murder to trot over, with a ten-ton bin on your back. Like a bloody donkey on the beach at Cromer, you felt like sometimes. Now my youngsters moan about Lord So-and-So not depositing his wheelie out at the end of his drive, or at the tradesman's entrance, or wherever happens to be most highly convenient for them. 'Do you really expect Lord So-and-So to lug out his wheelie along three hundred yards of deep gravel for your bloody convenience?' I snap back. 'Work!'

About a week later I get a letter from the union, with the appropriate regulation in nice italics, done on one of their bloody computers. I'm supposed to use this one, but I won't. I'm told to make what they like to call 'spread sheets', whatever that is when it's at home. The only sheet I spread is a nice clean one on the bed, now the wife can't bend over. My grandson knows what it means. He does it for me at the weekends. He's just eleven. Bright as a button, Toby. I'm very much looking forward to retirement, and I think the management are too. I'm not even supposed to smoke in here. It's a non-smoking zone, only I can't see the sign that says as much for all the smoke. That's my joke. Some other silly bugger in a grey suit and flash tie complained about the saucy calendars. What else am I supposed to look at all day? Experience isn't valued, that's the trouble. A couple of these courses and you're set up for life. They tried to send me on one of these courses and I said, 'Keep the money.' Because it must cost them, those posh hotels. You pay for your own drinks, though.

I'm a pain in their neck, that's about it. I'm the last one left of the old lot. Jim, Phil, Terence, Bob, all the old team. Val, before he got his shingles. Nerves, that was. Old Valentine, always complaining about his nerves. Little round spectacles. We were dustmen, you see, covered in

6

dust. I don't mean dust the way you're thinking of dust. History. Dust didn't mean dust, once. It meant rubbish. History, isn't it? We drove a dustcart. It'll always be the 'cart', to me. I've had letters from the higher management about my language, or one of their juniors who wouldn't know what a dustcart was if he was under her, gets on the blower here and tries to correct me. 'Refuse collectors', that's what they are now. Even women can apply. *You* could apply, for one, if you so wish to. It'll be dust*persons*, then. What a load of rubbish, eh? Literally. I've always believed in calling a spade a spade. If you don't call a spade a spade you won't know how to use one, will you?

Talking of spades, I haven't had a game of cards in years, not at work. We used to play for the tips, now and again, in our afternoon tea-break, on the front seat, or the bonnet when fine. Top winnings for me were twelve quid, the whole lot, the whole lot unclipped and in my overalls pocket by the end of ten minutes. Lightning. We only played for the tips if the tips were sufficiently ample and there was no racing, and we didn't always have a tea-break in the afternoon. Sometimes we just went hell for leather in order to leave that much earlier. Knackering, but you appreciated it when you rolled up on your bicycle at home and the wife's gob opened with surprise.

Love in the afternoon. You know what that is? I expect you do, even at your age. I thought you were here from one of them schools, can't tell these days. Then I see them coming out of school and think how old they look. Flouncing about. Odd that, isn't it? Them as are adult look too young, like the coppers always do, and them as are kids look adult. There's a saying in there. Like that one on the wall. The lads gave me that one. For when I left the beat, as we called it. A bit rude, I know. A bit of a laugh. Love in the afternoon, oh yes. When we were a bit younger. Always a temptation, if I happened to turn up twenty minutes too soon. She was quite a one, was the wife, in

those days, as it were. Kids still at school. It was the fact that I *ought* to have been at work, you see. Playing truant. I did quite a lot of that, that truancy lark, when I was a kid. I could have done a lot better with myself, really, if I hadn't, I suppose.

I wasn't skiving, though, when I rolled up early. We'd earned it, hadn't we? Going at it hell for leather, just to have that bit of time off. Roaring up to the depot over in Dropside Lane in those days and then off home on the bike, tinkling the bell when you get in earshot, still all covered in grease and wotnot, other people's filthy muck, and she'd open her gob in surprise and if there was so much as a sort of twinkle in her eyes I'd be out of those overalls quicker than Jim Wallet losing his fingers at Highfield Farm. Amazing, when you think how knackered I must have been after all those hours on the bins. Once or twice I'd actually lug her onto my back, it's a technique you learn *very* quickly, and carry her up squealing all the way to the master bedroom, as it were. Like she was a bin. A squealing bin. Don't write that.

She didn't mind the smell, no. Nasty stuff in my hair if my hood hadn't been up, body all manky from sweat. A bit of spice, I suppose. Some of you lot go for milkmen, don't you? In their uniform. Smelling of dairies. Or whatever they smell of nowadays. After-shave, probably.

Those were the days. Now her arthritis has got so bad we've had to move the bed downstairs. Anyroad, she doesn't like the way I smell of smoke. Cigs. Even after I have a good long bath, I smell of smoke. I'm like a kipper in here, I suppose. Smoked eel. But I can't be giving up, not now. And if I open the window I'll freeze. It's the damp. Since Tesco's put that warehouse bang next door the damp's stuck in. I reckon this whole area's built on a marsh. That's what I read somewhere, once. Can't remember where.

I don't suppose your readers will want to know this, but

we've not had what you might call proper conjugal relations for about a year now, when I come to think of it. As it were. I was thinking it was a few months, but it's a year. The leaves had dropped off pretty thoroughly, I recall. Couldn't have been much before November. Time does fly. I'll be out of here and on my pension before I know it. Twiddling my thumbs in front of the telly. A lot of rubbish these days, isn't there? The wife's hooked on the soaps. Her life-support machine, I call it. We'll have to be having two tellies, I suppose. Two beds, two tellies. Not much of a future, is it? Take out what you can. You don't get a second stab. Like the horses, I suppose. A bit of a flutter, and then it's rain stopped play. Bang.

Interesting incidents. I can certainly give you those. Plenty enough of those. Keep your readers happy.

Interesting incidents. Well, we've had one or two mad members on the team. There was a bloke, ex-army from Northern Ireland, who certainly had more than a screw missing. He'd empty the bins and throw them back across the lawns if he was upset about something. Lids rolling all over the shop. Used to fight something terrible with Terence, Terence flying out of the cab, this bloke – Trev, his name was, Trev something – yelling and screaming. Yet the next minute you'd see him pick up this little kid and bounce him or her on his shoulders like he was the nicest dad in the world, in front of the mother. And chatting up the mother, too. Butter wouldn't melt in his mouth, sometimes. I steered clear.

Another time – this is quite amusing, it's against me really, it's your own rubbish emptied on your doorstep, isn't it? – well, I'm running up to the cart with a very full bin before the days of compulsory liners, heaving it over and the cart goes off. All over the road, it was, the muck and rubbish, heaps of it with what looked like cat's vomit perched on the top like a cherry. And I had to – there was no second thoughts on this one – I had to scoop it all up with my bare arms and run after the bloody cart like I was late for my wedding. Get me to the church on time. Nice film, that one. Nice uniforms in those days, didn't they? They'd leave it these days, of course. Litter. We get complaints from the general public, these days. I shouldn't be telling you this, but I don't mind if I do. I tell the youngsters as they'll be going back and clearing up the mess they left, if this goes on. No pride, that's it. We'd pick up a toothpick if it dropped out of a bin we were engaged on.

I can't really tell you about the blind bungalow.

You did used to wonder sometimes.

Alan, Alan Hall, he had to do his own house. That was one thing we all didn't like the idea of one jot. Doing your own house. Like being present at your own funeral. Can't explain why. But he was the only one. The rest of us were lucky, our homes were always on someone else's run. Used to rib him about it. Bob planted a pair of fancy ladies' knickers in Alan's bin one time, back in the sixties I suppose it must have been. Alan was ever so straight. These fancy knickers, all lacy and black, you know, just under the lid. Bob playing it up ever so funny. We all laughed, until Alan's missus comes out. She wasn't very pleased.

We had a queer student with us one time. Always read a book when he could. Even at Mrs Talbot's, stopping for tea. We'd all troop into her living-room once a week, getting what filth we could off of our boots on her tiny little mat, and drink our tea and talk a bit, kept her company I suppose, all six of us squeezed into this warm little room, gas-fire popping, immaculate it was, antimacassers on the easy-chairs, ever so posh really after looking at all that filth and muck, and this student type would get out his book and read it, actually bloody read it. Like drugs, I suppose. We don't take students now, of course. Union regs. They used to be quite entertaining, though, those student types. Filling in the gaps. You ought to have a week on it, really, if you want to know about it properly.

Mrs Talbot. T-A-L-B-O-T. Passed away now. Edith, I
believe. Always called her Mrs T. 'Hello, Mrs T.' All of us
in that little room, greasy overalls and mucky faces, yet we
never left a mark on her belongings. Or her cat. Kept her
company. Something to look forward to. Big event of her
week, probably. Little cottage in a wood. Very isolated,
really. Not like Miss Rainer's on the Longridge Estate. It
got so rough there towards the end. Bricks, you know. Miss
Rainer. R-A-I-N-E-R. Deirdre Rainer. Poor old soul. She
did go on, though. We were her ears for ten minutes,
really. We didn't just empty bins. Interesting incidents.
They all run away just when you're trying to think of them.
All those adventures. I've told you about Jim Wallet's
fingers, haven't I? Eh?

The bungalow?

No, I don't think I can be telling you that one.

You did see things, of course. One of the other lot
caught some burglar or other, breaking in. Silly bugger.
Broad daylight. You'll have to see Jack Watlington about
that one, if he's still alive. Believe he is. Sometimes you did
hear folk rowing at each other, of course. Kids screaming.
Especially if you had to go grubbing about in their backyard
for the bin. Sometimes you did wonder if someone wasn't
getting done in while you were whistling away over their
rubbish. You always had a couple of runners as we called
them, going ahead and putting the bins out onto the
pavement for the convenience of the infantry, as it were. In
those days folk weren't always able to put their bin where it
was convenient, you see, because the bright spark who
invented the wheel had not so far thought of putting one
under a dustbin, had he? So there was a lot of scrabbling
about in backyards and back gardens, in those days. Or even
inside, for those folk who liked to keep their rubbish in the
dry. Then you did hear things, sometimes. But you don't
want to believe everything you're told, if you go and have a
word with one or two of the others. Especially when it gets

a bit saucy. No one I know ever saw anything that might put a blush to a maiden's cheeks, as it were. The blind bungalow doesn't count. No one else knows about that one, anyroad. I should never have brought it up.

The things folk throw away.

Very intimate, sometimes. Feminine articles.

Old Steve Hollis would have told you about the baby in the plastic bag, if he were still this side of the fence. But you don't want to go putting in that sort of stuff into a family paper, do you now? A sort of column, is it?

No, there are certain tales that would not go down suitably at all. Very unsuitable for family consumption, I'd have thought. Most unsavoury.

I slipped on the ice, once. A long time ago, went flying in one direction and the bin in the other, a bit of a clatter. Nearly broke my arm. A superficial fracture, they called it. A sort of crack, up here. A fortnight off. Did the garden a bit. The wireless.

Interesting incidents. Well, we'd always dream of going into the yard of one of those big houses and having a gorgeous nympho type instead of a bin standing at the door, of course, beckoning us in, like this. Didn't have to be a big house. Small one would do, as long as it were clean. Well, you're all the same underneath, aren't you? You don't have to be Lady So-and-So to be desirable, do you? Plenty of lonely wives or widows out there, but they always went for the plumber, for some reason.

The plumber, not the milkman. Or the thatcher. Thatchers are well known for that. Don't ask me why. Maybe it's the type of person who likes to be thatched, as it were. And it takes a time, you see. Thatching. My father was a thatcher, as it happens, but he ran out of work after the war. No one wanted thatch, then. I don't think the same type as likes thatch now were the sort of type as he had to thatch before the war, were they? Old Mrs Lampton's cottage, she was as poor as a church mouse, but by the time I was doing it, by the time I was servicing its waste, as we're supposed to say, I had to squeeze past a very large Rover parked where she'd had her cabbages. Up Sandy Chute way. Folk never threw anything out, before the war, not round here. They used to do their doings in the garden, I remember. Both types. Big and little. No plumbing. Nobody had bins in those days, not round here. It all got used up, somehow, the rubbish. And what wasn't used up was chucked into a dark corner, under a bush. God's muck, we used to call it. The worst thing they ever invented was plastic, to my mind. You can do things with a piece of metal. Recycle it, as they say. Cover the holes in your wall if you can't afford the bricks and plaster. Pans, colanders, what have you, hammered flat and nailed up to keep the wind out. Daft bloody idea, plastic. Kept us in a job, though.

Ash. Whoever thought of leaving out ash? And when it was wet, it'd turn to concrete. My old man swore by ash, for the vegetables. My old ma used to make what we called lye out of it, for cleaning the clothes.

There's less ash now, of course. Practically none. These youngsters don't know which side their bread's buttered, do they? You youngsters.

No, I won't go telling you about the blind bungalow. Private. Like on that door. 'Private. Staff Only'. They still walk in like they own the place. Nobody ever knocks. Not these days. Barging straight in like I wasn't here.

Birds. Thousands of birds on the tip. Seagulls, crows. That was always a sight. Emptying it all out on the tip up Alderfield way with all these birds. Reminded me of ploughing in the old days. Horses and gulls following, going for the worms. The tasty titbits.

Funny, that was the first one. The first one that was left out. *Titbits*.

A magazine. Saucy title but it wasn't, not at all really. The wife took it years ago, don't know whether it's still going. She is very proper, very proper. Interesting stories, mainly, mostly a pack of lies I suppose. But it was *Titbits*, left out on the top of the bin, like the other ones.

Them others.

You won't be printing this one, will you? Put your pen down. Just between you and me. Strictly private. You and me only. Not even the wife. All right? If a pretty face is an honest face.

The blind bungalow. That one. Rather extraordinary. Abnormal, I'd call it. Not for family consumption, this one.

Titbits. That's how it started. Innocent enough. Not left on the lid, no. In the event of it raining or the wind blowing. Just on the top of the rubbish, inside the bin. Waiting. Like it was waiting. First thing you did was take the lid off, then grab the bin by one handle and swing it up, like this, left arm on the handle and right down by the rim, at the base, and swing it up and onto the shoulder, see? One movement. Or you're sunk. Like a fireman learns his lift, we had to learn ours. Copy the others, we weren't taught. No training, none of that nonsense. Heavier than a body, some of them. Heavier than a grown man. Typewriters. Folk threw out typewriters, now and again. Weighed a ton, they did. And folk'd put them in the bin, squeezing them in like they had to hide them. That sort of object. Old wirelesses. But you didn't know when you lifted, did you? What might be inside. Though I'd always throw a quick glance at what was coming out of it into the cart when I was tipping out, just in case there were a few gold bars thrown away by mistake. Or limbs. A human head. You'll hear all the stories. Don't believe a word. Plenty of dead kittens, though. Full-grown felines, too. Mice. Even a hedgehog, once. A lot of the animal species, when I think about it. Ought to be buried, to my mind. Everything has the right.

Titbits. Very neatly laid. That quite often happened, though. Magazines and such like, left out for us. Folk thinking we were fond of reading. Sounds ungrateful, but we let most of them be mashed up. Unless it was one of those car magazines, for Phil. *Auto* this and that. Never the dirty magazines. That was Terence's dream. He'd always be sniffing out for them. But folk were too shy, I suppose. And you can keep them by, can't you? As it were. That saucy type. For a rainy day. They don't date. Flesh doesn't, does it? Not when it's from head to foot. Those calendars behind your head are only half-cock, as it were. If they were completely nude, you wouldn't know the year, would you? But they made a fuss about the last lot, so I've had to go for the polite version. Have I told you that? Some silly bugger in a grey suit and flash tie, probably gets up to all the tricks in the privacy of his own home. What else am I supposed to look at? Tyres and trucks and a bit of nipple. Nice smiles, though. Good teeth. All the same these days, teeth, on the young ones. Let's have a look at yours.

What did I tell you? Very nice teeth.

My mistake was to take it. *Titbits*. For the wife. She'd only buy it when the housekeeping allowance allowed, a sort of little luxury. So that's why I took it, in case she hadn't had that one. It was quite recent, as far as I remember. I didn't even look to see if the folk who'd left it there might be watching. A lot of folk would watch us. Passed the time of day. Hold up their little ones to watch us. You'd wave, if you felt like it, if you weren't feeling over-knackered, a little bit fed up of the job, as it were, by the afternoon. You'd take the trouble to be a bit polite and friendly, it costs nothing. Does it? Costs nothing. Give a little grin. Friendly word. The weather. The state of the economy. It always paid at Christmas. Or folk'd come out with a piece of cake, sometimes. A biscuit or two. It didn't have to be Christmas. Don't know if they do that now. Maybe they do. I don't ask the youngsters. And old Denny's too much of a bloody grump to ask anything of, even the bloody time. And that Charlie Soames, who's getting on, he's ever so queer. Hunchback, but not from the bins. Strong in arm and weak in mind. But don't go quoting me.

I did glance about, though, pocketing the *Titbits*. It was a bungalow. We'd only just got this circuit, this was a fairly fresh round to me, so I didn't recognise it as familiar. But I did note how very large its front window was, large and a very black colour, like a sort of visor, like they wear these days on their motorbikes. Blind. Can't see a thing through them. Could be monsters behind, couldn't they? Green from outer space.

Huge, it was. That window. Oh yes. Very large indeed. I don't think it was a new bungalow, but it was set back quite a bit. No garden. No proper garden. Just a bit of grass and a lot of mud, like the builders had left rather a long time ago and nothing else had touched it. Just a bit of grass. No weeds, though. Quite neat, when I think about it. And the bungalow set back and sort of empty.

Queer, you see, because the bin was nice and full, and that *Titbits*. I'm not sure I reckoned as a body was watching me, not that time. But anything could be going on behind a dark window, couldn't it? No curtains, as I could see. Just a lot of blind glass, gleaming but with this very black colour to it, a bit of sky reflected. Very quiet.

Stuffy in here. But you open the window and the drains come in. Tesco's. The hypermarkets are the worst, I'm told. For rubbish. After my time.

As far as I recall, I kept the *Titbits* to myself, inside my bag, behind the seat in the cab. It was a rule among us, sort of unspoken. We never noticed each other's booty. Unless we showed it or had to show it because it was too large to conceal. That way we avoided fights, didn't we? The runners were first at the bins but we all took it in turns to be runners, didn't we? So it all shook out fair and square in the end.

The wife already had that number. So I read it and found

it fairly amusing. Nothing saucy in it at all. A load of nice
gossip and tall tales. No different from the daily papers, is it?
Load of rubbish.

The next time, I wasn't a runner, so I don't know what
happened outside the bungalow. I wasn't interested, was I?
A couple of weeks on, then, it must have been. Frost. A bit
icy. Worst hazard for us, ice. Think about it. Half a ton of
metal on your back. It was a little bit icy that day, if I'm
recalling rightly. Slowed one up a bit. Had that burn of the
metal each time, right through the gloves. Shoulders aching
with it, because the bins are somehow heavier when it's
rather nippy. A really hard frost and the rubbish drops out
like an ice cube, doesn't it? Or freezes to the bin. Very rare
event, fortunately. 1963 was bad and then more recently,
'81 or '82, was it? Skin'd stick to the metal if you were to
lay your cheek too close. Rip it off, practically. You
appreciated the hot ash, then. Val got hot ash on him, once.
Embers. No consideration, is there? Thoughtless.

It was certainly on the nippy side when I got to that
bungalow, the second time. I was the runner again, you see.
I got to that bungalow and the lid – it was a black rubbery
type, not metal, much quieter all round when you discarded
it – this lid came off and there it was.

I shouldn't be telling you this, should I? Not for the
young ladies, this one. Private. Just you and me.

Men Only. Honest. Not even old. Mint condition.

In those days they were allowed to show the upper storey
nude, weren't they? On the front, I mean. These days it's all
covered up in case it gives some old bloke a heart attack.
Like me. Corruption of youth. Daft. But there it was, this
time I'm talking about, two enormous bubbies on this nice
and gorgeous-looking blonde type, female of course, and
there was me staring at her, hands gripping the rim on the
bin, sort of a bit surprised because it was so carefully laid,
like those reps lay their coats on the back seats. My son's a
rep, so I should know. Up and up, he's going. Sierra GLX,

J reg. Was always bright, he was, and a bit pushy. My old man's a dustman, he tells them. Proud of it. He doesn't tell them that I'm stuck all day in this dingy old hole, bloody supervising a cat's mess in a teacup. Bending the truth. You have to sometimes, don't you?

I ignore it. The *Men Only*, I mean. You know why? The bungalow lot are watching me.

They must be. Or maybe there is only one, I'm thinking. Having a good look at me through that big pane of glass. Maybe it's how he, you know, gets off on himself. Folks are very queer, you know. You'll learn.

Plate glass, like on a shop. Picture window, they call it. Not much of a picture out of it. A few blades of grass in a flat load of mud, the road, and a big green laurel hedge over the other side. It was sort of in the country, this place. Long straight road, you might know it, between Vernholt and Dipley Cross. All built up, now, of course. Back then, around the early seventies we're talking about, it was a bit out in the sticks, but there was a big garage up the road and quite a large housing estate further down, a farm or two, a couple of posh houses, the type that used to paint its name on the bin. Coat of arms, practically. They all do that now, don't they? Theft. Theft of wheelies. But it wasn't over-endowed with bungalows, round there.

I did take a quick glance, because folk have been known to play tricks on us dustmen. Kids, mostly. Mouse-traps. Bangers of course. My nephew totally destroyed my sister's toilet with a large banger, many years ago. Doings all over the walls. No doubt she binned the bits and us poor bloody infantry had to put our noses in it. Interesting incident, that one certainly was. One time I did hear a baby. Inside a bin. Crying from inside it, next to my ear, when I was lifting up this bin. But it turned out to be one of them plastic dolls.

So. I did take this quick glance back over my shoulder, but nothing untoward. Just the big window. The size of a couple of snooker tables, I should think. Unsanded frames, mind. As if no one had moved in yet. But they had, hadn't they? Or I wouldn't be staring at a pile of ordinary domestic waste up to the brim, with a *Men Only* placed on top of it, ever so neatly. Deliberately.

Blind, you see. A blind window. You could hardly see through it. You know how houses all have faces? You'd know that, if you were in the line of delivering or collecting. Some nice, some nasty. Watching you run up towards them, running up, rubbing your gloves and thinking of how many hundreds are still to go. But this one was sort of not looking. It was more sort of, sort of *smelling*. Like a mole. Blind, but with an extremely keen sense of smell. Good ears, too. It sort of knew when I was coming up to the gate, if there had been a gate. There wasn't, there was nothing but a little low wall of bricks and then a gap and a splat of cement for a car to park. But you get my point. It knew when I was standing there, by the cement, feeling a right fool, looking like I was about to throw up in the bin, I should think.

Blushing, too. Ridiculous. No one else about, I was nicely ahead of the cart and Trev – I think it was Trevor, the mad army bloke – was about five miles in front as usual, hurling the lids about.

Blushing like a tomato, I was.

I knew their game.

Or his game. Or hers. Little old lady, for all I knew. Witch type. Cackling away. I knew a real witch, as a little lad. In the village. Stopped the sheep dead. That's another story.

So I pick the bin up and put it down out on the pavement, for the infantry. If there were too many and the cart had caught up then we tipped them straight in, of course, we were all on the same job – but there weren't many bins on this road. It made life a lot easier. Then at a certain stage we'd run back and help tip out anyway. That was the system. So I've dropped this bin down when the cart appears round the corner and I don't know what to do with this *Men Only*, sitting there on top. I had no desire to leave it for Terence. He'd spend the rest of the day with his nose in it at every opportunity, talking smut. Never my favourite chap, Terence, he was always a bit like the cat that's had the cream, I couldn't have stood him spending the day shoving those bubbies and private bits at us, and for all I knew he'd pull it out – the magazine, I mean – at Miss Rainer's. As it were.

I'm just explaining why I pocketed it, you see. Sort of crouched down over the bin, so the ones in the bungalow couldn't see. Big pockets, those overalls had. I made a tube of it with the blonde rolled up in the middle and the Marlboro advert on the outside, then slipped it into my bag at the first opportunity. No point in throwing it away, was there? We'd just have it thrown back in our faces, as it were, the next time through.

Well, when it was the next time, I made sure I was the runner again. Volunteered. Worst job. I got to the bungalow, no change, blind as a bat, but I could feel myself being smelt. Alert. Lifted the lid with this very cold feeling crawling down my back like I'd got something nasty leaking out of a bin down inside my overalls and there it was. Clear as day.

No, a manual.

Blue. Pale blue. Stapled. Could have been one of these bloody efficiency reports or progress wotnots they keep shoving through here, except for its title. Here's the title. *Your Guide to Interesting Sex.* Can't get more straightforward than that, can you? Just that. *Your Guide to Interesting Sex.* Daft, wasn't it? The type that's sent in the post, plain brown envelope. Don't you go noting anything down, now. Just between you and me, this one. A pretty face is an honest face.

I looked out of the corner of my eye, like this, at the bungalow.

Nothing moving as I could see. Bloody cheek, I thought. Laughing at me. You see? For all I knew it was Candid Camera. The telly bods had hired the place, perfect it was, and had all those cameras trained on the bin, zoom lenses and all, just the other side of all that blind window, to see what my old man the dustman would do. I got very hot under the collar at that point, not scared at all, not then. I just jacked up the bin on my shoulder and strolled out and dropped it down on the pavement outside with a bit of a crash, very normal. Straight face. As if I'm too shortsighted to notice anything awry. But I can't leave *that* there, can I? So I do what I did last time, crouched over, over the bin. Only I'm keeping it about my person this time. Nice large inside pocket. But it felt like a bloody ferret, scratching at my ribs sort of thing for the rest of the day. That manual. Like an auto manual, really. I was extremely concerned by the possibility of one of the others spotting something untoward, but they didn't. Hell bicycling back home with it, though, after the shift. Waving to all and sundry.

It was fairly saucy. With drawings, illustrations as it were, but no photographs. Extremely saucy, in fact. Not one for the vicar. The mind boggles, frankly.

The wife did wonder what had got into me, in the private line. I don't know your inclinations but I do hear as how youngsters these days know it all. Try everything once, I suppose. No National Service. Earrings. I don't suppose you would be very shocked at the contents, not these days. Switch on the telly and you have it all served up before you even get to the news, don't you? So I don't suppose you would be very startled, as it were, if I was to describe the contents. All that gymnastics. It's all right at your age, isn't it? But she hasn't got the suppleness, she was always a bit on the heavy side. The wife, I mean. Could never touch her toes, even at twenty-one. Rather on the fleshy side. The more the merrier, I used to say.

Put her off it. That's probably what put her off it. Me

getting over keen. Around that time. Or, you know, the woman's change of life. Hormones. That programme last week. Your whole approach changes. As a female. She had to take anti-depressants. Still does. That's not surprising. She can't hardly move, now. She can't go up the stairs, now. Arthritis.

I never exactly showed it to her, though. The manual. She would have got totally the wrong end of the stick. Kept it under my tool-box, out in the shed. Eaten by mice, most of it. All in my head. Private. Staff only. I wanted them to put my name and position up, but they wouldn't. Nice brass plaque.

The next time through on that road, between Vernholt and Dipley Cross, it was me as runner again. The others were a bit bemused, I should say. A bit bemused at me volunteering every time. So I gets to the bungalow panting like a bellows and lift the lid but all the while looking calm as soap, the bungalow in the corner of my eye and just the same, big blind picture window, colour black, sort of gleaming but nothing moving, no lights, just sort of *sniffing* me, a sort of game I suppose, good for a laugh, a game I'm winning so far as I thought of it. And what do you think I see? Interesting incidents.

Now then. Guess.

Heart beating fit to bust. Looking calm as soap. Lid in my right hand, like this.

Guess. Go on.

No, no videos in those days. No. But close.

Photograph. Wasn't it? A photograph. As in snapshot. Sitting neatly on top of a load of stinking rubbish. Banana skins, dinner-time leftovers, soiled tissues, yoghurt cartons, a lump of what one hopes is porridge, you name it. But it wasn't an ordinary photograph, was it?

Polaroid.

And this is the thing. This is it.

It was still coming out.

22

Developing. It was still in the process of development. Polaroid, you see. Slowly growing lighter, exposed to daylight. Still wet and sticky. As they were in those days. Couldn't have been taken more than a few minutes previous to my being on the scene. A few minutes previous, then laid smartly under the lid. All very neat and clever. Just for me.

Very frank scene. White pinky bodies, red eyes from the flash. Appearing like sort of ghosts, you know, out of the black. Slowly, very slowly.

And the background. Now that made me step back a bit. Or rather, look a lot closer. You know what the background was?

What a body would see if he was to look out the picture window. True as I'm sitting here.

I could even spot the bin. That was very clear, a sort of dark bump through the glass. The road, the hedge. No sign of myself, of course. Not yet. A few minutes previous to my appearing on the scene.

Corpulent. The two bodies involved. Privacy of their own home. About my age, as I was then. Forties. Late forties, even. Very frank, what they were doing. Very very frank. Filthy, I would say. Sheer bloody filth, if you'll excuse my language. A man and a woman, but sheer bloody filth. For my delectation. Very frank.

I can see it now, clear as day. Boggles the imagination.

I must have been stood there at least a bloody minute, watching it develop out of the black, holding this lid in my hands, crouched over like that.

Couldn't help looking over my shoulder. Could I? Instinct. Sheer bloody instinct. Terror, I should say. I felt quite frightened, actually. I couldn't help looking at the bungalow, not when I saw the background coming out clear as a bell. Just where I was stood, the background was, if you get the picture. For all I know, they were taking some more, snap snap, with me in them. Writhing about with me in them, behind that glass.

So I glanced over. What did I see? Nothing. Just that bloody window. That was all. Blind as a bat. There could have been a whole naked orgy going on behind it for all I could see. A whole naked orgy writhing about. And there was myself, reflected in it all small and far away, like a bloody little idiot, holding up my lid. All I needed was a bloody sword and you could have had me as one of them knights of old on the telly.

So I gets a bit angry. Yes I do.

I look down at the bin. Filth. Wasn't it? More filth. Filth and muck. Wasn't it? Nothing but filth. Ordinary domestic filth. Full to the brim, banana skin on top, what looked like dog-food next to it, with mould on. Yoghurt cartons, tin cans, rotten cabbage. Paper, all smeared. Dirty cotton wool balls, that type of thing. Ear picks. Fish. The usual. And more filth on top. Very frank, in full colour, still wet. Little red eyes in the flash. And red shiny bits. You know.

Disgusting. Like I was looking into my own head. Clever lot, they were. Ever so kinky queer types obviously but very clever. Very very clever. Evil.

I did actually touch the Polaroid, as far as I recall. Still wet. Sticky. Smell the chemicals. Fresh out the pot, as it were.

You know what I did? Interesting incidents. Don't you dare bloody note this. More than my old job's worth.

I dropped the lid, picked up the bin, and chucked it at them. Bloody *hurled* it. All over the place, all over the front there, in the mud. The contents. That muck. Big crash and clatter. The whole lot, all over the place. Leftovers and all. Ear picks, fish, soiled tissues. You're not supposed to do that, of course. I wait a second or two. Silence. This gets me more narked. So I try to open the front door – I run up to the door and try to yank it open, catch them by surprise, tell them exactly what I personally have to say about it all, get them quite clear on what I have to say about it all, even if they're still struggling with their fancy undies. Very very clever and evil, people like that.

Locked. *Cobwebs* over the lock. I go round the back. All firmly shut. Like it's been shut a very long time. Cobwebs and grime. I go round the front.

This is very private, now.

I pick up the bin and chuck it again. At the window. Straight at it. I'm in a blind rage, you see. Other chaps would have had a little chuckle and left it at that, but I'm picturing a pair of very kinky queer types having a good old clever giggle the other side of that visor and am consequently in a very blind rage. One has one's pride. The bin hits the glass, smashes it just a bit, like a giant bullet hole, a few long cracks and the hole just big enough to poke my head through without getting slashed. Strengthened glass, I suppose.

A mess. An absolute bloody mess, inside. I can see that. Builder's mess. Cobwebs, mouse droppings, cement bags, spars of wood, the lot. Very damp smell. Wet floor. Like the roof's got a leak.

Not like in the Polaroid, you see. There was a carpet in the photograph, a leather chair, the edge of a telly, a magazine rack. Definitely a magazine rack. Smart. Their bare bits and bobs on the carpet, deep-pile, I could see that. All gone. Don't tell me how. Gone in about six minutes. Not even interior walls, they hadn't even got that far, just a stack of plaster board in the corner. But I couldn't check the snapshot because I'd chucked the contents all over the place, hadn't I? Of the bin, I mean. I'd have to go scrabbling in the filth. And then there was the cart approaching, hiss of the hydraulics, the lads whistling. So I scarpered. Pulled my head out of that bungalow and ran, fast as I could. Because I'm a little bit scared. Don't ask me why. Something at my back. Nicked my neck, too. On the broken glass, pulling my head out. Terence asked who'd gone and granted me a love bite. What lucky bloody piece of young skirt fresh out of the Badedas bath. That was Terence. *Things happen after a Badedas bath*, he'd say, waving an empty one about in front of his zipper. Sort of turned him on.

You explain it. The blind bungalow.

You asked for interesting incidents and now you've got one, just between you and me. I want your word on that. The blind bungalow.

I want your word on that. The bungalow. Leave that one out. All right?

Next time we passed by there, the bin was still lying on the ground with bits of broken glass on it. No occupants. Breakage not even boarded up. No change whatsoever. Like it was frozen. Sort of in a state of shock. I felt utterly ashamed of myself, seeing that hole in the glass. Then our round was changed. Never went that way again. You explain it. Didn't tell the wife about the incident. Private. Too frank. All in my head. Nothing shocks you youngsters, though, does it? Still fresh. At your age. Still fresh and pretty as the morning dew.

Other interesting incidents, now.

BUSINESS

She called me up at the worst possible moment, of course. We'd launched the new line, Easyplunge – a day's installation, cedar surround, double-strength lining, portable filtering system. Much more than a paddling pool, incredible value, but it gets them hooked, it's a lure – the next thing you know, they're ordering the big one. She calls me actually *during* the launch – soft music, champagne foaming, Sylvie doing the demo in her slinkiest thong, the reps boggling under their tans. My portable goes in the middle of Henri's speech and stupidly I answer it, you never know, it might just be the mayor ordering Olympic size for every park in Montpellier, ha ha.

'Hallo?'

'It's Marie.'

'Oh God. How are you doing?'

'It doesn't matter. I want you to come, it's urgent.'

It doesn't matter? That sounds ominous. Marie always played the sacrificial lamb, even as a kid.

'Is it Mum?'

'No. She's fine. It's about the sale.'

She wouldn't tell me any more, but my inner alarm was going. I felt the static go right up my spine and over my head. I actually had to pat my hair to see if it hadn't frizzed. Looking around at all the reps and assorted odds and sods that make up the company, hearing Henri drone on about the revolutionary filtering system that's basically the same with a handle and a couple of buggy wheels, I suddenly felt like going out to the farm. So of course I said yes. Marie is not going to handle the sale, I said to myself. Everywhere there are sharks prowling, Swiss, German, Dutch, English, Parisians, Belgians, even Russians now – we'd been selling pools to Russians recently, the personally tailored mega pools that need the diggers to gouge down twenty feet, and they'd always pay in *cash*. Terrifying.

I drove out that same evening, taking in a client on the way. He'd ordered the Tahiti Blue for one of his terraces and we'd had to uproot an olive grove and dynamite out the back rock to fit it on. We should have got the pros to do it but Henri said that his dad'd show the builders how, he was in the bloody Maquis or something, and we ended up with about twenty-five tons of schist on the poor bloke's patio and an unstable cliff-face. I shouldn't be telling you this, but I'm about to retire and what the hell, I've got more than comfortable on it and I'm allowed a story or two. I don't want to give you the impression that it was all a smooth ride on a lilo with a jug of pastis, as Henri would put it. Half of my job was calming the waves, I can tell you. Oil on troubled waters. I had a nice face and took care of myself, but I never let anyone push me about. No client was actually violent, not dangerously violent anyway. No guns or anything of that sort. Not like farm life. Not like life up in the mountains.

Every time I'd go back, I'd forget just how long that last stretch took and get impatient and start cutting the blind corners. Up and up and up. No one has a right to be reared up here, I'd be thinking. I mean, it's so lost, so remote, so bloody *high*. From the top windows you'd have got a view of the sea and the Alps simultaneously, if it wasn't for the damn hill in the way. Always black, that hill, facing north, too steep to catch the sun most of the year. The farm's on the opposite slope, facing south. But there were hardly any windows on the south side, can you imagine? Even as a kid

I'd ask Papa why and he'd say, 'Do you want to get fried in the summer? Do you want to be grilled, my little sausage?'

But he liked Marie better. That's because I was naughty, I didn't run after him pulling up leeks when he told me to or feeding the chickens or milking the goats. I actually hated manure on my boots, while Marie loved it. It would have been all right for a summer holiday or something, but I was actually there for good. We were both born in the big bedroom, so you can't say it was because of some difference there. My first breath was full of the stink of the farm, like Marie's. And then our brother came, and he was always odd. Did whatever I told him to do, even from Amsterdam in the last years, until he overdosed or whatever. Papa had to kick him into action, and then he fumbled about like he was half asleep, though there was nothing that was ever wrong with his brain. Maybe I was too bossy with him, when he was tiny. Maybe I was a cuckoo right from the start.

Well, I drove up that evening and sat in the car for a bit just where the track curves round to the house. It was early summer, so the light was still on it but the valley was plunged into black, as usual. There's a stream at the bottom but we hardly ever went down there, it's more like a ravine than a valley and choked up with holm oak and stuff and anyway the animals scared me. The wild animals, I mean. Boars and badgers and bats. That sort of thing. The house hadn't changed one jot, just crumbled a bit between the stones. Mum and Marie held onto it like a vice. Even Papa's horrible extension, all grey concrete, they didn't want to get rid of. Imagine! Everyone had told them how it'd bring the price right down, the place was disfigured, an old stone farmhouse with this ugly scar right across one side, but they still wouldn't touch it. Obsessive, that's what Marie was. She needed therapy. Hardly ever left the place, didn't see the world, reckoned Montpellier was another planet. No electricity, no running water, no flush toilet. Marie should have been a nun.

As I'm sitting there, thinking, trying to relax because it's always hard coming back and putting up with Marie's hold over the place, and Mum, and my memories – it's my place too, I've a hold on it too, I wasn't actually unhappy, was I? – I suddenly see the upper terrace before the meadow and think: it's exactly right, of course. It's the right size and shape for one of our mega pools – Olympic Cool, for instance, 12m by 6m; or the smaller Pompeii Mosaic number with a generous sanded slate surround plus automatic thermal safety cover, Roman laurel-and-grapes motif – complete innovation, at the time, that was. A nice antique metal table, barbecue, the lot. A couple of palm trees, why not, if you covered them up after the summer, because even the winds up here seem to carry frost. The balmy southern image, that's what I pictured – not like it was now, all grim and enduring. And it struck me how bloody ridiculous and actually bloody typical it was of Marie not to slap it up in every estate agent in Montpellier, or stick it in one of those glossy magazines full of chateaux and stuff, where we did a lot of our advertising. Instead she noted it with the *notaire* and had old Eduard put it in his window – the same Eduard who sold about one house a year and spent the rest of his time in the café opposite, doing deals over ridiculous morsels of land. He didn't even have photos, just hand-scrawled cards yellowing in the window. Hopeless. Another era.

Marie was in the kitchen when I went in. Mum was in the chair by the stove, of course, even more like a wrinkled date. Marie had got wrinkles, too. She was very pale under her windburn, and although I didn't show it I was shocked by how much thinner she'd got. I could hear her wheeze. She looked more like seventy than fifty. And I looked more like thirty-five than forty-five! We stared at each other for a moment, before kissing. It was like she was challenging me to a duel, or maybe summoning up her last bits of strength left over by the cancer. Because let's not make any bones about it – she was bloody strong. Like rock. Stubborn as stone. Maybe Papa slipped a bit of concrete into Mum's womb, because he made that terrible extension the year she was born.

'Thank you for coming,' she said.

I established immediately that I couldn't stay the night. As usual, Mum didn't make any protestation. I was the enemy, I suppose, and always had been. 'Just like your Oncle Jules,' she'd say. Who of course scarpered to America with the family jewellery before the war. Thank you very much, Mum, for the hint. But where was the jewellery? All we had was a couple of silver candlesticks and a lot of antique farm implements I had to auction off eventually.

Marie rustled up some goat she'd personally slaughtered and we sat around the table. I was the only one who ate anything, practically. Made to feel guilty even about eating, but I was hungry and Marie did a good goat stew, that I'll give her. Along with some fine home-made *muscat* the colour of piss. Well, not everyone can do that sort of thing. I mean, somebody has to sell swimming pools. What's wrong with swimming pools? One of the pleasures of life. Marie was basically a Calvinist – it must have stayed in her blood, for all her besottedness with nature. You're only here once, I'd say, and you might as well enjoy it. You might as well go for it. You might as well take the plunge and hope Peacock Pools are controlling the water.

But Marie – she arranged things so that they were as hard as possible for her. She only washed all over about once a month, you know. I understand her love of all things green and hairy and rotting but I think there's a limit, and that limit's personal cleanliness. I'm not saying she was dirty, because she'd scrub her face and hands all right, but she was a touch neglectful and you knew it when you got close, if you know what I mean. I'm not just talking about the last years, either, because the cancer took a very long time to eat into that particular boulder. I'm talking about all the years I knew her, which was all the years I've been around, until she died. She had that stale smell old nuns have, she had it even as a kid. I'm just putting her into context. Because I've had to suffer for what I did, since. I've been given the cold shoulder, since her death, from the rest of the family and quite a few mutual friends. I haven't given a toss, frankly, up to now – but when you begin to get on a bit yourself and you're all alone (I've never wanted kids, let's get that straight), that cold shoulder starts to bruise a bit. You feel like taking dynamite to it, but you know you can't. All you can do is explain.

Anyway, to get things going, I mentioned our new line, Easyplunge, but Marie went on about water shortages, about how the *sources* were drying up and somebody or other had screwed up the water table in Ste-Agnès by drilling down eighty metres for their pool water – but it wasn't one of ours so I nodded dutifully. Some people do bugger things up, they're greedy, they suck up water like it was made yesterday and not laid down over thousands of years – but they aren't breaking the law, are they? The trouble is, Marie had never broken anything in her life. No wonder no bloke would ever touch her, and she wasn't unattractive. In fact, I was sick to death of grown-ups saying how pretty she was when I was a kid, then looking at me running around and thinking I was her brother with my cropped hair and trousers, if they didn't know better.

Then she gets down to it.

'Estelle, there's this very nice young couple who want to buy the house.'

'How much?'

She barely blinked.

'They're farmers, they want to be farmers, they want to keep the land as it is except for the twenty hectares towards the village, we can sell that separately because it's too much for them –'

'You mean the hillside full of scree and stuff, that even Papa didn't know what to do with?'

'Yes.'

'So you're going to lower the price because of that scrappy piece of –'

'Estelle!' This was Mama. She was gripping my wrist. 'I like them. I want them to have it. They are good people.'

'She knows everything about plants. She's a sort of healer. He plays the accordion. They want to have goats and donkeys –'

'Donkeys!'

'They understand the farm. They love the place for what it is. I want them to have it. Mama will be happy down in the home, she's told me, if they have it.'

'This is what we call *talking up*, in the trade, Marie. How much?'

Marie looked at me. She had about a month to live, we all knew that. But her look was the same as it always was. Contempt. That's what it had in it. Like a bad smell. Like green algae, like scum floating about on the pupils of her blue eyes. Contempt and strength, even though she was dying.

I looked away, out of the window. Dusk, the same old view of fields rising up, the smell of the green rotting earth, the whiffs of the goats – still a few of them, shuffling about in the barn. But she'd managed to grow cabbages and leeks and stuff, I'd seen that as I drove up. Such strength and stubbornness. Such contempt for everything outside her little world.

'Estelle, I will die happy if they have it. It doesn't matter for you but it does for me. I was born here. This is my whole life. I don't need money in the next life.'

'You never did in this one, did you? Anyway, I'm not

planning on joining you there for a long time. Neither is Mum, for a bit. How much?'

When she told me, I laughed. I actually laughed. It was *half* the bloody asking price! Then I walked out, but saying I had to think about it. The fact is, I was so angry I might have hit her. In front of Mama, that would have been the last straw. And Marie's final triumph.

I can't stand people taking unfair advantage, I never could. Marie had this idea that most people weren't selfish, weren't out for the best deal, as if the farm wasn't built up over generations by tight fists and hard deals and the best price for everything. She'd rotted up there in the hills, while I'd got out and freshened up, expanded, deepened. Understood how things worked.

She saved my life, once. She came out into the field with the big stone *bassin* at the far end and saw me wobbling on the lip. She was seven, I was two. She kept very cool and ran inside and told Mum, who came out and saw me toppling in. She hurtled across the field and I was lying there face down in the water, still as a log. She breathed the stinky air back into me and I woke up right as rain, pretty well. Another minute or two and I'd have been as dead as a burst lilo. The trouble is, I had to be eternally grateful. It never occurred to them that it was their fault for having no safety cover on, or checking where I'd waddled off to. Oh no, I had to be eternally grateful for something I couldn't even remember happening.

But it was obvious, wasn't it, that my calling was there from the start. You've no idea what deep satisfaction I still get from seeing an acre of scrub turned into a shimmering pool, the sunlight on it, the opulence, the lovely slap of it on the sanded slate surround when the client slips in for the first time, the cool scent of water on hot stone, the flap of the filter gates – I'll get carried away, at this rate. I love my job. Frankly, I'm *terrified* of retirement. I suppose I'll have to build my own pool, now. But I haven't got any land, have

I? And you won't catch me ending my days in a villa out in the wilds, like half of them do, lonely as hell. My flat's bang in the centre, where it's all at. That's why I've kept young. Chemical free water treatment, as Henri'd put it, when we were going out together. Sex, we're talking about, now. Chemical free water treatment. I often think of that joke, these days.

I do think Marie lived up to her name, in that sphere. Not good for anyone.

I was so busy for the next three weeks, I didn't think about the sale. Then Marie was in bed, dying. I mean, really dying. We had to visit her, me and my junkie brother and various other relatives. She asked to see me alone, while the others wandered about outside, in the heat, trying to look sober on a couple of glasses of Marie's *muscat*.

'Well? Have you thought about it?'

Her voice was a wheeze. She looked like an onion with a face scribbled on it. She was born in this bloody bed, I thought. I used to bounce on it, its huge wooden bedhead cracking against the wall. She held my fingers. Hers were freezing. The smell was awful.

I nodded. She'd pulled the shutters half-to but opened the window, thank God. It was a good summer, even hotter and dryer than usual. Orders were flooding in. But I'd switched the portable off outside the sick room. That was unusual for me.

Then she started to smile, that was the trouble. Green algae. Scum on the surface of her blue eyes. It was a smile of triumph. She assumed I was backing down, like I'd always backed down. She used to tell on me, can you imagine? I'd have to confess to Papa. Get belted because of her. She told on me when I was taking my plunge in the *bassin*, and she went on telling on me, even when I smuggled in the boys. She'd say they were a danger in the barn, with all that hay and their cigarettes. Imagine even thinking like that. Sad, really.

So I said no, they couldn't have it unless they paid what we'd asked. I'd have said no anyway, even without the smile. Who wouldn't have done? What did it matter to her? Whoever heard of anyone giving away their only assets because they like the *look* of someone? Anyone sane, I mean. Anyone normal. I was protecting her from herself. And Mum. I was protecting Mum, because Marie had an influence over her that wasn't healthy. What Marie liked, Mum liked. All that graft, and to give it away to a couple of hippies on a donkey. I had no bloody choice. It wasn't anything personal, it was business. This is what I said, now, to Marie. But she didn't want to know.

'They can't buy it at that price,' she said. 'They're like us. They're poor.' She was wheezing, in a panic. I had never known her in a panic before. Speak for yourself, I thought. We'd be rich, selling this place for its proper price, to someone who'd appreciate its finer qualities.

'It's the right price,' I said. 'It's the market price. And you'd sell it tomorrow if you knocked down that bloody awful extension of Papa's, with all that junk in.'

The junk was tools, of course, bits of old machinery. Her face went into a spasm. I could hear the rest of us outside, wandering about in the heat, chatting. I so wanted to be somewhere else. Tahiti, say. Here it was all bloody rock, hard earth, not even much shade. My face was sweaty. I was looking out of the window now – I could just see the upper terrace through the gap between the shutters. This is what made me say what I did. It's normal, to dream, to imagine things better. To imagine a bit of luxury in your life.

'I want to build a pool on the upper terrace,' I said. 'The one with your leeks in. I want to sell the house to someone loaded enough to build a pool where I advise them to. I'll do it for them at near cost-price. A couple of palm trees. A barbecue. Nice slate paving. Chemical free water treatment, if possible. A decent garage in the barn for the equipment. Lilos and stuff. And they'll come every summer for two weeks and have a good time, Marie. They'll keep the grass down. They'll look after the place. They'll love it. They'll dream of it through their horrible northern winters. It'll be a happy house. It'll be a palace of leisure. Their kids will play all day in the pool and sleep like logs. The grown-ups will eat big meals under the hardwood gazebo and talk late into the night. Philosophy and stuff. If you ask me, Marie, you won't know it from heaven. The only difference between heaven and here will be money. Where you're going, you won't need money. It'll be free. You said so yourself.'

I was quite chuffed at my speech. I'd not even rehearsed it, really. I'm used to this sort of thing, though. Talking up. Painting a picture for the clients, reassuring them. Breathing a bit of humanity into the deal. Enthusing. That's why, if you don't mind me pointing out, we've grown to be Number One in the luxury pool line down here. Fruit of our expertise – and my personal enthusing, everyone knows it.

But Marie just gave a sort of groan and turned her face against the wall. Maybe she started to cry, I don't know. I have to admit that it was the first time in my life I'd won against Marie, and this did flicker through my mind for a moment, but the net result was a feeling of anger, and then total emptiness. Drained. Nothing uglier than an empty pool, of course, all that horrible glaring concrete and dried-up scum, but that's what I was. A big cracked emptiness. So you can't really say I'd won anything at all.

She died the next day. Earlier than anyone had expected, her face still against the wall. Stubborn as rock, you see. Knowing she'd lost, I suppose. Lost for ever. Never saying another word and sulking with her face against the wall, like she sometimes used to sulk if I teased her too much. But I hadn't teased her. I'd tried to negotiate, hadn't I?

It was because she'd lost for the first time, against me. Though I don't personally see it that way. And everyone thought her sulk was despair. And they found out why, of course, because Mum had been listening at the door. She always did. I never had a moment's privacy until I got out.

I did get to do the pool, for the Swiss-Germans who bought the house at near top price, but only because I wanted the heaven angle to be kept intact – to stick to my word, really. Funnily enough, I felt I owed it to Marie, in some way. I didn't want any fly-by-night crook of a builder putting in some crap concrete trough, did I? So I did do them a top range job, quality craftsmanship, slip-resistant slate surround and hardwood changing rooms, laurel-and-grapes motif on the safety cover, six metre deep end and sloped approach to the shallow. The palm trees didn't take, though. Frostbite. Too high. That was the only disappointment. That, and the colour they did the shutters. But that wasn't my domain, was it? It's no good Marie going on about that, in my nightmares.

IRON

I read about this fellow who was mowing his lawn the other day when a car jumped the hedge and killed him, right in front of his children. The driver was returning from a big business lunch, took the corner too fast. Of course it brought it all back. Helmut said I shouldn't read the newspaper if it makes me cry. Then he goes on to tell me about this fellow who was run over with his wife while lying on a blanket in his *own garden* – a lorry smashed through the little fence and squashed them flat. 'This was also his *own garden*,' I replied. Helmut never likes to think I have the better story. Also, he's going deaf.

My leg's getting worse. That too is age. I don't mean the leg that isn't there, I mean the other one, the one they managed to save. They saved it, but it's been a load of trouble. Thirty years of trouble. It's like my mother's left hand, the one that got squashed in the rubble when our flat was hit. She was lucky it wasn't her head or her heart, like Manfried and little Claus and Baby Inge, my sweet little siblings. Not that I truly remember them. I was only six. I remember voices and ribbons, pink ribbons in curly hair that felt as light as silk. One of the boys broke my doll's arm. Claus came out of a cupboard with a hat and made me scream. Manfried had boots too big for him and our neighbour said that they were taken from a dead boy up the street. I remember being hungry.

Helmut can't believe that I can't remember the explosion or being trapped in the room, under the bed. All I can remember, I tell him, is dust in my mouth. It burnt my mouth. It was like eating limes raw. My eyes, too. It burnt my eyes too. Perhaps that's why I can't remember anything until the nurse gave me a glass of water in the hospital. I can hardly remember Hamburg at all. We left so soon after, with my poor mother and her broken hand in bandages, like a white mushroom. She had some bits of the children's clothing in her bag, I don't know who had recovered them, maybe some clothes were found in the rubble. They were wearing their nightdresses when the raid happened so they can't have been taken off their bodies. At any rate, she would hold them and murmur to herself with tears rolling down her cheeks, expecting me to sympathise. But I was excited by the trip. I was excited by the train ride, by the idea of living in the country with Aunt Greta. Anyway, I thought, they are lucky up in Heaven, Claus and Manfried and Baby Inge. Nobody bombs them up there, they are laughing in the sun with Daddy.

I don't remember Daddy, either. He left for the war when I was three. He was killed in Russia, I think.

All my memories belong in the country, except for bits from Hamburg. But I don't like to think about those too much. I mean the flat when the children were alive, the smell of it, the burnt fat smell and the smell of the drying clothes on the rail above the stove. The brown rugs with their corners curled up, the black floorboards, the old clock that belonged to Daddy's father and was made in Austria. Its tick scared me. How can I enjoy remembering those things when they were all destroyed in one moment, along with my brothers and my baby sister? Why don't I remember my brothers and my baby sister as well as I remember those silly brown rugs and that clock?

You tell me.

Helmut, by the way, says the dust tasted of limes because it was the dust of limewashed plaster. I have no idea whether he is correct, it sounds like a joke. He is always playing with words. He read his grandfather the Bible as a boy and his school reports said that he was good at reading, better than normal. He might have done something more with his life than banging away at metal. But then, in our time the blacksmith was a most important occupation. Our time. Iron. Now it is all steel, Helmut says. Steelbashers. I don't know. Iron was not much good, either. There was too much iron in the world and now maybe there is too much steel. Our son works for Miele, he does something with plastic, with the plastic parts. He has a diploma in plastics. He wears a white coat. I think I prefer plastic to iron but that is hardly surprising. When I look at my mother's hand, when I visit her in the home and look at her terrible hand twisted up like a bit of old wood on an apple tree, I think: both of us, we have been hurt by iron. I once told Helmut this but he got angry and said that bombs were not made of iron. It's not surprising he got angry, when you think of it, but by saying this to him I did not really mean to make him feel guilty.

Aunt Greta's farm was on the edge of the village down a white road. It was hidden behind apple trees. As soon as we got there, I ran about on the soft wet grass and met a large dog the other side of a rickety door. I could see it through holes in the wood. We became friends. It belonged to a man who helped on the farm. He had a funny accent. He was from France but he wasn't Aunt Greta's new husband. They told me that. They told me also that I must be careful of him and the dog. I became friends with him, too, until he went away after the jeeps had come through, full of American soldiers. Before they came there were our young boys, covered in lice and in ragged clothes, some of them weeping and a few with wounds that smelt bad. They went all over the farm looking for eggs. We didn't mind because they were our boys. We gave them potatoes to put in their pockets, then they went away, leaving one of them who was wounded and sick. I had seen them pushing him in a wheelbarrow with a sack over his legs, then he was put into the barn. I think he died in the barn, because I didn't see him again.

'Why can't he come into the house?' I asked.

'He's infectious,' my mother said. 'He has a bad disease. He's better off out there. Don't go into the barn.'

I went into the field where our cow was and from there crept up to the back of the barn. I peeped in through a hole in the wood. It was dark at first but soon I saw a person lying on the hay, it was almost a shock to see this. There were strange sounds. Whimpers. *Mutte, mutte!* He was whimpering, that boy, calling for his mother in the hay. The sun picked him out in the haydust. Sometimes in church it looks like that and I think of him even now. I could see that he had something wrong with his legs, that they were all black or very dark red and too short, that there were no big boots on him like the other men. This made me interested, but when I tried to creep round to the main door I met another of our boys, who asked me to fetch him some milk. I don't remember what happened after that, but I think the wounded boy died in the barn because in the years afterwards, if I tried to ask about it, Aunt Greta would just shake her head and say, 'I don't know what you're talking about. That was the war.'

My friend the Frenchman left us the next day. He'd chase me around the apple trees and teach me the names of French rivers. Loire, Hérault, Rhône. He'd take me for rides on his shoulders and show me how to juggle balls he'd carved out of wood. My mother disapproved. He kissed my Aunt Greta on the cheeks and myself on the nose and walked away with a little bag on his shoulder and some cake in his pocket and his dog trotting beside him. Down the field they went. I stood in the doorway with Aunt Greta and my mother, watching. He had also carved me a doll out of wood. 'Good riddance,' said my mother. 'He was a good boy,' said my aunt. I broke away from her arm and ran after him and caught him up by the stream at the bottom of the orchard.

'Where are you going?' I asked.

'Home,' he laughed.

'France?'

'Yes. Far away. The other side of the big river.'

'The Rhine!' I shouted.

He smiled. 'I'm going to walk every day and every night until I get there.'

'Why don't you stay with us?'

He looked at me, not smiling suddenly, and he said, 'Do you know what a slave is?'

I shook my head.

'You ask them what a slave is. When they tell you, that's what I was. That's what your people did. But never again.'

The apple trees were coming out in blossom, it was April and quite warm. He looked at them. They hid the farm. I heard my name being called. There were tears in his eyes. 'Six years,' he said. 'Six years of my life.'

'I'm more than six,' I said.

He looked down at me and put his hand on my head. Then he left. He didn't turn and wave to me, though I was calling his name. The funny thing is, I can't remember his name. Maybe it was Rémy. The things you forget. Maybe he didn't hear me, I had a weak voice, my voice was never right again after the bombing, it was always a bit hoarse. I think it was the dust, it burnt something in my vocal chords.

I went back and asked my mother what a slave was. She was suspicious. She wanted to know *why* I wanted to know what a slave was. I shrugged my shoulders. 'That French-man!' she said. She told Aunt Greta about it. Aunt Greta told me that a slave was a man who worked for no money.

'Why should he work, then?'

'Because he has to.'

'Why does he have to?'

'Because if he doesn't, he will be shot.'

'Who by?'

'The people in charge.'

'Who's in charge?'

My mother was really furious, tutting away, but Aunt Greta just held my mother's hand that was resting on the table and said to me, 'I don't know. Now I don't know who's in charge. Perhaps God.'

My mother said, 'You and I are slaves then. We work for no money.'

Perhaps it was at this moment that I knew that I didn't want to be like my mother and my aunt, working for no money. I didn't want to be a slave.

That evening there was a commotion in the village. There were two of our boys in dirty uniform waving guns about, with wild eyes. They must have been left behind. My aunt and myself, we had gone down into the street. They kicked at the dungheaps in the yards and shot at the straw in the barns. We sheltered in Frau Enser's house and she told us that they had shot a Frenchman the other side of the village, in Herr Kessel's field. They were mad. What is the point in shooting anyone now? Aunt Greta was very upset. Frau Enser said that it might not be our Frenchman. I felt nothing, because I knew it was not our Frenchman, our Frenchman was walking to France. When the two soldiers had gone, Aunt Greta went to see the body lying in the field. When she saw that it was our Frenchman, she organised his burial in the village churchyard and made the stonemason carve a cross for free. She was very strong. Her eyes were red for a long time. Her room was next to mine and sometimes I would hear sounds through my wall, like the seagulls in Hamburg. I missed the sound of the seagulls when I came to live in the village, I missed watching them flying around in the sky above the chimneys.

Although I went to lay flowers on the grave every week, I could not believe it was my friend's. I pretended to, though, for Aunt Greta's sake. I don't know what happened to the dog.

When the American soldiers came a day or two after, they took Aunt Greta's ornaments and all the cider and Uncle Gerhard's favourite bottle of schnapps which was waiting for him when he came back from the front. They found Hitler's portrait in the drawer where Aunt Greta had hidden it when she heard them coming and they put it against a tree and shot it to pieces. They kept taking me on their knees and laughing. They smelt strange and smoked a lot of cigarettes. They chased our hens and took all the eggs and killed our one pig. It wasn't the time to kill it, and I loved the pig. There was blood all over their hands and on the white wall of the farmhouse. They were laughing, making jokes as they cooked the meat on a big fire, singing and making jokes. They gave us some and we ate it carefully, to make it last. They gave me chewing gum and I swallowed it by mistake and nearly choked. They left us some bags of noodles that they said had belonged to the German army, and made some joke we didn't understand.

I forgot to mention that when they arrived they broke the front door off its hinges with their boots, though it wasn't locked and we were sitting quietly at the table, Aunt Greta and myself. My mother was poorly upstairs in her little bedroom but they made her get out of bed because they thought there might be treasure hidden in the mattress. They ripped up the mattress with knives. One of the soldiers was very drunk and drove his jeep into the barn door and smashed it. Their jeeps had white stars on like the yellow stars on Jews and the silver stars on our Christmas tree in Hamburg. That made me cry. My mother complained about them to Aunt Greta.

'You should be thanking God they are not Russians,' Aunt Greta replied.

We'd heard what the Russians were doing in Prussia on

Uncle Gerhard's radiogram. My mother could not understand why the Americans and the British would not help us
to fight them, to fight the Red Army who were Bolsheviks.

'At least the Bolsheviks don't let the Jews run everything,' said Aunt Greta.

Now I know of course what the Russians did to the
Prussian women, what terrible things the Russians did to all
the women, even the old ones, but back then I thought that
they only sent you up to Heaven to sit with God and look
down at the smoke and the noise. Even so, the idea of the
Red Army coming to the farm kept me awake at night;
they had red faces and red uniforms and their eyes were like
hot coals. They were like the devils in the storybooks. Then
huge tanks came up through the village and the Americans
went away behind them in the jeeps, like pet dogs. My
mother has told me that the Americans were shot at from a
clump of trees in the next valley by the two mad boys, but I
don't know if this is true. All I know is that the clump of
trees was set on fire somehow and burnt to nothing.

The war ended as the blossom was falling like snowflakes.
I remember Aunt Greta and my mother and the people in
the village being very happy but also crying for the ones
who could not be there. Laughing and crying at the same
time. Some of them were sure that Hitler was not dead, but
there was one old man who was normally very quiet, he
suddenly burst out shouting that he was glad the villain was
dead, and he took a portrait of Hitler off someone's wall
and smashed it and stamped on it in the street shouting
'Murderer, Villain, Bandit,' while some people clapped and
others swore at him and my mother held her head and
cried. My mother loved Hitler like she loved Daddy and
her brother and her own father.

It was around then that she started having her fits. I think
she thought that my brothers and baby sister had died for
nothing. She hated the British. I don't know if she does
now, she's forgotten so much. It was the British who

bombed Hamburg, as you know. I forgot about Hitler quite
quickly, he wasn't important to me. Uncle Gerhard came
back with a hole in his head and a funny hand, but not like
my mother's. It looked as if his fingers had been melted, but
it was the cold that had taken them, he told me. He
remembered me as a baby, I had the same eyes, he said.

'That's because the baby was me,' I replied.

This made them laugh. My mother still tells me this story
when she has forgotten a lot of other things, much bigger
things. I asked where the cold had taken his fingers away – I
was thinking of the Frost Queen, who had always terrified
me in the stories. The cold was outside a city called
Stalingrad, a long long way away.

'I have walked back,' he said. 'All the way back. I dreamt
of this place. I dreamt always of the blossom falling on your
hair, my dear.' He was saying this to Aunt Greta, but she
told him to shush because my mother might hear through
the floorboards and have a fit. We knew Daddy had been
killed, by now. The hole in Uncle Gerhard's head was
made by shrapnel, I could put my thumb into it if I
promised not to press. It meant that when we took a train
to visit family in other places, he had to sit facing the right
way, with his back to the engine, or he would faint. We
only took a train about once a year, until things got better.

They took a long time to get better, about twenty years.
When Uncle Gerhard sold the bottom field to a firm
making parts for binoculars, to build their factory on, he
bought a smart car and did up the farm so that I could not
recognise it. I was working in the office in Leisenfeld, then,
about twenty miles away. I had a room which I shared with
a friend. I came back each weekend and every time there
was a new window, a big one, a big sheet of glass like a
shop. The old beams were hidden and the floorboards were
taken out. The farmhouse looked like new, by the time
he'd finished. I felt sad, but also proud. Only the attics had
not changed. There was so much room under the roof, full

of lumber and rope and old sacks, with a wonderful smell I cannot describe but that had a lot of wood in it from all the crooked beams.

He sold the field in 1965. Aunt Greta died in 1969. I liked her very much. She was marvellous. I never expected my mother to survive my aunt. Now my mother will be a hundred next year, and I am old, and my son is middle-aged. I think the bitterness keeps my mother going, though these days in the home she has a reputation for jollity. She likes the home. Everything is done for her there. She sings all the old songs, like she used to on the farm, and maybe before. She says to me that she has no photographs of her children, they were all destroyed in the bombing. But I'm your child, I say. Then she looks at me and says, 'You are Aunt Greta's child.' I know what this means: Aunt Greta brought me up as her own, she had no children of her own, Uncle Gerhard had a problem – perhaps the hole in his head, I don't know. But sometimes I wonder if what she says is really true: that maybe I was a love-child and my father was the French slave – the forced labourer, I mean. But when I think about the dates, it is just not possible. Unless I am six months younger than I am. It may be so. All the records were destroyed in the bombing, along with the clock from Austria and my toys and dolls and everything, everything.

I met Helmut in Leisenfeld. He was also working for the mine, mending all the iron tools, the picks and shovels, making the teeth for the diggers, all that. He made the hooks to keep the sleepers in place, for the pony rails. He was the only blacksmith in the mine, apart from the boy who operated the bellows. Then the bellows were electrified and he was alone in the forge. I was a typist in the office. I hardly spoke to any of the miners, I only worked with the administrative staff. I worked there for twenty-five years, from 1956 to 1981, before I opened the shop with Uncle Gerhard's money. The shop sold hats but now fewer and fewer people wear hats and Helmut didn't like serving in a shop. We closed it in 1990.

One morning in 1961 the blacksmith came to the office because he had some error in his papers. He waited to see Herr Kramer, my boss, in charge of wages. Herr Kramer was very short-sighted and always held papers up close to his face. I had to help him find the blacksmith's papers because there were several Schinkels and even another H. Schinkel, and poor Herr Kramer got in a terrible muddle. During all this fuss I noticed that this blacksmith fellow was squeezing himself close to me, pretending to look as well at the papers in a muddle on the desk. I had Herr Kramer on one side, so I couldn't move away any further. My hip kept touching this Schinkel fellow's hip but I couldn't help it. Anyway, he was a big good-looking chap then, you know, with just a slight stoop from working all day at the forge. He was seven years older than me. When he was leaving, he gave me a wink. I went very red.

A bit later he invited me to a dance in the town hall. We had a lot of fun. It was a year before we got engaged. When the mine company held their annual dance, he took me over to the forge and showed me around. It was huge. I had imagined a little place like the forge in the village, but this was like a hangar. He worked here all alone. It was full of big sheets of metal and very long iron rods, and had a compressed-air machine he was in the process of mending. He lit the forge and the electric bellows soon blew the coals red-hot. While the band was playing in the distance and all the miners and their partners were dancing in the yard under the fairy-lights, Helmut took off his jacket and rolled up his sleeves and made me a mattock. I can't think why he chose to make me a mattock, it doesn't seem very romantic. In any case, I gave it to Aunt Greta, for her vegetable patch on the farm.

I was a bit tipsy, but I enjoyed watching Helmut make the mattock, the way he bent the iron rod round to make

the forks and flattened the square he'd cut to make the blade, hammering it softly, heating it and shaping it, as if it was made of putty. When he welded the parts together, he gave me one of those masks to wear because otherwise the glare would blind me, he said. The forge looked very dark through the eye-slit, but the welding still burned a bright green. Helmut was different, working. I liked the way his skin looked in the flame of the forge, I liked the way it shone with sweat, the way the muscles on his brawny arms were polished like stone. The way his face was set in silver and gold, with diamonds for eyes. He reminded me of the men on the posters and magazine covers during the war. That is why I had been so surprised when the soldiers had come in their ragged uniforms, dirty and exhausted and some of them weeping, covering their faces with their helmets to hide their tears. Helmut was not like them. He had been in the Hitler Youth at the end of the war, but he never talks about it. Everyone of his age was in the Hitler Youth. It was normal. I can't imagine he ever looked like those poor boys.

But he was delicate, too, when he worked. He kept giving the tool little taps to shape it, little taps with his hammer, always away from the centre, towards the outside, making it sharp and strong. Then he said, 'Now we will temper it. It must be cherry-red. It must be the colour of your lips.'

It was heating in the flames, going very red. Then he pulled the metal out and watched it. My heart was beating. Perhaps I had drunk too much. I had sometimes watched the blacksmith in the village, but I didn't like the din and he was always banging horseshoes, it seemed. This was different. Helmut Schinkel was the blacksmith of the Leisenfeld Zinc and Lead Mine, working in a huge forge with electric bellows. I thought: yes, I could marry him. He has a good future. I had pink lipstick on, but Helmut pretended to study my lips to check the colour. Then he plunged the tool into a bucket of cold water. It gave a short hiss. Then he pulled it out.

'Look,' he said, 'now we will see the iron go blue and green. We call it pigeon's throat. It means that it is very strong. It will never break or bend. It will last forever.'

We watched it go the colour of a pigeon's throat, my arm around his waist, while the band played and the employees danced and shouted the other side of the wall. That was the happiest moment of my life, happier even than the wedding day. I saw life as going on and on, like tempered iron or steel. Then he handed me the mattock. It was so heavy! I knew all the tools of the farm, I had been brought up with them, but watching this one being made, seeing how easily it bent around the form, how soft it was, made me think it would be light. The weight almost frightened me. I thought: if this dropped from the sky, it would smash my skull. I could see it dropping out of the sky. Helmut wondered what was the matter with me. To this day, I don't know. But I started crying. I think it was the drink. I have never drunk very much. Poor Helmut didn't know what he'd done wrong. He had to take the mattock from me.

The mine closed in 1970, but the administrative office stayed open to deal with the pensions and claims and so on. That too closed eventually, in 1981. It was strange, working in this little building surrounded by quiet. Herr Kramer said it was like working on a bombsite. I was glad when we moved into an office in the centre of town, because the local youths were using the yard for their fun and games. Now there is a mining museum, but they have filled in the workings and made a nice park full of trees where the spoil was heaped. It is quite pretty. It has a real pond with rare ducks and a man comes every summer giving puppet shows in a beautiful red-and-yellow gypsy cart.

It was a hard few years. First Aunt Greta died, then the mine closed, then I had my accident. They built new factories in the town but none of them needed a blacksmith. Also, my mother was worse and worse. She left the farm and came to live with us. Soon she was staying in bed all day. The doctors said she was paralysed, I don't know how. I think it was in the brain. She still had those scraps from the flat in Hamburg, those scraps of clothing. They were so worn now that the patterns on them had faded, they were all grey and greasy with her touching, but she kept them as if they were holy relics, like the Catholics have, mumbling to herself and touching them like they do with their beads in their churches. My only joy was my son. He was five when I had my accident. This was in 1973.

I think that God gives and takes away in equal measure. Sometimes he takes away a lot. He took Hitler away but most people now say that was a good thing. I don't know, I'm not interested in politics, but I remember at the time how it was as if God had gone away behind the clouds, abandoning us. That's what people said in the village. That's what my mother said. Uncle Gerhard's youngest brother was in the SS and he still says that there is only one people apart from the Jews that should be wiped from the face of the earth, and that is the British people. If we had taken Britain, he says, Hitler would have been content, we would have had all of Europe and the Bolsheviks would have stayed in Russia and the Americans with their Jews in America, far away. But those bloody British had the devil on their side. Now we have drugs and graffiti and Jews running everything again. I don't know why he gets so angry: he has a big farm and a big car and a lot of money in the bank, down in Swabia. He smells of expensive perfume and gives us expensive presents. I don't like to visit him, but family is family. Besides, he paid for me to have the best treatment, the best surgery. If it wasn't for Uncle Verner, I might have no legs at all. Now that my leg gives me such trouble, such pain, I'm thinking that maybe it would have been better not to have saved it, after all.

I was saying about God, how He checks and balances. When we had the shop, I totted everything up at the end of each day. Incomings and outgoings. Each year, the figures had to balance to the last pfennig. I was good at this after all those years typing in Herr Kramer's office. I am sure that losing my leg meant that my son did not lose his life. I must explain this.

This was long before the shop, nearly ten years before. The office was open three days a week. The miners' pensions were good, and they spent it; Leisenberg did not become a poor town when the mines closed. But there were always problems, paperwork problems and disability claims and such things, and when an ex-employee died there was his widow to deal with, and more paperwork. Herr Kramer would look almost happy when a miner died, because it meant that the office was kept busy. He used a magnifying glass now, but he could not be easily replaced; no one else would understand his system. Eventually the operation was taken over by the company who had bought our company, and moved to their headquarters in Essen. Herr Kramer and myself were retired. There have been a lot of problems with company pensions in Leisenfeld ever since, even with my own and Helmut's! We have to write letters quite often. Helmut blames the computers. I blame poor Herr Kramer's system.

In 1973, Helmut was doing odd jobs, mostly in the building line. He had set up a little forge in a shed in a friend's yard, and turned out a few things to order: gates, wrought-iron fences, security bars for windows, names or numbers for houses, tools, sometimes a little chair or table for a child. He used scrap from the mine, it was lying all over the place. We had bought a house in the smarter part of town, it had once been a shop but for the moment we used the shop as our front room. There was a huge window and we could watch the world go by. The house was set a few metres back from the street at the bottom of a hill, and had the sun all morning. I planted a little garden between the house and the pavement and dug a big hole for an apple tree. Helmut thought I was mad. I told him that he wouldn't think I was mad when the blossom came out and filled the window and made the front room smell of the countryside. For Helmut, the countryside smelt of dung, though not many people put dungheaps in front of their houses now. Even my old village was cleaned up by this time and had pavements and lighting and the new church that looks like an army barracks.

When summer came, I put a chair out by the front door and sat under my little apple tree whenever I could, watching the people go up and down, up and down. Normal, they were. This life was normal. People going up and down, quite happy, saying good morning or good afternoon as they passed the other side of my little white wooden fence. Helmut kept promising to replace it with metal, as if I wanted him to. I knew many people through my work, and my happiest times were spent sitting in the sun when I could, even if only for a few minutes. Helmut said I was like an old woman, sitting out there. I was only thirty-five. Why shouldn't young women sit out and enjoy the sun? Why should they always be washing their husbands' vests and ironing their sons' trousers, cooking and cleaning and sewing? Slaves. Working for no money.

Then one day in May, after lunch, Helmut made me stay in the back of the house until afternoon coffee. I was not permitted to go into the front room or the front garden. I could hear hammering and sawing and drilling from there. I thought, maybe he's cutting down my apple tree and putting up a big iron fence. I will pull it down. I will leave him. Since the mine closed, Helmut had become rather difficult, as if he had not enough iron to hammer and shape and so must beat at everything in sight. He never used violence on me, however. He's a good man, really. You can't blame him for anything.

I got very worried during the afternoon, and when he came in for a drink of water after two hours or so, I said that I must go and see what he was up to.

He held my arm and looked into my eyes and said, 'You will like it. Please wait.'

I trusted him. I could see the apple tree making shadows on the drawn curtains in the front room. Mother was calling for me from upstairs, and Claus my little boy had started crying in the kitchen over something. '*Mutte, Mutte!*' This reminded me – something in the way he said it – of the sick boy in our barn nearly thirty years before. Maybe it was a premonition, because the boy had had something bad with his legs. I went up to Mother and she asked me to change her. She could only move her head and one arm now, and made messes. It was like having another baby in the house. It was all in the head, the doctors said. Now she is in the home she is better. She is nearly a hundred and she is singing and talking and even moving a few steps and waving her arms about. She was punishing me, I think. I don't know why. I looked after her really all my life, or since I was six years old.

Then a bit later Helmut came in wiping his hands on a cloth and said, 'I am finished.'

'Is it a nice surprise? It isn't my birthday!'

He smiled at me and said, 'Do you remember that mattock I made you in 1961?'

'Of course.' Then I thought: where is it? I should have put it in a glass case and hung it on the wall. Maybe it is in the shed, with all the other tools. That is a shame.

He gave me a little squeeze and a kiss and then he picked me right up and carried me out squealing a bit to the little front garden, in front of all the people passing in the street. They smiled when they saw it was not a violent domestic situation. It's good when you see two people who are not very young still loving each other. Now and again I see old people walking arm in arm, and I feel very glad. Always arm in arm, never holding hands. Why do old people never hold hands? Only their grandchildren's hands. The young people in Germany are always touching each other, as if there is no one looking, but that makes me feel sorry for them when I think of Helmut and I, how romantic it was when there were rules.

Helmut carried me out in his strong arms and showed me what he had made. It was a bench of wrought iron. Its seat was of spirals and the arms were like feathers curved back, and he had set it into the wall of the house, supported by two bars underneath.

'A place for two', he said.

I kissed him and he put me down. People were passing, not many, but I felt a bit shy. I would have liked to have hugged him. But I didn't really like the bench, I only liked what Helmut had done. He had taken us back to the past, to the good time. I liked my old wooden chair with its cushion tied to the back, I liked taking it out each time and leaving it there if it wasn't going to rain. I liked the way it squeaked when you sat on it, the way it wobbled, the way it was so light when you picked it up by the back. It was one of Aunt Greta's chairs, one of the chairs in the kitchen over at the farm. It wasn't very smart, but I liked it. I loved it, even. But how could I tell Helmut this? I would grow used to the bench. It was hard and cold, but I would warm it up. I was selfish, preferring my own chair with only room for one. My own throne. We sat on it together and I felt foolish, in front of the people coming down the hill, passing along the pavement. It was like we were in the cinema. I never felt like that on my old chair, because in the old days it was normal, sitting in front of your house or cottage on a kitchen chair, maybe with some knitting or lace. But you have to get used to things, then they are normal. Soon, I thought, I will like it. It is always hard, accepting presents. Even Helmut didn't know what to say, sitting next to me. I knew it was beautiful work. Everything hammered out by hand, very delicate and strong. Cherry red. Pigeon's throat. The iron feathers were cold and hard, but the sun would heat them up like it heated the iron chairs in the park.

'Thank you', I said.

I didn't know that it would be warmed by my own blood, soon.

'It's very strong,' Helmut said. 'As long as the house stays up.'

He laughed, and bounced his behind on the bench. He is very heavy, big-boned, but I didn't feel a single shiver from the iron. He was grinning at me. I felt a bit frightened. Everything should move a bit. It is not normal that something should not move at all. If something is too strong, it can hurt others. It will not get out of the way for you.

Helmut would say, 'Tell that to a miner underground, with only his helmet and a few beams between him and a thousand tons of rock!'

Claus says that plastic can now be very strong, as strong as iron. Helmut says that is rubbish, nothing is as strong as a beam of tempered iron or steel.

'You are still in the Iron Age, Daddy,' says Claus. This is always his joke, but Helmut doesn't mind it. 'Better than the pansy Plastic Age,' he mutters. He's proud of his son, really. That big brain. And Claus is very well paid. Like my mother, Miele will be a hundred years old this year. They are giving every employee a three-hundred page book on the history of Miele, and a month's salary. Better than the mines.

'Three hundred pages?' said Helmut, when he heard of this. 'You can write the history of the human race in three hundred pages and still bore my boots off.'

'It's very interesting,' says Claus. 'It's social development.'

'Social decline, more like,' says Helmut. 'Give me the Iron Age. Give me the old days.'

Then the quarrel stops, because Claus knows what he means by this and can't stand it. Once as a schoolboy he came back full of rubbish about the war and wouldn't talk to us for a week, as if either of us were old enough to have done anything. Now there are films and programmes every day, everyone talks rubbish, you believe what you want to believe. All I know is that Manfried and Claus and Baby Inge were killed, and many of my friends, and Daddy, and my home was destroyed. I don't know any more. I don't know who was good and who was bad, as I can't blame Helmut for what happened to my leg. Only God sorts it out. It is fate.

I remember exactly the day it happened. A Sunday. July 25th, 1973, at twelve minutes past five. Uncle Gerhard had called round with some cream cakes and a horrible furry devil for Claus. He had been to Bad Wildungen, to 'take the waters', as he put it, in the big hotel there, and they sold these devils in the souvenir shop. It was red with pointy ears and held a bunch of twigs. I ask myself sometimes whether that devil was responsible for what happened, but the pastor says that is superstition, I'm sounding like a Catholic. Claus loved it, anyway, and I do believe that children are sensitive souls, like dogs. If the little devil was evil, Claus would have dropped it like a hot coal. But it had a horrible feel, all bony underneath the fur. I found it the other day, in the back of the cupboard in Claus's room, all mangy and with an arm broken off. It was made of plaster, you could see that, white plaster. The eyes and teeth were hand-painted, it was all hand-made. They don't make things like that any more. Even at our Christmas market in Leisenfeld you don't see stuff like the old days, though all the craft people are out. It looks foreign, these days; Indian or Chinese or African, expensive knick-knacks really. Claus's girlfriend fills her house with such things. But we are glad about her; Claus brought her round along with his washing one day last spring. We were so happy, Helmut and I, because one did ask oneself why Claus had taken so long to have a girlfriend. She is a child psychologist. So clever. But they don't believe in marriage. Imagine!

As long as they believe in having children, I don't care. They'll get married in the end.

We had finished tea, on this famous Sunday. Uncle Gerhard had spent two weeks eating only carrots, swimming and sweating in the sauna and walking in the forest or whatever, and then he gobbles down so many cream cakes!

'I don't think it's healthy to be so thin,' Helmut said.

I laughed, because Uncle Gerhard could not be described as thin, even though he was nearly seventy. This was before he was ill.

'Why are you laughing?' asked little Claus. He had cream around his face like a white beard.

'Your mother thinks I am a pig,' said Uncle Gerhard. 'She is a cheeky monster.'

'I like pigs,' said Claus. 'They can fly.'

Everyone laughed. Claus had a plastic toy pig with wings on it which whirred when you wound it up. 'Pig Angel' it was called. I don't know who gave it to him, it was a silly thing. Claus looked upset when we laughed at him. I explained about the toy to Uncle Gerhard. Helmut said he was glad pigs couldn't fly because if they could they would drop on your head when you shot them, and they were very heavy.

'Then I suppose you're glad that I can't fly,' Uncle Gerhard said.

We laughed again. He was flapping his bad hand about. It was very jolly.

'You'd even break the special bench,' piped up Claus.

We told Uncle Gerhard about the iron bench. Helmut had only put it in a few weeks before, and Uncle Gerhard had not called on us since. I wish we had changed the subject, but of course Helmut wanted to show him. Claus kept saying that he musn't sit on it. I think he was really worried in his little child's way. But when I think of what might have happened, what much worse thing might have happened, then I can only thank God. It might have been Claus sitting on it instead of me.

We went outside and admired the bench. I still didn't like it as much as the old rickety chair (Helmut had thrown this away), but I pretended to like it. Uncle Gerhard started to sit on it but Claus wailed so much because he was really afraid it might break, so Uncle Gerhard stood up again. Helmut was a bit angry with Claus. I sat on it, and took Claus on my knee. He shut up immediately. The men chuckled and went inside. I closed my eyes in the sun, it was a beautiful warm day. The apple tree had one apple growing on it, even though it was hardly a tree yet. I had planted bulbs in the autumn and they had come up in their neat rows full of colour under the little wooden fence. There weren't many people around, the hill was empty of traffic – it was much quieter in those days, especially on a Sunday.

Claus was quiet against my body. I always feel sleepy after cakes and coffee, if a bit jumpy too from the caffeine. It's a mixture, but on that bench that afternoon I didn't feel jumpy. There was no warning, not even from Claus. Certainly not from God.

I started to drift off with the hot sun on my eyelids. I have always liked to lie with my face in the sun – I was told as a child that the sunlight was full of vitamins, and that I must catch it whenever I could. I must stimulate my metabolism by running about and jumping. We did a lot of exercises at the village school. The teacher said they were Swedish, but they would make us into good Germans, strong and healthy and agile. I was always running about on the farm, anyway. My legs were strong and brown, my knees were skinned and bruised like a boy's. There was no television, only the radio. Aunt Greta listened to the English BBC on it, but only for information about the war. They put out propaganda in German. She said she had two ears so she must listen in two directions, when my mother complained. You could get executed for listening to the BBC. Claus believes she was against the Party, handing on information to the Frenchman. He can think what he likes, he never knew Aunt Greta. If he wants to make her into his type of saint, he can. She was just normal. Wonderful and normal.

Maybe I was dreaming of myself running about on Aunt Greta's farm all those years before, while sitting on the iron bench with Claus on my lap that famous Sunday. Maybe. I don't know. All I know is that something made me open my eyes. A sound, maybe. I saw the bonnet of a car facing me and growing bigger. I thought of my flowers, it was in slow motion, I could see the tyres crush my flowers. The car's radiator was like a horrid grin. I threw Claus off my lap so he landed in the patch of grass but I didn't have time to get up myself, the apple tree snapped and the car was enormous, I put out my hand to stop it and there was a huge sound like a whole shelf of pots and pans was falling down and then the car was half on top of me as if about to eat me. There was a man in the windscreen who stared at me as if *I* was the monster. I heard screams and it was myself screaming. I wanted to faint but I couldn't. Claus was screaming too but he was sitting on the grass where I had thrown him clear. I was stuck, I couldn't move, the car was pressing my leg against the iron bar underneath the bench. More than pressing. I couldn't see how my leg could have fitted in between the car and the bench. My other leg was crooked. Blood everywhere. So much blood. My right arm was free and pulling at my thigh but my left arm was smashed, terrible cuts that hurt. I thought: this is a nightmare, I will have a hand like Mother's and Uncle Gerhard's. I didn't think about my legs. I just wanted to get off the bench but I couldn't. It was as if Helmut had welded me to it.

The others were crowding around me and there was a man sobbing and saying, 'Sorry, sorry, oh my God.' Helmut shoved him away quite violently and started pushing the car with the others and swearing like I have never heard him swear. No one was with Claus, I wanted them to be with Claus. I heard my mother at the window directly above me, she was shouting out of the window and I thought: she is having a fit, oh my God.

So much blood.

Why didn't I faint? I couldn't see yet what had happened to my legs. Then the car was pushed away and I looked down. The left one was squashed against the iron, it looked like the inside of a sausage, I could see the toes where they shouldn't have been, they were all mixed up with my ripped-up stocking, and there were white bones sticking out. But I couldn't feel anything. The right one was more painful, its pain was spreading up my body into my smashed arm, but the arm and the right leg still looked like an arm and a leg. They were no worse than those of the wounded soldiers who came to the farm that day at the end of the war. Everything was swelling very quickly and turning blue and green, and the helpers were splashed in blood. When the car was pushed off a really horrible feeling came into my leg, as if it was a tyre being blown up too much. An ache that was the real devil, the real devil. Worse than the sharp pains everywhere. I could see blood and skin and muscle stuck on the chrome of the bumper. This made me shudder and want to faint more than seeing my leg made me, but I couldn't faint. My body did not really feel like mine any more, but that lump of stuff on the bumper did, it belonged to me, I wanted it stuck back on me. This is what made me feel so bad. I had come off the bench now, I could see it dripping with blood, and there was blood all over the wall behind. It was like the killing of the pig on the farm at the end of the war.

They laid me down on the grass and there were a lot of

people now. I saw Uncle Gerhard's white face, I thought he must be getting giddy. 'Take Claus,' I said. 'Don't let him see this.' Helmut held my good hand. He was very calm now. 'We'll get you to hospital,' he said. 'We have phoned for the ambulance.' Then he looked around and shouted, 'Where's the bloody doctor?' Worse than that, his language. I was ashamed, but I was swearing too, to myself. Terrible words.

I felt sick, I felt I wanted to be sick. I didn't want to be sick in front of everyone. The ache in my sausage leg was awful, someone had pulled my toenails right back, and my toes too, and they were still pulling, they wouldn't let go. I tried to see but they had put a blanket over it. All the faces were white. Then I started floating a little. I started praying to Jesus in a little whisper. A man came up and said he was a doctor. He seemed rather shocked. He gave me some brandy but it burnt my throat – I have always had a delicate throat, since the bombing. I closed my eyes. This is a nightmare, I thought.

The sobbing fellow was the driver, I recognised him. I swore at him. That is awful, but I did. I swore at him. I was like the old man in the village who stamped on the portrait of Hitler. He bent down and said he was sorry, he was going to kill himself now. He smelt very strongly of alcohol. 'Go and kill yourself,' I said. It wasn't me talking, it was my vocal chords without my brain. I didn't know which part of my body was where – only my right arm. I tried to touch my left arm with it but the wounds hurt too much. I saw the watch on my right arm. Helmut had given it to me, it was quite smart. The face was not even cracked. It was at twenty-one minutes past five. The ambulance took nine minutes to come, Helmut told me later. So I know exactly when the accident happened.

Then there were men in white coats. They gave me an injection, or maybe the doctor did. The pain was pushed into the background. Everything was white and silver, a bit blurred, and I thought in very fast thoughts how I would wake up the other side of it, completely all right, like Daddy and Manfried and Claus and Baby Inge in Heaven – only I would be in my bed at home. I wasn't sure which home. I even saw the flat in Hamburg, the Austrian clock ticking high above me, and I heard these seagulls, they were flying above some bare branches, round and round. At other times I was running down the field through the apple trees, towards the Frenchman.

I was in hospital now, on a trolley. Lights in the ceiling moved past me. A horrible smell of bleach and antiseptic, which reminded me of Claus's birth. I felt suddenly worried about Claus, but I was too sunk down to say anything. Helmut's hand in mine, squeezing it. A door swinging. Then this voice I will never forget. It must have thought I couldn't hear. It said: 'We'll have to operate on the leg, Herr Schinkel. It's beyond repair. I believe we can save the other one.'

I don't remember any more, until I woke up after the operation. Helmut was there, smiling encouragingly. It was so quiet around me. He had a patch of dried blood on his forehead. I remembered the voice first. There was a steel cage keeping the blankets off my legs and I felt down inside it and the left leg had gone. I could not believe it. There was my thigh and then the bandage and then nothing. I started to cry. It was a bad moment. It was a nightmare. How could I look after Claus? How could I look after my mother? How could I look after Helmut? The left leg was still there in my mind, I could feel its foot hurting, the toes, a terrible ache in the knee as if someone was pulling at the kneecap very hard – but none of those things were there. I was given another injection. Helmut was saying good things. I couldn't stop crying. Just lying there with tears rolling down my face, a mess in a lot of bandages. A terrible mess.

Oh, I managed. I have had different types of prosthesis,

some metal, some wood, now a plastic one, a special advanced type and lighter. They all hurt a bit. But it's the other leg that hurts more, these days. All twisted. It had to carry me about for so long, and now it is going on strike. I'm too heavy. I have grown too big, like Uncle Gerhard. I don't eat cream cakes, but I can't stop growing larger. The less I move about, the larger I get. The more it hurts.

I was only a young woman, still. Helmut put up an iron fence which would have stopped a lorry, in case anyone else came down the hill too fast, completely drunk. But no one has in twenty-five years. The car was an old Volkswagen 1600 and the driver was put in prison for one year. He had been out for a drink with his mates and lost control on the hill. He blamed his brakes. He was thirty-six and lived with his mother. I don't care what happened to him, or if he's still alive or not.

The job saved me from going mad. Two days a week. Helmut took over at home for those days. He felt ashamed doing the job of a woman, but he shouldn't have. He was a hero. He changed my mother's linen and cooked and cleaned and amused Claus. Some things can't always be normal.

I couldn't understand why this had happened to me. I felt angry, hobbling about. I couldn't dance properly any more. I couldn't forget the pain. Helmut painted the front of the house to hide the blood but I couldn't forget it. The bench stayed because we never thought of taking it out, it wasn't really the bench's fault. I was told I must try to sit on it again, and after two years I did manage to sit on it without feeling sick.

Then God showed me why it had happened.

Claus became quite difficult after the accident; he had to see a psychologist. Perhaps that's why he fell in love with one, later. He became a bit wild in his teens. I felt he never accepted me, after I was damaged. I understood this, because I had never accepted my mother after she was damaged. Parents must be perfect. He bought a motorbike when he was sixteen. One day, I had a phone call from the hospital. Claus had crashed.

'Is he alive?'

'Of course he's alive, he's OK, but he's very lucky.'

I fainted. Isn't that strange? I fainted with relief.

He had cuts and bruises and a bit of concussion, that's all. This is what happened. It was on a little road between Leisenfeld and our old village. He missed a corner and crashed very fast into a gate. The gate broke as the barn door had broken when the American jeep drove into it forty years before, and Claus ended up in a soft patch of mud.

The farmer was very angry, because it was a new gate. He had just replaced it that morning. Helmut went to see him afterwards. He showed Helmut the remains of the new gate. It had been especially made by the old carpenter, in beechwood, and had five coats of varnish on it. It had only hung there a few hours! Can you believe it? Now it was matchwood!

'Where's the old gate?' Helmut asked.

The farmer showed it to him, still lying where he'd dumped it, in the field. It was a rusty iron gate.

'Nothing wrong with it, apart from a bit of rust', said the farmer. 'Who cares about appearances? I should never have replaced it.'

'I'm glad you did,' said Helmut. 'You saved my son's life.'

'How did I do that?'

'Iron doesn't break. It doesn't give way for anything. I should know. I'm a blacksmith.'

Helmut told me this, afterwards, sitting on our bench. The bench never had a scratch. It was as firm as a good tooth. Uncle Gerhard for one always reckoned it should have been removed, but why remove a good tooth? I might have been killed, sitting on my old chair. Though I don't think I would have been. I might not even have lost my leg. Maybe it would have been better to have joined God, I often think when the pain is bad. But I survived the bombing as I survived this, He must want me to stay alive for a reason. Helmut finished telling the story of the farmer's gate and took my hand and squeezed it.

'So there you are,' he said. 'Claus was lucky.'

'That's God's doing,' I said. 'Checks and balances. The wood for the iron.'

Helmut didn't say anything, he just frowned. He would reply, now, because he's got very crotchety in his old age. Rusty, as Claus jokes.

I spend quite a bit of time now, on the bench, knitting or sewing. The psychologist who treated Claus said I should do this, all those years ago. I think a lot, I plan things. They say Hamburg is very smart now, very beautiful. I think I will take Mother there on her hundredth birthday. She has never been back. It will do us both good. We can sit in the park in the sunlight and close our eyes, feeling peaceful. Sit on a park bench in Hamburg and close our eyes, together.

STONEWORK

'Doug?'

Doug turned and I could see his age suddenly. You know that? That kind of omen of age? Jeeesus, he said, under his breath. I'm not putting it in quotes, that one, because he didn't really even say it under his breath. He more kind of mouthed it and you could see all of his bottom teeth, practically. He looked a bit like a really old string puppet that used to frighten me half to death when I was a kid. We left that behind, too, when my folks went out.

'Christ, Doug,' I said, 'you've got a load and a half on there!'

It was true, what I'd said. There were more breeze-blocks than you could count, unless you wanted to be a heck of a time counting. Bloody huge piles of cement breeze-blocks! I banged the door of the van shut and it swung open again. I didn't kick it because Alabaster was in there and I don't like to show a kid violence. Anyway, it was hot. Like a bloody oven, in fact. There was dust all over. Doug's face was kind of talced, like my old mum slapping it on after she hit sixty. At least in Sydney the rain lays the dust now and again, I thought to myself.

'At least it rains in Sydney,' Doug said then. Amazing. Sometimes we didn't have to talk. That's what the palmist in Wollongong'd pointed out. You're chalk and chalk, she'd said, making a joke out of it but with a mica of truth, as Doug'd say. Granite was always his favourite stone.

Come to think of it, it was really that palmist's fault we came out in the first place. Or *went* out. Depending on your personal geography. 'Your personal geography's a fuck-up, Linda,' Doug'd say. 'You're a has-between, Linda.'

Well, now we're both bloody has-betweens. Get out of that one, Dougie! The thing is, that loopy palmist was so *hazy*. About the future, not about us. Handling dressed stone's never that. Hazy, I mean. If you're hazy handling dressed stone, you get a bum wall and probably a crook toe. Doug never dropped a single rock. If you think the Ancient Gyppos were classy, with all that pyramid stuff about not slipping a razor in the joints, then you ought to've seen Doug in the good old days. Doug was bloody *obsessive*. He'd get a spalling hammer and a lump of limestone ('limo', Doug'd call it) and it'd be rough-dressed in, well, about as long as it takes to say 'it rains in Sydney', slowly. And then he'd stroke it, sort of fondlingly. Great big hands, Doug had, the kind that can hold a couple of tree-trunks with room to spare. Yet he'd stroke that stone like it was a new-born baby or something.

I stood there and blinked a bit after Doug'd said that about Sydney. It was like the real low. Only I felt it could get worse. He could clout some local guy and get hauled off by the local gendarmerie and leave me high'n'dry. Or whatever. Not knowing a word of the lingo. ('All French to me, mate,' Doug'd say.)

Then Alabaster started to scream and I couldn't even go get her, I was so depressed. I could see her banging the window and I couldn't even go get her. She was only, what, two and a half then but she never stopped. Talking, I mean. Questions. Like life was a quiz-show or something.

There were others on the site: Moroccans, Doug'd said. They were whistling and laughing and they all seemed to have one tooth that was silver or something. Doug was just about as dark but he was a yard taller it seemed like and of course his hair was blond as a beach, done up in his pig-tail

Indian squaw look with the little scrap of ribbon he'd
filched from the Hopis. Well, not filched: he'd found it by
their temple thing with that great big ladder stuck out and
reckoned it must've got torn off a mask or something.
Looked like a scrap of Barbie ribbon to me but it meant a
lot to Doug. Doug collected bits from all over, especially in
his nomad days. Carted them all out with us in an old tin
from out his dad's lock-up, the one his dad did himself in
in. (Ugly as it sounds.) Even in the tent all through that first
lousy summer I'm trying to get over to you right now he'd
yank open the tin at sundown and lay them out neat as his
stonework tools. You know what I mean – that kind of
classy authentic junk your mum'd want to chuck if you
were a kid. A heap of really old pot bits you'd still see the
antique nail scratches in, birds' bones from the Great Sandy,
flint spear-heads that weren't, a smatch of grass from out the
Himalayas, way up, and of course all the flaming pebbles.
My favourite was the little blue glassy tear-drop, off a beach
in Guam or something. It was the shark's tooth for him.
Reminded him of surf, the big classy Aussie surf he
practically lived in after leaving college early. He never
wore a lot round his neck, though. Only that stringy snake-
skin thing from the camp at Tennant Rock. He used to kid
me mad about my feldspar. I was kind of touchy about that.

It was the Moroccan guys had the stuff, but we didn't
have the francs. Clean and dark it looked too, nice thick
cakes they'd cut with a fancy bone-handled knife and wait
for the campers to stroll over. That was the worst of it:
sitting outside that tent in over forty degrees with it sort of
wafting over all sweet and tender from the German bike
gang. If it hadn't been for the vino we'd have gone mad, I
reckon, though neither of us'd ever been ones for the
booze. That's one reason why we left Sydney. 'Come on
over and crack a tinnie, Doug and Linda!' But they didn't
really want your soul. You could leave that behind for a
start off, mate.

In the old days even the sauerkraut-munchers would've given us a flake or two for free, we both agreed, Doug and I. In the good old days. Just enough to get the dust blown off.

Times they are a-changing, all right. (Christ, we're so bloody antique!)

Doug didn't work, canned. I don't mean he couldn't hold a hammer steady or smooth out a curve or get a polish off granite that'd blind you when the sun came out – cos he could, even after an all-night barbie on Palm Beach, once. I mean his rhythm didn't work, with booze. He'd end up with this sort of snarly dog-in-a-teacup mood each night, and the booze'd leave a kind of tarty smile on his upper lip, like the shit the surf dumps up onto nice white Bondi. Wrack, to be posh about it. He'd sit with his wrists on his knees and his head hung down, like a pissed-off Buddha, and do these really loud sniffs that started out in his chest and finished up practically in his hair, hunching his shoulders high then hawking it all out. Mainly towards the sausage-munchers.

But actually, I reckon in a funny kind of way it was really at his Linda. And Alabaster. He'd look at her like she was a piece of garbo, and she'd scream so big half the flies on the camp site'd fly right into her throat. I reckon now he was getting at his dependants. As the admin guys called us – in French. 'You'd think they'd learn some bloody English,' Doug'd say, and then tear the papers up. 'You'd think they'd fuckin try!'

Anyway, there was Doug and these thousands of breeze-blocks and it almost made me want to cry, seeing him just stand there holding one like it was burning his hands to a blister. He held Alabaster like that in the first few days, but that was a kind of fear of something so bloody soft and slippy and frail he didn't know where to park himself. This was different.

I mean, Doug handling breeze-blocks. Lousy cement

breeze-blocks a kid could pick up with one finger. I ask you!

Some huge new barn or something. It was in the middle of a whole load of vineyards so I think it was meant for those really huge grape-pickers, the same as they have back home. It was depressing, stuck out there with a whole load of vines stretched out as far as the eye could see, even without Doug holding his breeze-block, and him turned to me saying at least it rained in Sydney. I really wanted to scream like Alabaster had started doing in the van, a real tonsil-whacker. Only I couldn't. And the van wasn't ours, either. Just in case you think we could've hitched up in it, instead of the camp site. The van was bloody Marcel's. It was about as bad as you could get. I said to Doug, the flaming Flintstones did better. It was like a jerry can on wheels, I said. Doug said you can't be choosy and Marcel joked about the string. It was done up like a parcel in string. Cut one knot and you'd have a nice pile of spare parts, he said. At least, that's what I think he said, his English was so bloody half-cock. We all laughed, at any rate. Laughed like there was no tomorrow or something.

The thing about Marcel, was that he gave us hope, the bastard. He fooled us stupid. Doug'd got his folder out about a minute after Marcel'd got talking to us, because it was early days then. Doug and his folder were like body and soul. They were real mates! I used to get jealous. Cross my heart, I did. Doug'd flash his folder before he'd flash me and Alabaster, if you get what I mean. We were kind of extras, while Doug's folder wasn't. It was his soul-mate, that thing.

Anyway, Marcel parked himself down on the dirt and flipped right through. This was by the camp site taps. He'd been getting some water for his jeep, he wasn't pitched there or anything like that. His jeep turned out to be one of those plastic types that shouldn't come off the beach, with no treads and about half a brake, a kind of dune buggy or something. Still, he was friendly enough, was Marcel. A native who spoke our lingo, at least, and about our vintage. A pair of rainbow thongs, cheesecloth kind of shirt, cut-away Levis. Well, he might have been one of us except he was short and scrawny and had a kind of wily French look you never see back home. And scent. Doug'd rather be dead than after-shaved, though he had a turn for patchouli oil once, behind the ears. But that was way back, when I first knew him. We were just bloody kids then, thinking the future'd be all surf and strumming. Night stars, crackle'n' pop of gum branches, cool gusts out the west, hot skin out the sea? Christ, it makes me want to weep and bloody laugh all at the same time! Doug's hair stiff and salty and loads of it then, his big hands laid on my breasts, like he was keeping them warm, zonked-out Wayne in his grandfather's bathers doing his cartwheels into the dunes and cutting his wrists on spinifex, the good dark dope, the red chunks of meat sizzling, Nan walking stark naked so the surf kind of creamed her thighs in the moonlight, then me having my visions and making up the songs, and that Tibetan wind thing of Bru's we lost one day out on Palm Beach. And it was always Doug who'd raise the tone, as my posh sister'd say. He'd always keep it kind of sturdy. The whole thing. Not just spaced out and stupid, like the Macquarie gang. But my old folks never took to Doug. He was just too Aussie native, I reckon, for them. Apart from not being mad about Jesus and all that. They'd still got half of their flaming toes in Gloucester, England. Has-betweens. Bloody has-betweens. Yeah, yeah.

Marcel had a gun, dogs, the whole works. That was weird. When we walked back with him to his vehicle the dogs barked like crazy, and it wasn't even the season. Anyway, he got Doug going at first by coming on real crazy about the stuff in the folder. He kept slapping the pages and shaking his hand all floppy at the wrist like the Frenchos do when they think something's bloody marvellous. He really seemed to go for the fancy limestone cornices on that city council pile and the granite bits Doug did for the Stock Exchange in '83, the ones that had to be curvy like billowing waves or the Opera House or something? He kept blowing on about a friend of his called Pierre and thumping his chest, so I reckoned Pierre was a bosom mate of his. I thought perhaps he was into guys, this Marcel. Then Doug went on about Pierre as well, thumping his chest like he was mad about this geezer, too. I thought, Christ, this is rather heavy – and they weren't really speaking any lingo now, only this kind of love-in for this guy Pierre. Then we went back to the jeep, as I said, and Marcel's Anglo kind of warmed up, and he was saying all the time how he could find Doug work. 'No problems', he said, and kept jerking his hand at this huge farmhouse over the road, and another the other side of the camp site, and a big old rubble-stone barn way off over the grapes, like he was saying every stone building this side of the Med is crying out for Doug to handle it, while those bloody dogs of his were wanting us for tucker and practically pulling the vehicle over, they were that keen.

I suppose we'd been about a month out by the time we met Marcel. A month's a heck of a duration, when the cash isn't coming through like you thought it would. I mean, we'd left home kind of on the hop, on a one-way ticket, just like that. You have to do this kind of thing when the energies are still high, we reckoned. We kind of woke up one morning and decided to go run for the whole thing before we could change our minds, and I suppose we'd thought the house would sell real quick, being an antique clapboarder from the time of the chain-gangs practically and the yard stuffed full of Doug's originals, the ones he'd make for his own healing, as he'd put it. I guess now people aren't as heavy on sundials and totems and runes and so on as we'd kind of thought, and the house'd got some worm or something, they said, some worm that gets really high on old timber.

Well, I reckon the real estaters were bloody Macquarie crims. Just wanted the land or something to build a poshie villa. Stuff the hippies or something. Hippies, Abos, beach-bums: it's all the same to a feller in a fancy tie and scent who hangs his shirts up. Anyway, these bloody egg-suckers did us. Just like Marcel did. And he wasn't even in sneakers.

He said he had this old van he could lend us but it wasn't for free. Oh no. Doug had to do a bit of, well, *work*. Just a bit. Like moving half a ton of slate to do up some Swiss geezer's huge vacation place near St-Jean-du-Gard, way up in the hills.

'Fuckin splendid, Linda,' Doug'd say, real knackered, 'splendid fuckin view, Linda! And boy, that slate – you should see it gleam after a soak! Blue and kind of purple – no, kind of green, kind of mulga green. Big hunks of first-class flaming slate. Snaps off the side of the hills like old bullock-shit.'

He would've laid the roof, Doug would, like a shot, but some Moroccan'd got there first and was doing it for smick, to use the French. Doug'd not had a lot to do with slate back home. It kind of gave me the heebies-jeebies, slate, the way it broke up flat as a pancake every time. I'm a limestone person myself. I think kind of soft and pale. Why Alabaster's called Alabaster, I suppose, though alabaster isn't exactly soft. Suits her, anyway, the way she talks back at me sometimes. She's, what, nearly ten now. Christ. Nearly ten. Doug'd say Doug was granite. Him and his twinkly eyes. Like mica in a block of granite.

Well, I don't know.

Doug just kind of delivered the slate and hauled it up in a bucket. That was his first job, pulling on a bloody rope, thanks to Marcel. It was all downhill from there, I suppose. At least in that one he got to handle the *real* stuff. I mean, real clean rock. The rest's dirt, Doug'd say. Bloody dirt. It had almost murdered him to see Sydney every day. All her bloody concrete and glass. 'I'm a shark in a sandwich here,

Linda. A shark in a bloody sandwich.' Then there was that
TV doc on the Med and Doug going crazy because every
house seemed to be rock, like they'd never heard of bricks,
and then the palmist.

Funny – I can't even remember what she said now, it
was so vague. But we hung on to it like a hat in a buster.

I suppose we'd still be kind of intact if we'd stayed. It's
like the whole bloody thing's just kind of split open. It's like
nothing could break us back home, down there. Out here
we went and got our faces at the wrong angle, as Doug'd
say Life just cleaved us straight through every bloody time.
That's what Doug'd start to say, anyway, flat out in the tent.
Then he'd get his hammer and big blue chisel and duck
through the flap and bash away at the dirt, just smack away
and raise a huge plume of dust. He'd make a hole the size of
a bloody rock! Then he'd put his head in. The hole, I
mean. Alabaster'd squeal like a pig. She didn't understand,
really. She thought it was a joke. She'd bang her little plastic
spade on his bum, but he didn't move. Like an ostrich,
Doug looked. The sauerkrauts'd frown. They thought he
was sick, I suppose, or canned. Them and their large bikes.
They'd give us a yell sometimes: 'Aussie Aussie Aussie, one
two sree!' Or something. They were making a joke, I
suppose. He'd stay up to half an hour like that, would
Doug. Just like an ostrich.

That was before he went on walkabout every other
bloody day.

Marcel. I was on about Marcel. Well, after that slate job
it was kind of blank for a few weeks, and Doug was going
around in the van showing his stonework folder and using
his hands. I mean, using his hands instead of words. He'd
stop at a builder's or a stonemason's or wherever he could
hear a spalling hammer at work and get out the van and find
the boss and sometimes the boss wasn't there and sometimes
they thought he was a tripper trying to find some place and
some of them didn't like what they reckoned was the hippy

look (Doug wasn't what you might call a regular user of the showers) and some of them just kind of ignored him as some type of spaced-out maniac or something and one or two looked at the folder. I reckon the stuff was too good in there, that was the trouble. It kind of freaked them out. That was stupid. I mean, it hurt Doug real bad to see a ruin. 'Look at that, Linda,' he'd say, 'it's crying out to be healed, Linda.' Or the dry-stone stuff. There was a heap of those tumbling down at the edges of fields and suchlike. Doug could've got every stone in the South of France back into place if he'd been given the chance – and enough dinero for all three of us to live on. But the stuff in the folder was too fancy, y'know? Limestone curvy cornices and billowing granite and inscriptions, that kind of stuff? Either that, or the photos had got really faded, and leaving it outside the tent one time didn't help. The sun was worse than Sydney in bloody March. It kind of just bleached out two whole pages, and one of them was that basalt deco stuff Doug did for the university library frieze in '85. Real nice detail work with the small chisel. All those teeny weeny toes on Isis and the others. I forget their names. And the Four Elements. And me up there where it went behind the Linguistics part for a couple of feet. My face. 'Like they did on the cathedrals, Linda,' he said. 'Where no one but God could see it.' My arms out wide, in a billowing dress. Behind Linguistics. He was really proud of that one. The whole frieze, I mean. He showed me my portrait in the workshop, before he fixed it up. 'Guess who, Linda,' he said, with a twinkly look. Brushing the stone-dust off it like it was a diamond or something. Me with my arms out wide, and a third eye on my forehead. Looking kind of wise, I suppose. That's when we decided to conceive. We just stood there and hugged each other like we'd only just met, and I said, 'Let's have a baby, Doug.' Christ! Tears dripping off my earlobe into the stone-dust like it was a funeral. Him with his chisel digging into my back, big and silent. Then feeling him nod. Yes, Linda. Yes yes. I bloody loved him, then.

I wouldn't have minded being seen, but there you go. Poke in the eye with a burnt stick and all that.

No, Doug's stuff was just too fancy. They could see that. It hurt their pride, I reckon. Out of their depth! Heck, just about every house out here looks as if it's kind of grown up all on its own, like a bloody cliff or something. Well, the old ones anyway. But that was what Doug went for, what he was kind of searching for all his life, really, that organic look. He'd never been one for straight lines!

Then Marcel pops up again like a bad smell. I can see it all now, of course, like it's hitting me in the face. I mean, see what I couldn't see then. The jeep sweeps up and scatters a few Norwegians or something and there's Marcel in a cloud of dust. Jesus, it was hot. I was feeling pretty stuffed off with the whole thing, really. Well, I'd kind of imagined the Frenchos all dusted over with stonework and waving their chisels or something and hugging Doug like an old mate and us gazing at the Med from a café table like they showed in the TV doc, with all these houses like cliffs in the background, making Doug feel he'd come home. But all we'd got so far was a lousy camp site and a whole load of bikers and you couldn't see the beach for the ten-berthers parked and anyway, the first time we went Alabaster picked up a syringe instead of a nice shell. And no bloody work. And only Marcel seemed to have what you might call the international lingo. We'd never have believed it. I mean, even the Krauts could say, 'We have a good laugh, yes?' Or something. But the Frenchos spoke French like they were fucked if they were going to speak anything else, mate. They made you feel like a real dag. Well, that's what I felt, anyway.

'Good on yourself, mate,' said Marcel, with his kind of slippery grin, and kissed me on each cheek about ten times.

Doug'd been teaching him a bit through that slate job. The lingo, not the kissing.

'Mates aren't Sheilas,' I said, checking up on my cheeks because Marcel wasn't what you might call a close shaver.

'Where ees your darling Dog?' said Marcel, glancing around and fiddling with his little wrist-chain thing like I was about to grab it or something.

'My Dog's gone walkabout,' I said. 'You've come for your van, I suppose.' I heard Alabaster start to scream then and I had to go over to the Danish family. They were kind of really helpful looking after her but they had this whole load of fancy picnic stuff, all royal blue china and so on, and Alabaster just couldn't handle it. It would've been better had they kept right out of it, really, because I just got so tense, watching them trying to keep Alabaster from yanking off the tablecloth – all of them trying to kind of distract her in a really nice way, which she always reacts badly to. Not that I'm strict or anything – it's just that I don't have any classy breakables around. People make life really hard for themselves.

Anyway, Alabaster had just smashed a Danish coffee-pot or something, and they were all kind of trying to calm her right down, bending over her and kind of flapping their hands like they wanted her to waft up like a feather and I could see the adults were really freaked out but trying not to show it. So I came up and started tickling Alabaster under the armpits and she let go of the cloth and stopped screaming. So that was all right.

Then I looked up and there was Marcel, standing right next to me with an arm out and a couple of dineros flapping on the end of it (there was a bit of a buster at the time, blowing the dust about). He was kind of like Napoleon or someone, looking real important. The Danish mother (Kristin, or Kursten, something like that) looked at the francs and then at Marcel and then at me, real puzzled. Then she shook her head and raised her hands up and laughed while Marcel kind of waved these notes around and kept on jerking his head.

Now this was a real sticky one, because our cash wasn't exactly what you might call fluid. I didn't want Marcel to bale us out, but I didn't want us to pay for the coffee-pot and go without a feed for a week or so sooner. So I just kind of walked out of it. Lousy, I felt, doing that. A real scumbag.

At any rate, I didn't see what happened in the end. I didn't want to know. But the funny thing was that the Danish crowd packed up that day and left without saying cheerio. I reckon they'd taken the money and felt kind of scummy as well.

Anyway, Marcel came straight back and sat down on Doug's little canvas fold-up.

I didn't say thanks or anything. I just left it.

He lit up a French smoke, the type that Doug reckons smells sexy, and did some coin flipping to get Alabaster laughing or something. He'd slap his wrist and the coin'd go right up, and Alabaster'd try to catch it. She'd be really whingy all day long, and then Marcel'd do his coin flips and she'd be like honey. He had a real way with kids. Anyway, I was folding up loads of clothes after the last wash. Well, it was hell to keep anything even half bloody clean then, with all the flaming dust around and the camp taps always looking like they'd just come out of a swamp or something. So we didn't say a thing for a good while and then he cleared his throat and spat and said he'd got a number one job for Doug.

'Oh yes?'

'*Oui oui*', he said, which always made Alabaster split herself. 'Zertenlee, Linda.'

I looked at him and I could see his hand was trembling, the one with the smoke in it. The other one was pushing back his hair, which looked a bit tinted, actually. He was a

real scrawn, Marcel was. He had rings in both ears, too,
now I think of it.

'What kind of job, Marcel?'

Marcel coughed and pulled on his cigarette and said it
was a Doug kind of job, some big barn in a vineyard or
something, with smoke coming out of his mouth as he said
it, kind of crawling out. I really hate that, I don't know
why. It's probably to do with my parents being far-out
Christians or something.

'*Ouvrage de pierre*', he said. Never any mention of bloody
breeze-blocks, I can tell you.

That bloke again, I thought. Even Marcel couldn't speak
straight Anglo for more than ten seconds. Well, I hardly
knew a word then.

'Who's this Pierre, Marcel?' I said. 'Who's Pierre?'

Weird, isn't it? – but I'd not asked Doug before. I forget
things. Doug blames the crazy days out in Adelaide, when
we used to take the little round white Bus Australia, as he
used to put it. My mind kind of hits blank patches. It kind
of lets go now and again.

Marcel laughed like a bloody hyena.

I asked him what was so bloody funny. Then Doug came
round the corner from wherever he'd gone to, first thing
that morning.

'Good on you, mate,' said Marcel, putting his hand out.
At least he didn't kiss Doug. Quite a few of the French guys
do that, even the old ones.

Doug just stood there. He was carrying a load of peaches
in a big brown paper bag. I could tell they were peaches
because of the wet kind of red patches where Doug'd held
the bag a bit too tight. Peaches were practically free just
then, and there were a whole load of stones around the tent.
Peach-stones, I mean. Doug'd just sit there and work his
way through peaches each night like he was going for a
competition or something. I mean, you only had to blow
on those peaches and the skins'd kind of wrinkle away from

the flesh, they were so bloody ripe! Anyway, he held the bag against his chest with his left hand and the other one took Marcel's and it was amazing – it was like Marcel's kind of disappeared for a minute while Doug gave it a good jerk. I thought that's how people see Doug and me, probably: I just kind of disappear next to this bloody huge monument. I've always been kind of small, but anyone would be small next to Doug. Doug was built too large for this world, that's what I reckon. That was half the problem, probably. France was like the Danish family's fancy picnic table or something, for Doug.

So Marcel's hand comes out again looking kind of stunned and then Doug says to him, 'Marcel, you're a fuckin sleazebag. Do you know that? A fuckin sleazebag, Marcel.'

Marcel kind of spreads his hands out like the Crucifixion and his lips go all pouty ready to say something I suppose but Doug says, 'Here, have a bloody peach, Marcel.'

And Doug plops a really huge peach onto Marcel's head, so it kind of sits there like a fat type of red toad or something, juice dripping off the end of Marcel's earlobes. Or rather, off the end of his nice gold rings. Alabaster gets kind of hysterical, of course, and Doug goes into the tent while I think: heck, this Marcel's going to have to handle this like bone bloody china. Though Doug's hardly ever swiped a soul before. I mean, he's only hit me once in his life, and that was after a really bad trip way back in the Adelaide days.

But Marcel just takes the peach off his head real slow and I think: hell, he's not quite such a dag after all, this Marcel. And he kind of looks at the squished-up peach in his hand, real sticky, and he just goes 'hm'. Just like that. 'Hm'. Almost like he was *agreeing* with Doug. I thought: I wouldn't like to be Marcel's barber right now. I really thought that! Stupid. Then Doug appears again with our pail half-full of frothy old smelly water from my clothes

82

wash and says to Marcel, 'Heck, Marcel, you look as if you
need a real good shower.' And I thought: Christ, he's going
to tip the whole lot over Marcel's head. We're going to
have a real heavy blue on our hands if this goes on much
further. And Marcel must've been thinking this too,
because he was already sort of half off the canvas fold-up
grinning like a maniac while Doug's raising up the pail and
Marcel ducks and sort of waddles away a bit with his arms
right out and he's not got that far when Doug lets him have
it – with all that smelly old water shooting out the pail and
most of it hitting Marcel's back, smack! Making him look
even scrawnier than usual.

'Why'd you do that, Doug?' I said, kind of lightly.

Doug said, 'I don't like pervs.'

Marcel was looking really hard at his cigarette. I think he
couldn't give a fuck about his wet clothes, because it was
real hot, but he was kind of upset by his damp smoke.

'What d'you mean, Doug?' I said.

'What I mean,' said Doug, 'is I don't like pervs.'

'I don't think he wants the van back, Doug.'

Actually, the van'd just gone crook, and sounded like it
had a pregnant elephant instead of a carbie, but we weren't
telling Marcel that just yet, or he might've gone funny and
blamed us.

Doug sat down on the canvas fold-up like he wanted to
flatten it. Some of the other campers were glancing over. I
guess things over our way looked kind of interesting.
Marcel started to walk away without looking back, which
rather surprised me. I didn't like him much, but he was
kind of our one and only friend. Well, if you didn't count
our neighbours and the weird old French guy with the
mangy goat on a rope we were always trying to shake off by
the telephone booth, he was the only bloody one! Marcel
was the only one who'd got Doug a job, anyway. And he'd
lent us the van. I mean, you've got to start somewhere. As

Doug'd say: 'We're on a one-way ticket, Linda.' Which was literally true.

I gave Alabaster a banana and parked myself down by Doug. We heard the jeep start up and leave like he had to get somewhere yesterday.

'He was only saying hello, Doug. Hello there. *Bonjour*. I know it looked like he was making love or something, Doug, but it's not like it is back home, out here. Anyway, I reckon he's into guys, Doug. That scent. Earrings. And all that Pierre stuff, Doug.'

I put my hand on Doug's knee. It looked bloody stupid, I thought, my teeny weeny hand on Doug's really huge knee. I wanted to cry. I started to wish we'd never bloody left Australia. Alabaster'd finished her banana and she started to whinge again, so I gave her a tiny slap and she went off screaming. I put my face in my hands. I felt depressed, actually, but I couldn't let myself go under. I had to support Doug. I screwed up my eyes and thought of that figure behind Linguistics. That was me. In basalt. Real strong and all that, arms out wide. It didn't matter if no one could see her. I was still there, fuck it.

Doug just kind of stared out at the vineyards, like a monument.

I stood up and spread my arms out wide and stayed like that for about a minute. Then I sat down again on the ground next to Doug. I felt better.

'He came to say he'd got you a first-class job, Doug. Stonework. A big barn. Some really huge barn for a vineyard or something. I feel this is it, Doug. I feel you've got to swallow your pride and phone Marcel, Doug. That's what I feel, anyway.'

He did. That was what was so big about Doug. He never kind of rested on his pride or anything. He got up and phoned him. Phoned Marcel.

SAWMILL

This was how Mason lost his arm.

He told me about it himself in the sweep-out from Mahongo, after the Mba rebellion spilled down from the mountains. Those were gorilla rather than guerrilla mountains, as a matter of fact. Big hairy creatures with liquid eyes – very cautious, only violent at the last resort – lived in there amongst the big leaves and liana. The peaks were in cloud most of the time, and the ground underfoot squelched on the lower slopes, where the rifts and folds were full of fog and a heat clammier even than Mahongo's. Then you'd get keen types going up in a T-shirt and almost freezing to death at night, soaked to the skin by a precipitation that was chill and perpetual.

From my window you could see the peaks beyond the forest, rising up into a lid of cloud. I'd found an old copy of Stanley's book on the Congo in the Club's cupboard, and read what he had to say about equatorial Africa (copying out the long words I hadn't heard before: I was educating myself). He said the light was solemn and frigid, and made the bush look flat, as if the equator's sun knew no angles, shining down from the mid-belt of the planet through a gauze of dust or of moisture. He said it made the bush look merciless, primal, pre-human. I couldn't see this; to me the light was part of the difference that Africa made to me. She made me grow against the harshness and the luxuriance of her, and the light was both those things. I mentioned this once to the DO's assistant, when the show was on the road and passing through Mahongo; he was an educated chap, and reckoned that Stanley saw in Africa what he couldn't face up to in himself.

'What's that?' I asked, still in my eager period.

'A total lack of human sympathy. Complete egotism. An unpleasant streak of sadism.'

I nodded. That was the first time I had ever thought of Stanley as anything but heroic. But Africa does that to her white visitors; it draws out of you what you had never even looked at back home.

That's why I'm not so sure about Mason's story any more. It sounds like a justification, a type of excuse. But I'll tell it to you anyway, because I've started.

Mason was by now the manager at our newest sawmill. He was in his forties. He'd taken a long time to get to this position. He'd come out very young – at least twenty years before independence – as a mechanic's mate; turning bolts, greasing gears, steel-brushing rusted bits. This kept him busy, as metal no sooner touches this climate than it starts to corrode. He was already a drinker, and spent most of his free time down at the English Club in Kasa, the next stop on the tooth-loosening dirt track coming south out of Mahongo. You know what they say about us: wherever there's an Englishman, you'll find a garden; wherever there are two Englishmen, you'll find a Club. Mason started this Club with Jack Mole, the sawmill's chief engineer. They both hailed from Matlock, by sheer chance, and had been brought up two streets from each other without knowing it. That Club was a kind of glorified Scotch Club, no more than an old dilapidated shack from the coffee-growing era with some tatty old wicker chairs they'd filched from somewhere; but it was legendary all the way to the coast for its conviviality and high stakes on the gaming table. It was finally closed by orders of the sawmill's manager, after Mason had lost his young *bibi* to Jack Mole at bridge. The manager could stomach money being gambled, but not people – not even pagans, because he was a young, up-to-date type. Mason's attitude was as cold and hard as Stanley's: these people were there to be used, and if they weren't used they were in the way. One day he struck a black worker several times over the head with a bamboo cane for some minor infringement, and the worker sued him, because suing people is as normal as eating out there. Mason was moved to another sawmill, nearer Mahongo, owned by the same company. Because this was a bigger affair, he was quite happy.

Why wasn't he sacked?

Because he was never sick, never wobbly one week out of every month, like the rest of us; took twenty minutes off for lunch to our two hours; could repair anything that moved, even without the necessary spare parts (which were usually sent out late or got stolen on the way); and never lost a certain cheery grin, even in the rainy season. Now and then, when something finally got to him, he would crack – disappear for a day or two with a couple of bottles of Scotch, or get violent. To the company, that was better than the sluggishness, the gloom and the nonchalance, the plop-plop-plop of the mind rotting down that afflicted the rest of us half the time.

I was the company's junior clerk, at the time Mason was transferred. Gleaming wet behind the ears, fresh from a bank in Chepstow, I was already training locals to take over my job. It was a strange era: there were all these nationalist movements, tribal movements, peasant movements, communist movements and so forth, which we were told was part of the process towards self-government. It felt like anarchy to me, and I feared what would happen when we left. But the clever, university types kept quoting the UN Charter of '45 and rabbiting on about democratisation and such things at parties (when they weren't fuming about something or other), so I shut up. The company had its concession off the government, which was by now an

87

executive council with an African prime minister and ministers, so we had to go along with the general policy. We assumed that this concession (and we had it for thirty years) would be transferred intact once proper self-government had happened; there was so much virgin forest at this time, it felt like we were nibbling at its hem. There was room for everyone. Felling the bush meant clear-felling for farming land: it was all part of the civilising process. We were helping the natives; even when a road was cut, it had squatters either side of it, cutting a mile deeper in to plant their millet. We didn't throw them off, but we took the timber. What I can't stand about ecologists is their hypocrisy: do *they* leave the brambles and nettles standing in their back gardens? Five thousand years ago, Britain was a great wodge of forest from end to end; the trees started at each cliff-edge, and met in the middle without a break. One great wood, as dark and humid as the rain-forest, if not as hot. God knows how it was ever cleared with nothing but antler-picks and brawn. Getting rid of a big tree, roots and all, is one of the hardest things a man can do, even with a caterpillar tractor and a donkey-winch. They got rid of millions, and it was just as wet then as it is now, so they can't have fired them. Perhaps they had Mason.

Whatever, without that great feat our island wouldn't be where it is now. And who are we to deny those fruits to Africans? If most of the areas we cleared out there weren't, in the end, farmed, but left for the rain to wash away, was it our fault?

After seven years on that sawmill, ending up as its chief mechanic, the miracle happened: a brand new site was established seventy-five miles west of Mahongo, where the forest had more than its fair share of ebony, mansonia, yellow-wood (West African teak), red-heart, and some big mahogany. There were no villages in that sector to speak of. And Mason was appointed manager.

He was the only one who could take it on. The place

was in a gloomy rift on the lower slopes, teeming with tsetse, and shrouded most of the time in fog. It was too wet to do any kiln-drying, let alone air-drying, and some of us wondered why they couldn't just pull out the logs and have them sawn down our way; but the powers-that-be decided that they would be trucked out of there as boards. Later, I learned that the whole project was Mason's idea in the first place, shared with a visiting director (Bob Clifford, I think) over a beer in the club late one night. Mason had driven over there one weekend, on a recce, and had climbed up above the mist. He could see the mahoganies sticking up out of the white, rolling sea like the grey masts of drowned ships. It was a beautiful sight, he said: he felt like he'd stumbled on gold.

Real gold – and diamonds – were being stumbled on, deeper into the interior; but we were timber men. The mining men were different. They were saggy and stubbled, spending their time scratching about in the dirt (or ordering others to). There was a pecking order, and timber came above gold or diamonds, and those came above rutile or manganese. That's the way we saw it, anyway. There is nothing in the mining line to compare with a big tree slowly crashing down out of the sky, letting the sun in like a blade.

All Mason's men were black, and pagan. He liked it that way: he could boss them about, rib them, chide them in the way he reckoned they understood and appreciated. They were good, well-trained men, because Mason had learned his stuff off the Canadians – huge, hard-drinking lumber-jacks the company hired in the early days to teach the ropes. He not only practically built the place single-handed, it was said, but hand-picked his team. Keeping the Christian ones out also kept the missionaries out. Mason's view of missionaries was unprintable.

But his real secret, I reckon, was to keep his cheery grin glued to his face, whatever – even when he was screaming

89

at someone. You know what the Africans say about the crocodile? They say it's the only animal that smiles when it kills. They called Mason *Pa Croc*, informally. But Pa is a term of respect, and the croc is worshipped when it's not being speared or shot, so Mason liked his nickname. Even his teeth, on the odd occasion he came down to Mahongo and met me for a beer, seemed to have grown bigger and yellower.

The timber that came out of there was stupendous: it was all the lorries' suspension could do not to crack under its weight, but that was partly because it was still green. He liked to drive the odd lorry himself, to Mahongo; then he'd hand over to the white tough perched next to him, who'd take it all the way to the company's big air-drying yard on the coast, next to the port at Korondi. They were incredible, those drivers: hulks who'd keep going twelve hours over roads more pot-holes than surface, splattered head to foot in copper-coloured mud or caked in dust (depending on the season), arriving at the port with a thirst for beer and whores sufficient to knock a sailor out of the running, plunging into the thundering ocean for a wash then sleeping in their cabs under the coconut palms like babies. We trusted them purely, even as we feared them. Mason knew some of those old trucks from his earliest days, and liked to have them banging and jolting under him occasionally, the timber stretched out for an infinity behind his neck. Mahogany and red-heart and mansonia and ebony, barked and sawn and gleaming under their chains, smelling sweet and rich and full. Our own two operations (I was head clerk for the whole circuit, by now) were pulling out saplings in comparison. Mason's team were clear-cutting up a valley said to be the haunt of a giant gorilla twenty feet tall. Looking at what came bouncing on the back of those Fodens down Mahongo's main street, I could well believe it.

'It's like the nicest, fattest, softest *bibi* you've ever had,' he

said to me one time, under the crooked fan at the Union
Jack Club. His big, red face (the only brown he ever
acquired was off the trees' juice) shone with pleasure as
much as perspiration. There were leaves in his hair, thinned
and paled from the bright ginger mop even I remembered,
and the hairs on his forearms were white with sawdust. He's
a completely satisfied man, I thought – in a land of chronic
frustration, sickness and resentment. Africa doesn't wear
him down: it plumps him. He draws her into his squat,
square body, and feeds off her greedy juices as mosquitoes
feed off the rest of us. (I never knew him once to get bitten
by anything except the touring DO's pet spaniel.)

I smiled, and asked him how, without real women, he
kept the team happy up there in that God-forsaken place.
He told me he'd introduced a recreational pursuit from
Derbyshire pubs – the Derbyshire pubs of his youth, I
suppose. There were lots of forest rats in the sawmill camp,
like there'd been lots of rats in Matlock, big ones from the
barns. You fastened a live rat to a hook in the middle of a
round table, giving it just enough run not to slip off the
edge. Someone tied your hands behind your back. The
spectators then laid wagers on whether you could kill the rat
inside so many minutes, using nothing but your teeth.

They kept the rats in cages, up in the sawmill. This
classified them as pets, and somehow appeased the more
fearful pagans, who were afraid they might be haunted by
the rat's spirit or double or whatever. Every Saturday night
they had a rat massacre, he said, and everyone's mouth was
bright with blood. They drank beer, but not too much. A
drunk man would have his nose bitten off. You drank
enough to give you courage. Mason said that his name, Pa
Croc, was more than justified by his performance.

'Do you have any fights between the men?' I asked,
feeling a little shaken.

'That's the point of it,' he said. 'Keeps us happy and

peaceful all week, like a lengthy bash with a top-quality whore. Takes the lid off.'

My own experience of the whores in Mahongo or on the coast was slight, but if it involved a bed you were lucky. By now I had a native girl, a *bibi*, so my seedy days were over. She was exceptionally beautiful, to my mind, and her skin was more indigo than black; she stayed in a hut behind my shack of a house and came to me at night. If it had been acceptable, socially, I might have married her. But I was keen to move up in those circles and had my eye on a colleague's sister, who'd come out to visit him recently. She was called Gillian, and was as white and cool as the inside of a cucumber, which for some reason made my blood pressure rise in the romantic way. We wrote to each other, anyway, and she was impressed by my long words, words like 'assiduously' and 'attenuating' and 'antithesis' (I logged them in my pocket-book, until the ants got it). I took her out to the films on my two-yearly leaves, just about getting to the petting stage – but she didn't know about my *bibi*. She married someone called Dudley Baugh in the end, when I was about to come home and propose with the help of a malachite brooch set in freshly minted gold. When I heard, I chucked it into the smelly creek where the mangroves start. Propitiation, they call it.

It was from my *bibi* that I heard the story of Mason's arm, that's why I mention her. I had got her brother a job as a cook up in the camp, and he eventually told her the truth. If it wasn't for certain other facts, I'd have assumed it was an ordinary accident: limbs, or bits of limbs, were lost like shillings on Club bridge night amongst the sawmill opera-tors. In those days, we were more lax about safety regs, I suppose. It was all part of the harshness, the luxuriance, as fever and the bloody runs were. I'd been hit by malaria five times, despite being careful with the chloroquine, and I looked older than my thirty-odd, by now. The joke went that you lost weight twice in our company – once with fever, and once by having a bit lopped off, so you had to make it up with your belly. Another joke: this worker sits too close to the head-saw and loses a buttock. Big Chief Barney 'Barking' Soames (the top man at HQ for years) comes up just after and wonders why the feeder's stopped running. The manager says: 'I'm getting behind with my orders.' We thought up lots like that over our beers and whiskies, but those are the only two I can bring to mind, at present.

Odd reports were coming out of Mason's mill. For a few months, the logs and planks had diminished. One week had passed without anything at all, and then a truck had arrived with a few lengths of poor quality, warped *musonga* banging about on the flat-bed. The driver reckoned that there were still enough big trees left in the rift to keep a saw busy for years, and that the forest track was in as good a condition as any track can be expected to be in a wet equatorial belt. But the machinery was in poor shape – at least the head-saw, the main circular one, kept breaking down, the feeder repeatedly jammed, the generator expired twice while he was there and even the gas cylinder in the kitchen-house had blown up (my *bibi*'s brother was unhurt).

I asked him how Mason was taking this.

'Badly,' he replied. 'His cheery grin's still on him, but I think he's going to crack.'

'Why do you think he's going to crack?'

'He told me to fetch him a white goat. It's got to be white. All the goats up there, the ones that haven't been eaten by leopards, are black-and-white or brown. Funny voice, he had, when he said it. Like he was somewhere else.'

This was certainly *not* a sign that he was about to crack, if the mechanical faults were sabotage, as we reckoned they must be. Mason knew what he was doing: he was appeasing the gods and spirits of the forest he was cutting down – in other words, appeasing his own men. All our sawmills had been through this fairly messy business, before they started operating properly, or when a big saw was replaced. The BOB, or Bloody Old Baptism, we called it. An albino goat was tied onto the feeder and fed alive onto the saw. To hear the poor animal bleat like pity as the feeder jolted it along, and then explode into blood and gore as the saw's teeth met its stomach, made me feel sick, frankly. It didn't even have time to scream. When I first came out, the DO would stay away from the ceremony. Now, with all this Africanisation business, he'd feel it incumbent on him to attend, his immaculate whites far enough away not to get spotted. The DO's pretty little wife came once, and surprised us by taking a photograph instead of fainting. 'A fascinating traditional custom' she called it. I called it barbarity, but not to her face.

The albino goat was sent up after a couple of weeks of official flaffing about (YCHA, or You Can't Hurry Africa), and then there was silence. I was asked to pay a visit, as the circuit clerk in charge of accounts and a personal friend of Mason's. I should have looked forward to it, but I didn't. I wasted a couple of days when my works Land Rover broke down after fifty miles and had to be towed back by a passing truck. The road was pretty bad – it was mid-May, and the first big drench had hit us – but the Land Rover made it a second time. What was worrying us was that Mason should have been sending down all the green stock he'd pulled out for the last two months, before it started to warp and the summer downpour made the road pretty well impassable, at least for laden trucks. Instead, there had been next to nothing since January.

I arrived in a more than light drizzle, and actually felt chilled. I hadn't realised it was so high above sea level. The valley stretched away and up like a fold out of Hell: coppery green gloom, full of writhing mist, a great ruck in the moss that was the far tops of a million trees so high that it made you giddy when you were underneath them, looking up. I thought of big black gorillas skulking unseen in there, and shivered under my umbrella. Running across the puddles to the main block – no more than the standard long tin shed on a concrete base – I thought I saw something white skipping about beyond the head-saw's housing. Well, if he hadn't sacrificed the goat, the spanners would go on being dropped in the works. But I couldn't spot a single worker. Not one. The place looked abandoned. This actually frightened me in some way. I'd expected to come up here into a welcoming bustle and screech of activity. Instead, there were soggy hills of sawdust, countless strewn branches, and rain-blackened logs casually thrown around the place, along with some green slabs and boards that were starting to writhe, they were so moist.

It looked as if something really extraordinary had happened: Mason had gone to seed.

I would have been surprised if he, of all people, had started this place with a team of pagans without baptising it in the native manner, but the ceremony hadn't been reported and none of us had been notified, let alone the DO's office. It had been going great guns for two years, this mill, until around January. The head-saw was the original one. So it should have been. Even this climate couldn't do much to that principal item of equipment, if it was kept properly oiled and greased – and all ours sharpened and cleaned themselves on the wood. These were the thoughts going through my head as I found the shelter of the main block. But if that white glimpsed thing was the goat, they didn't add up. Nothing added up – but that was not an unusual situation for Africa, even for the chief clerk in charge of accounts. As long as Mason hadn't run off into the bush, or been carved up by the insurgents who were already active, so we were told, a hundred miles to the north of here, I'd presumably have the adding up done for me by the man himself.

I couldn't find him.

The generator was still happily humming, which reminded me of the German helmet I'd found rocking by the chessboard during our lot's advance through Normandy some ten years earlier. So I radioed HQ.

'I know it sounds what you might call preposterous, but I can't find Mason.'

'Can't find him?'

'I think he might have gone bush-happy for a bit. He's done it before. The trouble is, there's no one else here but the albino goat. If he does come back, he'll have to hire a whole team and recommence.'

HQ were both furious and heartbroken, of course. By the time I'd made it back with a raging fever that sprang onto me halfway along that bloody awful road, all sticky clay and brackish puddles brimming into rivulets you could drown a kid in, they were elated. He'd radioed at dusk, just as I was staggering into the mission hospital on the Mahongo road for a shot. (I'd driven, there and back, in a single day, one hundred and fifty-five miles, give or take a pot-hole the size of my bed.)

He'd cleared up a sticky matter, he claimed. Or he was about to clear it up, in a couple of days, at dawn. There was no question of getting another team: his team were all there, present and correct. HQ probably doubted the tightness of my screws for a moment, even before they knew the state of my temperature, because they double-checked with him that the place had been left empty. He agreed that it had, but only for the day. If the timber wasn't all delivered by the time the storms were on us, and the road was a stream (if there was a road left at all), he'd offer his resignation.

I'd sweated out my malarial bout (brought on by the camp's chill, I suppose), by sundowner-time the following evening, but was still a touch wobbly when, a couple of days later, the rumour circulated in the office, confirmed in the Club, that Mason had been brought into the mission hospital with his arm cut off at the elbow. A rough tourniquet of oily wipes and a bandage of same had saved him from bleeding to death, but he wasn't in a fit state to be talked to after the bone-rattling journey in one of his own little bush-wagons, thrashed nigh to its component parts by a terrified chief mechanic. The oil had acted as a disinfectant (Mason was legendarily careless about his medical equipment, and had nothing more than a packet of Elastoplast and some Epsom's beyond the resident stack of chloroquine), and he was up and about within a matter of days. He was pretty jolly, given his trauma and permanent handicap, but his cheery grin had changed to a sort of knowing smile. It made me wonder if he hadn't got his own supply of hashish. He hadn't had that sort of quiet knowingness before: a cheery vigour, yes, and what the supply manager at HQ referred to as Mason's Mania (meaning an incredible ability to work in torpid heat without wiping one's brow, let alone dropping – usually the first sign that the 'bitch' had got you, and you were about to go bonkers), but not that deep sort of knowingness, not that eerie kind of quiet smile.

Sure enough, even before he was back at his post a week or two later, the timber started rolling in. By the time the rains were playing the devil's tattoo on our tin rooves ten times over each week, the bulk of it was stacked in the kilns and my accounts were looking very rosy, thank you. Now, I assumed that Mason had done something really extraordinary: I assumed – and my version took the Club by stealth, rather than storm, so I had it told back to me by seedy old bores like Bill Price the cocoa trader, or 'Ambling' Ambrose from the manganese-ore outfit past the scruffy lean-tos on the edge of town – that Mason had baptised the blade with his own blood, had sacrificed his own limb. Incredible as this seemed to anyone who didn't know Mason, my version was mostly met by modest nods from those who did. It turned him into something truly legendary.

Then my *bibi* received a visit from her brother just before Christmas (all the workers had a couple of weeks' leave a year), and my version was proven quite dull, compared to the reality. By cobbling together her brother's account, and dovetailing it with Mason's own story (told to me while fleeing Mahongo in poor old Ambrose's Humber Snipe), I've reached a pretty reliable explication that adds up in all essential details.

This, then, is how Mason lost his arm.

There was a huge grey mahogany in the centre of the valley, easily the tallest, reaching up for the light and, once there, carrying on for another few floors so it ended up towering over the rest. It was the big cherry, was how Mason put it. It was the big prize, one for the timber-trade's record books. It made you giddy just looking up at it, and took two minutes to circle – running. There was a snag: the locals – there were a few pigmy-like locals, scattered about in the hills, in their tatty little clusters of huts, without even a loin-cloth to their name – told one of the workers that this tree was sacred to them. Mason had clear-cut right up to its outlying branches. Everything was ready: the chains, the saws, the ropes, the vehicles, the grabs, men, the lot. He'd heard rumours, of course, for some weeks, that there might be a lot of palaver if he cut this particular tree, but he'd been confronted by this nervous type of superstitious-ness before, and had overridden it by a mixture of guile and sheer white-man's will.

Then the locals appeared from the trees. They had their sorcerer with them, dressed in a devil's mask that came down to his knees, who actually spat through the mouth-hole at Mason before going into this mad, wild dance around the mahogany. The workers fled, and since the pigmy types were armed with poison-tipped arrows, Mason retreated too.

He waited a few days, clear-felled right round the tree and for a mile into the tangle beyond – and then offered his men a deal: if they cut the mahogany, he would protect them with his own magic. He produced a wad of greasy old pound notes from his wallet and waved them in their faces. Greed vied with superstition, and greed won (as it always does). Of course, he had to add to the cash-till magic with a touch of indigenous stuff, some home-made mumbo-jumbo involving a strangled cockerel and mashed palm-leaves and milk, but it was the extra pay that did the trick.

Very early, just before dawn, the air still chilly and the mist just stirring from the ground or the air or wherever it comes from, the team crept out to the big tree, tied the chains and set the teeth of the biggest two-man handsaw against it. Not using a mechanised saw was Mason's wheeze; he didn't want to be a poison-quilled porcupine. But just in case the locals noticed the tip thrashing about, or a sudden absence of their 'steeple' (as Mason himself described it), he set a few workers about as guards, clutching rusty old Lee Enfields sent up from the company store.

The double handsaw squealed and squeaked, others took over, it jammed, Mason fixed the problem without even swearing, the tree moaned and groaned and shivered, then fell down with the most colossal crash that made the ground bounce under their shoes like rubber. Its resident bird-life fled in great flocks, leaving only a few multi-coloured feathers floating down. What seemed like a hundred screeching monkeys had leapt as it fell, finding no nearby branches and so mostly breaking their necks – or finding a softer landing on some of the workers, who screeched likewise, picked themselves up, and fled. Caterpillars, moths, spiders the size of plates, armies of ants – these all spilled out in an instant panic, causing consternation among the men. A little bush-baby was picked up, petrified with terror, clutching Mason's thumb with its miniature mitts.

(He kept it as a souvenir, but it died a couple of days later.) No locals appeared, however, and the tree was cut into lengths, to be hauled away.

The saw jammed. The chains broke. The biggest caterpillar tractor steamed to a stop. A donkey-winch somehow slipped into a swampy patch, bubbling under for good. By twilight, in a dense rainy fog, only one section had made it over the clear-cut's churn of mud to the stack. The next day, a bolt behind the gang-saw flew off and practically brained one of the mechanics. The feeder jammed on a perfectly ordinary load of red-heart and then, when started up again, smoked like a charcoal fire. Three of Mason's best workers were suddenly crippled by yaws, and the chief hauler appeared to have yellow jack. The camp overseer was bitten by a green mamba and was only saved by prompt action from his boss. Then the gas bottle blew up, setting the kitchen alight, while my *bibi*'s brother was stirring the *fu-fu* in the yard. On the third day, the generator clicked and gave out, plunging the camp into darkness. The paraffin lamps were extinguished in a bone-chilling down-pour at midnight, some actually losing their glass to thermal shock. The black clouds broke dramatically and revealed the most enormous full moon above the nearest peak, which loomed in the shape of a vast and hairy man – a gorilla, Mason thought, complete with gleaming eyes from some effect of moonlight on the canopy's leaves, or the rocks beyond the tree line.

The workers knew what it was, of course. But you can't put a felled tree back. As Mason himself said, it's like sticking back a limb, or going back in time. Two, three, four centuries, perhaps more. He found himself waking up at night, sweating like a pig behind his mosquito net, out of a real corker of a nightmare involving spiders, leopards, and gorillas with devil-masks. A storm cracked over them like the sky was a giant nut, and blew the tin roof off the saw-housing; the tin roof beheaded the camp mongrel and embedded itself in the mahogany log. Lightning lit up the scene and workers claimed to have spotted blood flowing from the log's bark and rippling towards them.

Basically, the whole site was a seethe of panic. Mason's very good in these situations: he offered to cleanse the place with a sacrifice. His resident medicine man consulted his oracle and reckoned that only the flesh and blood of something white would do. Mason nodded benignly and ordered up the albino goat. The goat arrived but on spending its last night in the compound, mysteriously acquired yellow patches on its flanks. The other resident soothsayer consulted his grains again and reckoned that only something black would do. The first agreed (he must have been in a bad way), and added that this something would only be found in the forest. Mason is a great layer of traps as well as an excellent hunter, and gambled that he could come back with something suitable. He went out to where he had set them a couple of days before, followed by the whole team, who were by now convinced the place was full of spirits intent on their destruction. That was, then, the day I arrived and found the mill and the camp deserted.

In the first trap they found the paw of a mongoose. It was blackish, but neither medicine man would accept it as satisfactory. In the second there was nothing. In the third, set quite deep into the uncut gloom, there was a small, black, hairy lump which whimpered. It was a young gorilla – not much more than a baby, caught by its foot. The workers reckoned it had been delivered by the mother, in obedience to the forest spirits, or the ghost of the mahogany tree itself. They were eager for their pounds, of course. The resident sorcerers nodded excitedly. It was black, and might be the child of the giant hairy man, who was in turn the mountain's child. Mason looked up, through a slash in the canopy, at the peak. A rare ray of sun had lit it. Its dark, bare crest had turned golden. He carried the whimpering bundle himself back to the camp.

'If I hadn't had to wait until the stipulated dawn, I'd still have the one to go with him,' he said, waving his right hand about, when he was telling me all this.

The Humber had stopped in a cloud of dust caused by a stream of trucks and mammy-wagons temporarily snarled up in our mass exodus. People were clinging to the sides, or on top of bundles and suitcases and other people where logs or cocoa sacks usually went, or gossips on their way to market. Mason leant out of the window to shout: great barrel chest, hairy shoulders, singlet black with exertion all the way down the spine. I suddenly found him repulsive – maybe because I was moving up in the world, and wearing a club tie even at the worst of times, which was now. I was fleeing Mahongo with nothing more than a spare set of clothes and my accounts books on the back seat, but I had donned my tie. That back seat was where Ambrose had had his heart attack in front of the Friendly Stores just the day before, when someone a few yards off had fired the old German cannon at the mountain. Now he was trussed in a sack in the boot, for God's sake, already smelling to high heaven. (We hadn't wanted to leave him there, to be kicked and mauled, and we couldn't find the time or the spades to bury him up in the cemetery.)

We got going again. I was waiting for the horrible climax. I like gorillas. I like baby animals. So the thought of a baby gorilla sliding towards that big saw made me want to throw up, frankly. Mason didn't like animals in the same way as I did. He only liked their skins.

All that night, the baby gorilla whimpered. It didn't sleep: its eyes stared at Mason mournfully in the glow of the paraffin, and Mason stared back. He talked to it, in the end. He tried to explain. It wiped its mouth and held its injured foot (which Mason had dressed and bandaged as if it was his own). The creature whimpered and clung to a blanket in the corner of the room.

'Funny thing was,' Mason said, 'it didn't *accuse*, if you

know what I mean. It didn't *accuse*. It was just frit. It didn't blame me for anything. It understood, see, the whys and wherefores of life. Dog eats dog. And the other way round.'

I snorted at his familiar joke, realising in a flash Mason's true secret: he was terrified of being blamed for anything. Anything. It was his one great weakness, but he'd turned it inside out, into a strength.

The next day, they tied the baby gorilla to the head-end of a heavyweight log of yellow-wood at the top of the feeder-table and started the rollers going without a hitch. Things were already beginning to function normally, in anticipation. Mason was hoping, for the first time in his life, that something would go wrong with the head-saw, but it didn't. It started circling smoothly and cleanly, building up speed in that majestic way, inevitable somehow, like the roll of the planet on its diurnal round and so on. The baby gorilla, just clear of the rollers, was moving slowly and steadily towards the saw's teeth, almost as if it was dragging the log behind it. The workers watched in a semi-circle, some of them close enough to be splashed. This was very big medicine. This was the biggest medicine any of them had ever seen. Then, from out of that glossy little bundle of black fur, those eyes peeped and found Mason's own. Huge eyes, liquid, much bigger than a human's. The creature was five feet from the spinning metal, by now; the eyes carried on gazing at him, as they had done all night in his room.

What made Mason run forward at that point was that the thing didn't know what was about to happen to it. It might have been on its way to its mother, for all it knew. That's what the eyes told him: he was delivering the most innocent of innocents to its bloody awful end.

He grabbed it about a foot and a half away from the blade and hung on. The workers were shouting at him. The rollers of the feeder slipped a bit then pushed the log against Mason's weight and strength. He'd somehow lifted the animal a bit but the rope tying it was biting into its fur and flesh as the log inched forward. It was crying out now, in pain from the rope. Mason screamed for a knife but no one could hear him over the saw's screech. The big log's tonnage was too much even for him. He held the baby gorilla tight and watched the rope on the feeder inch forward and fray against the spinning blade. The instant he felt it give, he yanked the animal away and dropped it on the ground. There was blood splashing and spurting over his boots and over its fur. He swore and screamed from sadness more than horror, but the baby gorilla looked up at him, got to its feet, and clutched his leg. There was nothing wrong with it at all.

He saw a hand and forearm on the ground, being pissed on by golden sawdust as the log carried on through. The arm's elbow-end was emptying its blood into the mud, like a tipped jug. It was a white arm. His own arm shot to where its partner should have been, hanging at his side, and found a mess of stump.

'Like putting your fingers into warm porridge,' he said. 'Like, if you were being a bit original as a kid, and playing up, you put your fingers into your oats of a morning. I don't remember much, after that. I found myself in my bed. First thing I asked was: where is it? Na arm cut off, some idiot said. No, I mean the gorilla, the little hairy boy. Dat small-small beef done be over dere, they said. He was, too. In the corner. Right as rain. We had a gingerly cuddle, he and I. Apart from his tics, he were like a big black teddy, only softer.'

'What did you do with him?'

'He was called Small-small, by the time I got back. Having the time of his little life. Stayed with me a bit, until he was old enough to be delivered back to the bush. Sad day.'

'You were trusting. I mean, of your men. Lamb to slaughter, I'd have thought.'

'I had said to them: if anything happens to this little man, while I'm away being mended, you no get your dash, dat clear? I thought they'd have another go at laying this curse, you see. Oh no, they said, na small-small beef done be safe too much, Pa.'

'That amazes me, Mason.'

'It did me, too, until I passed the head-saw, with all that blood on it. My blood. Pa Croc's blood.'

He was quiet for a bit, then he said: 'Big medicine for a big tree, see. Dog eats dog. And the other way round.'

'Not quite, Mason,' I replied, smiling at him through the red swirl kicked up off the road by the fleeing populace. 'Not quite. Not that time. Most times, but not that time.'

I expected him to turn round and edge his mouth into its usual grin. But he stayed looking straight forward, with his mouth turned down, the skin of his face veneered in dust.

Propitiation, I thought. Propitiation.

Well, we're all in need of it, at times.

TYRES

My father started the business in 1925, the year of my birth. It was a good business: roads were rough and tyres were punished. In those days, there was the inner tube, and the outer casing of hard rubber. I always saw these as the body and the soul. Don't ask me why.

The main road is very straight, and always has been: Roman, they say. In those days there wasn't much traffic, although at the time we thought it was busy. Life would go by us, and now and again stop. We were proud that M. Michelin was a Frenchman: for once we had invented something useful, instead of making a lot of noise about nothing. No, really, I am proud of our business.

I started helping my father as soon as I could stand upright, just as he had helped his father, who was a blacksmith, hammering hot iron tyres to wooden rims. I was at first scared of the hiss of the compressors, of the great blade that took off the rubber, peeling it like an orange. I learnt to see a tyre as sad, when its chin lay flat on the ground, melting away – and when it was fat and full it bounced, it was so happy. My father could roll the tyres like a man I once saw in a circus that came to the village. The worn, sad ones lay leaning each upon the other like old men one side of the yard: my father would roll another so that it fell exactly into place against the end. He called this 'playing his accordion'. Some of the farmers would take these old tyres away, for use on the farms, where they would have a second life under a trailer, bouncing behind a horse or perhaps a donkey over stony fields. In very hard frosts, they would heap up the old, dead tyres at the ends of the fields, so that the evil smoke would scare the frost away from the vine-buds. Not everyone did this: it was my father's idea, I believe, and they didn't like to think he could tell them things, a man who had turned away from the land.

My father would tell me, when I was old enough, how one must never fall short of the highest standards, in this job. The road was getting busier, and the future looked rosy. But, he said, if you fall short of the highest standards, and start 'cutting corners', or grow sloppy, and let a man drive away with a set of tyres unevenly inflated, or with an inner tube that – from the very kindest of intentions – you have pretended to yourself is passable, though frayed in one spot, or with a tread that is smooth as here (he'd smack his furrowed brow), you might be sending that man to his death. Every time we heard of a local accident, our hearts beat faster, and not only because this unfortunate occurrence might have involved someone dear to us; many, if not most, of those running around on the roads at that time were putting their faith in our rigour and honesty and skill. Even I, a pimply young lad handling the bicycle trade (how much more considerable it was in those days!) knew that my hands were capable of bringing injury or even death, if I let my attention wander, or felt too lazy to triple-check a pressure or a repair or a bolt or the depth of a tread.

The blessed Trinity, my father called it: the check, the double-check, and the Holy-Ghost-check. Who was a Protestant through and through.

Even the local *curé* would use us. My father and he drank together, in the little office with its Dunlop tyre-clock, talking about Verdun or other things closed to me, while I dealt with the *curé*'s battered old bicycle – a Raleigh, from his time in Flanders. M. Dunlop and M. Michelin: these were my father's gods. I would like to say that my father

107

was like the Michelin man, but he wasn't: I was always, from maturity, bigger than he ever was, but he was never fat. His face has always had an emaciated look, perpetually sucking on its dead cigarette, glossy with grease and seamed with dirt. Tyres pick up the filth of the world, they are not fussy. In their treads I have found the hair and blood of small, hapless creatures. In the great chasms of a giant truck's treads I once found a shrew, intact but quite lifeless, its tiny paws folded as my mother's were on her death-bed, in the room smelling of camphor and candles.

So the road passed by us in a blur, and now and again would come the tell-tale sounds of tyres turning into our yard, scrunching over the grit and dust, and we would lift our heads to look, squinting in the heat and glare or rubbing our hands in the cold.

André Paulhan et Fils. That sign was painted in 1942, when I was seventeen. I was very proud.

The next day, we saw our first German limousine. We had seen German trucks before, passing through the unoccupied zone, on their way to elsewhere, but never before had we seen a big, black Mercedes, with a little flag fluttering on its bonnet, and motorcycle outriders. It did not stop. There was much less activity on the road, after the country was defeated, but my bicycle hands were kept busier. Our old tyres were soon used up, and new tyres were only fitfully available, until my father came to some agreement with the local powers in the town. We had no family there, except some distant cousin of my mother's: we are all from further up, in the mountains, the Paulhans. There is a tiny village in the chestnut country, about ten kilometres from where we lived at the time (when we weren't sleeping on the job, as happened two or three days in the week), which is mostly bats and ruined walls, and a simple church. That was our village, once. At least, the *mas* was ours, and the *mas* was well nigh a village in itself. I won't go into the reasons for our dispersion, or we shall be

here all night. Suffice to say that it was not for wanting to
see the world, or the descent of the Holy Spirit one
Pentecost! We go at each other hammer and tongs, still, the
Paulhan clan, until we are threatened. Then we hold as fast
to each other as one of my tyres to its rim. We don't meet
much, these days.

One time, in March or April 1943, my father came back
from town one day, looking very pleased with himself. He
was scrubbed clean and in his best suit. He had left very
early, before I had even shaved. He had spent the morning
in the *gendarmerie*, he told me. 'There are a few new faces I
don't know, but there is Jules, getting along fine, with his
own office. He is in charge of regularising.' 'What is he
regularising?' I asked. (There were no clients about, I might
add.) 'The STO,' he said. My heart came into my mouth.
By this he meant the latest bad idea of Laval's, the *Service du
Travail Obligatoire*. Jules – an old schoolfriend and card-
playing companion of my father's – did no more than type
out lists and send out letters, but he had a certain control
over things. Jules had shown my father round, 'and I shook
a few hands.' Just as well he had scrubbed his own, as best
he could. That is why I escaped the fate of certain others of
my age, amongst them several friends. When I was twenty,
I spent a few not unpleasant months in the Vosges cutting
wood and gathering charcoal and getting very cold with
some young people from places like Lyon – smart, educated
people, who had never cut wood in their lives before. But I
never went to Germany.

Whether it was because of this visit, and his odd evening
with Jules playing for small money and drinking, I do not
know – but the Germans used us. That is to say, they used
us when it suited them, for they seemed to have their own
mechanics, even their own tyre people, like they had their
own newspapers and their own films and their own
language. Maybe they would have used us anyway, in that
case, but my father saw it as his doing. The odd thing is, he

hated the Germans – they had, after all, given him his limp, in '17, and the itch would come back with heat. When the *maquisards* really got going, he didn't turn them away, when they came as clients. He served them and pretended that he didn't know, but somehow those boys never paid, only shook hands. But he said to me, one day, after the famous 'Petit Ours' (tall and elegant) had had a tube repaired on his motorcycle one evening, late: 'Don't get mixed up in all that. These boys, they are free. You are not. When all this is finished with, and those bastards are back in Berlin, that sign will have your name on it, and your son will be *le fils*. I will be the old fellow who stands watching the world go by, and getting in your hair, and proving, at ninety, what a damn good grip I still have at the expense of your clients' knuckles!' He laughed uproariously at this, but I think he was nervous, inside. I suppose he was playing a delicate game. He was a man who could never take risks. It was moulded into him, it was part of his job.

When old Mme Renouvin slid off the road in her little blue Peugeot, in 1938, and was found dead as a log in a wild rose bush, where she'd been thrown, and the report in the local paper blamed it on a 'blow-out', my poor father did not eat for days, like a fast of repentance. The fact is, Mme Renouvin was the worst driver anywhere, and in those days you could smooth out a tread in months if you took corners poorly, the surfaces were that gritty. But she was a client, and the last man to have dealt with her tyres was my father. Surprisingly, there was no decline in custom. That, as I said, came with the war, when the road traffic died away to near silence, and everyone went hungry. If we hadn't had the chestnuts, in our area, I think we might have starved to death. So my father's visit to the *gendarmerie* certainly put things straight.

I was in love, if there is such a thing. It was a girl who passed by on her silver bicycle every morning and every evening. She was a clerk in the silk-works, further up the road. She would work all day in the roar of the river-race and the typewriter clicking away like a mad nuthatch, and I would work in the hiss of the compressor and the clatter of my tools and the intermittent gossip of our clients, dreaming of Sunday, when I could walk in the woods and mountains, and breathe good air, and forget the war. I noticed her first as a very young girl, just coming into womanhood, when she arrived in the yard with a tyre in ribbons, and caught her ankle on the pedal, walking the bicycle towards me. She was nothing much to look at then, except for a mass of beautiful, glossy black hair, but she spoke in a very sweet, soft voice, and had a winning smile. She hardly looked at me, and (both being shy, I suppose) we exchanged only a few commonplaces. But some dart must have wormed its way in, for when I saw her pass on her way to work (as I surmised, and soon confirmed) I recognised her immediately. This must have been just after the war broke out, in '40. I remember poppies between the vines, and the white asphodels that came up always (and still do) in the good-for-nothing field at the back, and the poplars on the river glittering like fountains in a wind – so it would have been late spring. The dust was on the road; the last of the big rains had passed a few weeks earlier. The whole stretch of the road, either way, was empty (just before all those refugees from the north trudged past, with their wheelbarrows, in June); the poppies thinned into one crimson thread of silk either side, and the plane trees dappled nobody but the birds, alighting while the coast was clear. Rubbing my hands on a rag, taking a moment's break between two jobs, I saw coming up from the west, from the town, a dark-haired figure on a bicycle. I stepped back as she drew nearer: I am naturally shy, as I have said, and in the long time it takes for a bicyclist to pass us from first sighting there is much that can happen in the head, and many possibilities for difficult exchanges of regard. As I recognised her from my slightly retracted vantage point, I have to say that I blushed; she was already hot in the face from the ride – but anyway, her skin was so olive that one never saw her blush. My skin is from my mother's side; my mother had red hair, which everyone claimed was from German mercenaries a thousand years ago. What rubbish people speak!

I nodded as she passed, busily washing my hands over the pail. There was a wealthy client, a local meat-supplier, talking with my father, coming out of the big shed. He showed me a three-inch nail that had just been taken out of his nearside rear tyre. I indicated my admiration and commiseration, as one always has to with these bores, and then looked after the girl, who had now dwindled to a dot. I forgot to say that as she ticked past, just before the bore opened his mouth, she glanced at me and smiled. Her lips fell into an open pout as they automatically described a *bonjour*, but mine stayed frozen. They are like that: the muscles of my face have a will of their own, at times. It is because I am shy, with people, unless they are clients. Also, it was because my voice had only just broken, and still threatened to be all at sixes-and-sevens. It was after this that my father gave me a lecture on treating clients as if they are the most interesting people in the world, with their tedious, repetitive histories of three-inch nails and roads full of sharp stones.

You cannot fail to strike up some relationship with those who pass you at definite times six days a week, but it took two years before I had reached a sufficient maturity to wave at her as she passed, and shout some innocuous greeting (I mean, more than *bonjour* or *bonsoir*). The final 'break-through' came after three years when, pedalling towards me at the time I just 'happened' to be wiping my hands on a rag at the edge of the road (which is also, of course, the generous entrance to our yard), she wobbled and wandered a little towards the middle of the road. Seeing, as I could, a large military vehicle bearing up behind her at considerable speed, I waved my hand and shouted at her to keep well in. The military vehicle swirled the dust so much that I was not certain for a few moments of her safety, but she emerged from the cloud, hugging the verge, with a somewhat shocked expression, which did not preclude her look of gratitude as she pedalled past me, thanking me very much. A look which I responded to with a clownish shrug, making her laugh. On her way back that evening, when I just happened to be washing my hands in the pail under the old Michelin sign, with its tyre-man pointing potential clients in, the ticking slowed and stopped before I had time even to look up. 'Thank you', she said. I stood, wiping my hands on my overalls (normally I would shake them dry, on such a fine day, because my overalls were of course greasy, but I could not shake them free of moisture with her so near). 'That's all right,' I said. We couldn't think of anything else to say for the moment, but it didn't matter. I was aware of my father hammering in the shed, and of a sleek black *Milice*-type car shooting past, and of a couple of motorcycles stinking of some home-made fuel – dung, probably – struggling to overtake a horse trotting with a cart full of hay and sun-blackened, nattering kids, but it was not to these that I attended with anything more than unconscious instinct. Yet I recall them all very clearly – along with the loveliness of her form and the sweetness of her face, her legs held either side of the bicycle, very straight (I imagined) under the pale blue dress, propping the rest of her body while she could think of nothing to say. What is there to say to someone you have known as a reliable face and form for three years, but with whom you have never exchanged more than a greeting? Someone you know you will see at a certain precise point twice a day, as one sees a tree or a house or even some discarded piece of metal rubbish in a ditch, too jammed in even for the floodwaters to snatch away? Someone who, if suddenly no longer there, can leave a hole in your heart, and a feeling of doom until the moment he or she reappears?

This is all very well, but it is recounted in the warm (oh so warm!) glow of hindsight. Look at me there, in the yard, still the boy who knows nothing of the world, or keeps mum about it if he does. I was filled, let's be honest about it, with a sense of helplessness and near-panic, for this might be the only opportunity I would ever get. Once I had seen her in the market, when my father had heard of an exceptional delivery of Normandy apples and sent me off in a client's 'borrowed' car to grease the vendor's palm. But it was so odd to see her then, stood like anyone else on the ground, and not on two spinning wheels, ticking past, that I failed to do justice to the occasion by positioning myself next to her with some joke at the ready, as many a lad of my age might have done. A few other times I had reckoned I had seen her, at a distance, in one of the streets or on the main square of the town, but she had never come for repairs, or a new tyre. That's what it was like, during the war: people dealt with their own problems, their own repairs, more than in peacetime. Everyone 'cut corners', from necessity. It was a difficult period.

So I was glad when she pointed at the nearest pot-hole and said, 'I was avoiding one of those.' This gave me an opportunity to open up. 'It's the military vehicles that do it,' I said. 'The roads can't take them. The surface is battered stupid by all the trucks.' (This was about six months after the German invasion of the southern zone, by the way.) 'We are all battered,' she said. She looked sad, then, and I noticed how her face had thinned over the three years I had watched her. If she lived up in one of the villages to the north, she must bicycle a lot of kilometres each day, on a diet of boiled chestnuts or whatever. There was something sinewy about her, though, that one could trust. I nodded. I was conscious of my father in the shed, and how he'd told me to keep my mouth shut. 'Petit Ours', she said, all of a sudden. I felt renewed panic, inside. I frowned. She looked at me, thoughtfully, as if reading my face. Then, because I didn't say anything more, she set off into the distance. 'Chatting up the skirts, then?' yelled my father, from the shed door. 'Hey, young Raoul's picking the cherries as they pass!' There was no one around, and his joke was lost to the air, after echoing as usual in the shed's cavern behind him. I told him to piss off, under my breath. I was exhilarated and at the same time very upset that the girl (whose name I didn't even know) was involved in some way with the Maquis. It never occurred to me that she might be working for the other side: that possibility might have been suggested by my feigned ignorance, but that was an automatic reflex. You've no idea on how many levels one's mind worked, in those days: isolated compartments of body and soul, with a lot of soft rubber in between.

I was upset not only because her existence might suddenly be perilous, but also because she had not stopped just for me, or for her feelings about me. In the end, I never knew how deeply involved she was, but I reckon it must have been on the simplest level of message-carrying, like a lot of kids and teenagers in those times. My position, on the main road, with the cover of the business, would have served the Resistance well. That was obvious. But I was not the one to make that sort of decision alone. Maybe my father did more than just give the *maquisards* 'God's credit', as he used to call it; but if so, I never knew about it – and trust between father and son would mean nothing, in that case.

The Germans – and, naturally, the *Milice* – started to furnish us with increased custom as the war dragged on and things became more and more difficult. Since many of our clients were paying us in blackmarket goods, the 'honest' cash of the occupiers was very welcome. One day, I was sitting in a café on a Sunday morning (the place in the tiny square this side of town), when a man in a peasant's overalls (but not, somehow, a peasant's bearing), sat down next to me and said, 'Try a nail or two. Otherwise we'll be thinking you are collaborators.' With that, he got up and left. My hands were shaking so much I spilt my drink. I imagined the other, mainly old, men in the café were looking at me. The wine tasted sour (it probably was). This was about a month after the girl had stopped to thank me. I decided to do something clownish, to make her stop again. My heart thumping like a drum all night, I rose early and started work before my father had shaved (we were 'sleeping in', that night, in the little rooms above the office). I had never missed her in the morning, but I wanted to be absolutely certain. The advantage of the morning encounter was that my father always did his paperwork until nine, and the thick net curtain across the office window obscured the view of the yard sufficiently to waylay any casual glance – even that of my father's. At a quarter to seven, with the sun laying broad stripes across the white road, so that vehicles seemed to appear and disappear as they approached, I saw the girl in the distance . . . to my relief, I have to say (*nothing can be relied on except death*, and so forth). There was nobody else on the road. I stepped out into the middle with a bucket full of stones and earth and started to pour it into the pot-hole, the subject of our former exchange. I was so nervous I nearly dropped the bucket, for my arms were very weak all of a sudden, but I was already stamping the stuff down by the time she stopped. 'You've no right to do that,' she said. I paused in my work, and my prepared grin froze into what must have been rather a stupid-looking grimace. 'You'll be arrested for overstepping the mark. *Les Allemands sont corrects.*' With that last familiar phrase, I knew she was 'having me on', and my grin restored itself. 'It's for you,' I said. 'I know,' she replied. She giggled (no, not quite – but there is no other word to describe such a sprinkle of delightful, teasing merriment) and pedalled off. I was left gazing after her, empty bucket in hand, little stones

caught in my boots. If a truck had not blared its horn, I
fancy it would have run me over.

Of course, all doors were open now. My father
wondered at my whistling gaiety that day. His eyes
narrowed over lunch – which we'd have, on those summer
days, at a little table set under the plane tree in the corner of
the yard (the road is too noisy for that, now). He poured
himself a generous quantity of wine and eyed me suspiciously over the tumbler. His face (no more nor less
emaciated than it was before the war, just a little sharper)
gleamed with sweat and grease. I smiled back, innocently.
Despite the heat, a bird was singing in the branches above
us. Or perhaps I imagined that. There was a noon stillness,
otherwise – though the Germans never respected our hours,
and would shatter the holy quiet at unpredictable moments.
I saw the wine go down his throat as I had seen it go down
for as long as I could remember, and the throat always
glossy and dark. He wiped his mouth and set the glass down
more energetically than usual. 'Wipe that bloody stupid grin
off your face,' he said. 'Or I'll think you're up to
something.'

There was no doubt that the game he played was a strain
on his nerves. I have no doubt that men like my non-
peasant in peasant's dress had approached him in recent
months, when the bolts were turning tighter on our world.
He must have felt cornered, in some way. He wouldn't
have liked that.

But if he didn't like what was happening under his very
nose, then he never said so. That evening she waved with a
merry laugh as she passed, and my father was in the yard,
jacking up a big white Delage (the one with the electric
gearbox that belonged to M. Coutaud, the footwear
fellow). I didn't turn to look at him, but neither did he
wolf-whistle, or yell something about cherries. The next
morning was a Sunday, and I spent it roaming the hills
around my family's village, making myself giddy from too

much exercise combined with a lack of proper nourishment. We never talked about the war as such around the table: only the lack of food. Now and again the Germans trundled up the little main street, knocking plaster and even stone off the corners of the old buildings, matching their exaggerated wheelbase against the donkey-cart dimensions of the village turns, but otherwise the war was something that went on either far away, or in the subterranean parts of the mind and the land – places one only entered at one's peril. Certainly – let me assure you of this – the Paulhans were never regarded as one of those *salauds* families who put all their eggs into the enemy basket. Many were the folk around us who looked upon the early days of Vichy as times of redemption for the poor, ground-down countryman, but they tended to be Catholics, who didn't even mind very much when the Jews (including a few of our clients, most of whom I had never even thought of as Jews) were taken away. My father disliked Catholics with a two-hundred-year-old force flowing in his veins. Thus he had no time for Pétain. Apart from anything else, he had put all his eggs into the basket of progress, which he saw as intimately connected with the automobile. Now we were living as people had been in his father's time, or even his grandfather's. To my father, the war was a personal attack on his business. Thus he felt no compunction in screwing what he could out of the enemy.

Do I make myself clear? There is nothing obscure about what followed. I will set it out like a spread of cards, as stained and smeared as my own, but no less honest. I lost, I lost more completely than most men lose . . . but let me go on. The girl and I, we slowly discovered each other; her name was Cécile Viala, she came from a small family that farmed in a simple, modest fashion two valleys west of mine, in a village I had never visited – yet we decided that we must have crossed each other's paths at numerous moments during our lives, if only at fairs and festivals, when we were to each other only another strange face under the trees.

She never again mentioned Petit Ours, or anything in connection with the Resistance, or even the war, very much. Twice a day we would talk, and she would arrive earlier and earlier, so as to talk for longer. She shook hands with my father, and my sisters soon learned of my 'affair'. They teased me about it, but I was happy to be teased. They said I should invite her over, for they had learned how pleasant and pretty she was from someone who worked on the machines in the silk-works – and how clever she was, too, and what a fine hand she had, and what a head for numbers. Far too good for a dolt like me! One morning, I said that I would be walking in her valley. (The idea popped into my head, just like that – really, it was not so far as the crow flies, but then I am not a crow!) She looked down, shyly, and said, 'I can be walking there, too.' So we worked out a place to meet, in very sensible tones, as if we were talking about prices, or bent wheel-spokes – and as she pedalled off I realised that I had made my first secret assignation with the one I adored. I felt giddy, and even a little sick. I spread too much grease on the wheel-rims, and dropped a ring spanner on my toe. I had to sigh, as real lovers do – as if someone had taken a pump to my mouth and overdone the foot on the pedal. Each hiss of the tyres seemed to express my own impatience with the ordinariness of things: no young man could ever have been in love as much as I, I considered. Where my palm had rested on the warm leather of her saddle, lay the cold arc of a jack's brace. I turned it with a ferocity that my father happened not to see, or he would have cuffed me on the ear, as in old times.

We met under a certain, ancient chestnut tree already dropping its life-sustaining fruit, on the path that eventually winds up to her village. We avoided the shepherds and their tinkling goats as best we could, and made our way deeper into the woods. Neither of us said much, I remember.

Without the long road, the yard, the trucks and bicycles, cars and horses, the dust or the puddles, the regularity of the moment twice in the day and the knowledge that it would not be extended beyond ten or so minutes, we were a little lost. The world was suddenly like an immense garden in which we could wander at will. Before a fine view of the higher mountains to the north, blue fold upon blue fold, I took her hand. Yes – we had not yet held each other's hand! Hers moved in my light hold, like a little rabbit, and I thought I was going to explode. I sighed as silently as I could, and then I said, 'You make me very happy. I would like to do this every Sunday, even in winter, until I'm so old I can no longer walk.' 'What an odd thing to say!' she cried. I felt very disappointed: I had rehearsed it all the way up the slope. Then she said, very quietly: 'Me, too.'

Oh, let's get on, let's get on to the inevitable horror, after God alone knows what happiness of embrace and gentle kiss up there in those lonely, lovely hills. It will bear only brief telling. First, a big truck – a Latil, huge for those days, six cylinders, a twelve to thirteen tonner diesel – passed us one morning, six-thirtyish, at a hell of a lick, scattering grit and clouding the yard in dust. Moments later, two German armoured cars shot past, clearly in pursuit, and I heard a terrible tearing sound, which I believe was some kind of machine-gun fired by the Germans at the truck. My father and I ran out into the road, only to see the Latil swerve as if to turn – in fact, it slewed to a halt in a great vortex of white dust and the Germans did likewise, if only just in time. A figure leapt from the truck and ran off into the vines, with the Germans following on foot, firing like mad. We saw, over some obscuring trees, black smoke rise up in puffs and heard several loud bangs. These, I assume, were the grenades later reported in the local paper as having been thrown at the driver (who escaped, for he still lives to recount it). The truck was full of dynamite, which any one of the many bullets fired could have set off at any moment –

and it was near enough to us to have taken our shed clean away. My father and I kept our heads down, as the Germans by this time (early in '44) were very nervous and shot at anything that moved, if they felt it threatened them. But I wanted to warn Cécile, who was due to pass at any minute. To run up the road would have attracted fire, and even to go the back way, through the vineyards, would have been assumed suspicious by the Germans. So I walked up the road. 'Where the hell are you going?' yelled my father. 'For a walk,' I called back, and then kept going, keeping by the verge, with my hands in my pockets, looking as ordinary as possible but with terror beating in my mouth. I had, I think, a fifty-fifty chance of attracting fire, but none came. When I saw Cécile, I waved, and she stopped. 'You're going to be late for work today,' I said. She held my hand. She was quite startled to see me out of my usual place. She took the long, winding back route and arrived safely. My return was easier: the German guards, looking minuscule against the Latil, hardly seemed to look at me. There is nothing worse than facing danger with your spine.

That evening (by which time everything had been cleared up), Cécile thanked me with an open kiss. My father called me 'a bloody fool' and gripped my hand. He was proud of me, for once.

Then the village, one Sunday, was crossed with the darkest shadow of war – that of blood. We were sitting down to eat when the rumble of a convoy sounded. 'Bloody Boche,' murmured my father, followed by something ruder, in *patois*. A few minutes later there was shouting, and sounds of gunfire from the northern end of the village, near the little crossroads. There was lots of banging on doors, and we were all told to pay a visit to the *Mairie*. In the larger room, on the big table there used for the meetings of the *Conseil Municipal*, were laid three bodies. Their guts were literally looped and dripping almost to the floor, ripped open by that brief burst of gunfire. One of them was a local man, the son of the butcher, a little older than myself. The other two I did not know. They looked surprised in death, and it was said later that, though all three members were of the Maquis, no one knew why they had taken that road slap-bang into the German convoy, and then reversed in such panic. I know why: because, for all their bravery, they were mortals, and felt mortal fear. I was sick in the gutter, immediately afterwards, to my shame. We all – the whole village – filed past the bodies and came out silent and pale. A few of us cried. I had never seen anything like it before, the only dead person I had ever looked at being my poor mother, at peace in her bed. The following week they looped a rope around the long neck of Petit Ours, whom they'd caught in a botched raid on the *gendarmerie*, and pushed him from the town bridge – over which the schoolchildren were forced to walk class by class in the afternoon, while the body swayed in the wind. The Mayor had to give a speech, thanking the Boche for keeping public order and so forth. The atmosphere was terrible. It crept up the road and cast my father and I, and most of our clients, into a deep gloom.

But some of our clients, of course, were Germans. One, in particular, was a large, friendly man – and probably the very chap, as an officer of the Gestapo, keeping an eye on things out here, who had ordered the execution of Petit Ours. His huge, soft-topped Maybach (of which he was very proud, and with good reason) needed a change of tyre about a fortnight later: a sharp stone had finally wormed its way in, on his way to the town. Both spare wheels, carried on each side of the bonnet, had been stolen, but we found the right fit. I remembered the words of the fellow in the café, and the ripped stomachs of the three good men, and the swaying body of Petit Ours, three days after his death, sending foul whiffs of gas up the river. In a shadowy corner of the shed, out of the bright sunlight, I took a brand new inner tube and quietly (though my father was in the office, talking with the fellow) shaved its rubber with a small steel file on a certain spot, until it looked frayed, but still just airtight. I placed this inner tube in the new tyre. The officer's chauffeur and some other armed minion watched me fit it onto the wheel – the nearside front one – but I could scarcely stop my hands from trembling. In those days we tightened the bolts by hand with a box spanner, not a gun, so there was no risk of over-tightening, but I kept dropping the tommy bar with a big clatter. Anyway, I was giving the disk chrome a little polish by the time the big man himself stepped out of the office. I saw him, in the mirror-finish of the chrome, advance towards me, all distorted, looming over my shoulder like a big bat, and I composed my face and stood up. He pumped my hand and boomed at me about the state of the roads, and my father handed him the bill, which startled him. The fellow patted the bonnet and began to discuss the future of the automobile, while the two minions leaned on the sweeping mud-guard and smoked. His black gloves did a little dance while he talked. He must have been some sort of technical engineer before the war, for he was full of this idea that would avoid 'grovelling in the road' with a jack and getting your knees dirty: some sort of crowbar lever that would work a fitting under the bonnet, and put up either set of wheels as desired, and bring the whole car into suspension with a final twist. (A few years later, in about '48, a British couple in sunglasses stopped for a puncture-repair in a 1.25 litre MG, and laughed when I searched for the jack. It had exactly the same system as the Gestapo officer had described, and I all but burst into tears. They did not understand my upset: they said something about the French having 'a different sense of humour' – which really means none at all, perhaps.)

While the man was boring us stupid with his broken French, booming from under his glossy peaked cap, his boots as polished as his coachwork, his jacket and breeches as black, I heard the ticking of a bicycle . . . but it cannot be Cécile's, I thought, for there is a grating sound behind it. I glanced at the road – and there was, indeed, Cécile, coming to a halt at the entrance to the yard. She looked tired and worn, as we all did, after the events of the last few weeks. When she saw the Germans, and the big car, she made to go – but thinking only of how suspicious they were, and unpredictably sensitive and vengeful, I made my apologies and went over to greet her. 'You should be ashamed,' she murmured. 'Don't worry,' I said. 'It's not as you think.' Her face brightened, and then looked intense and question-ing, and then spotting something over my shoulder, she as quickly disguised her interest behind a soft laugh. The officer had evidently been staring at her, for he then boomed his own greeting: 'And might a fellow take a lift on the saddle from a pretty damsel, like a stick of bread?' – some such tripe. She shook her head, adding: 'No. My chain is loose.' That explained the grating sound, and I offered immediately to mend it. We were nearly six kilometres from the town, and more again from her village. I noticed how sinewy her calves were, to the point of being wasted by effort and lack of proper food. She shook her head and pedalled away, without so much as a blown kiss or a wave. 'Till Sunday!' I shouted after her, recklessly. 'Till Sunday, Cécile!'

There was a banging of doors, and the Maybach purred like a black, evil cat out of the yard, and turned to drive towards the town. It was at that moment that I saw Cécile, in the distance, apparently shudder to a stop. Her head bent down and I could just make out her hand between the wheels. Clearly, the chain had come off at that moment. I began to run towards her, my father shouting after me. The Maybach got there first. As I ran, an ominous sense of doom came over me: a kind of terrible chill, that made my heart slow, though it was pumping hard to keep my speed up. With a hundred yards to go, I saw the luggage locker opened, and Cécile's bicycle placed in it. She appeared to be in conversation with the officer, for I spotted his black glove waving through the side window, like a little black snake's tongue. The long and the short of it is that she was forced – I can only think that the appropriate word – forced by circumstance (my belief is that she hoped to extract something useful from the enemy in that brief drive into the town) to accept his offer of a lift, gallant gentleman that he pretended to be. (Or perhaps was, in another airtight compartment of his brain.)

I was left coughing in a dust-cloud, for they accelerated away at great speed, as was typical – dwindling to a dot and out of sight in no time. I had not even had time to turn on my heel when there was a distant bang and clatter, as of heavy pots and pans falling off a shelf, and smoke began to drift above the plane trees. I ran as fast as I could, in the silence, but could not finally approach the spot for all the uniforms ringing it already, waving their guns – like excited kids around the blazing effigy of the *Petassou*. For myself, though, it was the beginning of winter, not the end. I leave fresh flowers every year, on the anniversary. The terrible scorch marks on the trunk have been long rubbed away by the rain and the sun and the wind, and the dent has grown out. The tree is well again – for we crop the branches close, here, as a matter of course.

I tried – I still try – to explain her presence in the car, but I am not sure, now, anyone really cares, or even remembers her very much. When my father 'retired', in '69, I did no more than touch up *André Paulhan et Fils*; I could not change it, I could not paint it out. Well, I have had no sons, of course, staying unmarried – and anyway, he still hangs around the yard, getting in my hair (what little I have of it left to me), and showing clients what a firm grip he has, at ninety-odd. The road is very busy, of course – business could not be better. But something went out of the job when it all went tubeless, to my mind. I don't suppose I will miss it. You'll see the flowers on your way in, to the left, tied to the trunk. When they begin to fade and wither, I replace them with the plastic type. To be honest, no one knows the difference – shooting past as they do, these days.

NEON

The best joke I ever made? I can tell you straight off, no problem. I made it about five, six years back now. After I took Tricia Gomme out on that date.

I'll have to go back to the start. Zero point and that.

First thing is, I'm late. Blame Arshad's scooter. I forget to push the choke toggle back in and the plug floods and then it won't go faster than about three miles an hour. Anyway, it's not really a scooter. This is the first thing she notices.

'What's that, then?'

'A scooter. If we need to go somewhere. Better than the bus.'

She sort of snorts. And that's when I first get a whiff, all hot and sweet. It's not spearmint but banana flavour, or maybe mixed fruit. I don't know, I'm not a bubble-gum specialist, am I? But this is a big problem for me, I see that straight off.

'That ain't a scooter, Mujeeb,' she says, chewing all slow. 'It's a piddlin moped.'

I look at it. Arshad's made it a bit flash with a windshield and mirrors and popped the silencer but it's still a 49cc moped. It'd only just get to the top of her hill, choke or no choke.

I lock it to a lamppost and we walk down to the Crown, on the corner at the bottom. I don't drink, so I have an orange and lime. I've never had one before, the name just pops into my head. She has a lager shandy. She only stops chewing if she has to take a sip. When she blows a bubble and it pops, I get the smell hotter and stronger and I start to click with my tongue. You know, inside my mouth. Click bang click bang click bang click bang. The same old beat. She says to me how she likes going out with me, though it's the first time and I'm getting a bit political.

'Why d'you call it home, then?'

'I go there every three years for six months, Tricia.'

'But you were born here, Mujeeb, like me. Sunny old Chesham.'

I shrug my shoulders. She's staring at me and chewing with her mouth closed. I can't explain. My eyes feel like they've got dust in them like they do in Karachi. The pub's a bit chill.

'You could get me another lager shandy,' she says.

Then she leans towards me. All I can see is her big red mouth and this bit of white pulp inside. Her breath is sort of splashing my face with invisible yellow paint. I feel sick.

Well, I can't believe her breath is so similar!

She's squashing up to me a bit now with her body, her thigh is touching my thigh on purpose, it ain't an accident. But my head goes round and round like her breath is coating me all over and I can't breathe. I have to close my eyes and hold onto my thumb as if it's opened up again.

'Here, are you getting all overcome, Mujeeb?'

Her hand on my thigh now, sort of rubbing it. Her mouth blasting out this hot sweet paint, the same smell exactly! And it's not yellow, it's white!

'Let's go for a walk.' Arshad's scooter can go stuff itself, I'm thinking. I'd crash.

We hold hands, walking in the drizzle. She says she's scared of the dark. We pass my house. She asks me how many people live in it. I tell her ten, halving it. Well, the ten on night shift don't really see the ten on day shift, do they? We just turn the pillows over, that's all. So it's half true, what I'm telling her.

We're heading for the park, but not on purpose. She's

probably thinking I'm taking her into the park to have some fun, but I'm not. I don't know what I'm doing, not really. Getting some fresh air, I suppose. We don't go into the park but cut along the back by the Methodist Hall and up past the youth club there and past the back of Waitrose where there are some stupid kids whistling and that and then along into the old bit by the river, with the crooked little thatched houses and posh cars. It's quiet except for people practising pianos and that.

'I want to get out of Chesham,' she says, sitting on this bench and looking at the water. Then she gives me a grin, but still chewing. I'm not taking her to Karachi, if that's what she's about, I'm thinking. The street lamp makes her mouth look a bit glassy and it's like she's still coating me with her breath, making me come out in a sweat. Mixed-fruit flavour – but it's never been near a real fruit, has it? Then she takes my fist and lifts it to her mouth and shuts her mouth on my thumb.

I scream. I can't help it. Sort of panic attack. The person's stopped playing the piano when I stop screaming. No privacy. Tricia's standing up and shaking.

'Like a friggin werewolf,' she says. But she's still chewing, like it's on automatic. I say I'm really sorry, Tricia, it was one of them flashbacks, it's to do with my job – but I can't say straight out why, can I?

Well, Tricia has friends in Rayvo but she's never gone in. So I have to describe my machine, don't I?

'You have to load the rods, the little filament rods, slipping them out of the packet into this sort of metal box behind the gate, Tricia. The gate's like two flippers on a pinball machine – only they're almost touching when they shut and they're made of steel or something. They're punched at by the magnet punch, click bang click bang click bang click, hammering in and out, Tricia. This punch picks up one filament rod each go and drops it into a hole on the rim of this cylinder. There are twenty-four holes on this cylinder. You following me, Tricia? This cylinder jerks round and dips each filament into a dish with this chemical swirling around in it. I don't know what this chemical is, but it's swirling around right under my nose and is sort of like melted toothpaste but it's not spearmint. Perhaps this chemical is what makes the filament light up when it's in the bulb. Maybe it's sort of liquid neon. I don't know, Tricia. Then the filament is covered in a glass tube and the glass is pinched into a little bulb. I have to load the machine with glass tubes. They get shattered sometimes. Bits of glass in my eyelashes, right here.'

'Don't you have safety goggles, then?' says Tricia. She's really calm, now, she's sat down next to me again.

'Rayvo can't afford them, can they? It's got to keep them managers in gin and cigars and Spanish holidays, see.'

She even laughs a bit, now.

I tell her how my old man's on the next bit. He just sits there and has to take out any bulbs that ain't jiggling along right. He just sort of slumps there all day long with his chin in one hand and his tweezers in the other. I don't know what he thinks about. He's been slumped there for twenty-four years or something, probably even before neon bulbs were invented or the stuff they get put in, amplifiers and that. They built the machine around him, the factory, the whole bloody place. She laughs again. It's going to be *all right*, once I've explained.

'But I ain't on that machine, not now,' I tell her.

I haven't said nothing about the problem, not yet. I'm working out a way.

'Why not?' she asks. 'Get promoted, did you?' She's sounding a bit bored, or maybe just fagged out. She starts early up at the egg-packing station. It would have been all right, wouldn't it, if she'd smelt of eggs, or even chickens and their shit and that.

'It was the accident, Tricia. When I got my thumb caught.'

'Caught?' I show her it, but the light's too bad to see the scar and anyway she sort of puts it to one side like it's a bit disgusting. 'What – industrial accident, was it? I hope you got something out of them bastards, Mujeeb.'

The water is sort of swirling past in the street light. I swallow like I'm swallowing a couple of neon bulbs. *This is it.* Go for it, Mujeeb!

'I was feeding the filament box, Tricia. They have to be stood all straight, packed together, or the magnet punch won't pick them up right. It slams in hard, then out, then in, then out.'

'Ooooh,' she says, and laughs. A sort of blast of her bubble gum, like it's a toxic ray, all over my face. So I have to close my eyes. Concentrate. See it all over again. *Feel* it.

Patting down them filament rods with my finger, me cracking a joke with Arshad and then my thumb's sort of yanked but it's like it's not really my thumb, I can't – I can't *believe* it, my thumb's trapped in the bloody gate and it's not coming out, is it? It's like the machine's yanking me in with this bloody evil laugh clicking and banging from it, like it's been waiting all this time to do it. Like it wants to turn me into a little neon bulb, starting with my thumb what the gate's clamped on and then the magnet punch punches into it anyway on account of the machine not having a brain or a heart, just an evil laugh, and I'm swearing and screaming but my dad bloody well just sits there frowning and I have to do it all myself – I have to think: yank it out or lose it, Mujeeb. So I don't know how but I yank it out and this friggin incredible fountain of red blood shoots right up out of my thumb, up and up and up right up to the girders nearly, then spatters down on everything – the machines, the people, everything. Alan's run over and is slamming his hand against the big red emergency stop button and my blood falls onto his white overalls and onto Saif and Abdul and Hairy Haz and Zafri and it's all over Arshad's face and he's practically fainting and then Mr Pryce the shop-floor manager comes up and he gets it like I'm this machine-gun with blood instead of bullets, little red bullets all over his powder-blue suit and white face.

'Poor sod,' she says. I think she means me, so I put my arm round her and she squashes her hair into my neck. But I'm all sick and giddy again, because her breath is floating up past my nose. Shock. That's what it is. I can hear her mouth working the bubble gum, or maybe it's the river.

'I couldn't go back to the machine, you see, Tricia. They put this safety guard on, told me how to be careful and that, but I couldn't go back to being the feeder operative. I'm on a shittier number now.'

'Oh come on, be a man, Mujeeb. It was only your thumb got caught.'

She lifts her head and stares at me, real close. Almost touching noses, we are. The way she's chewing now, slower, is sort of inviting me in. If only it was spearmint. If it was spearmint I'd snog her until I was dead. I stare back at her. Now, Mujeeb. Tell her.

'I can't, Tricia. It's that chemical under your nose, Tricia. The smell rises up all stinky hot and sort of fruity from the dish and makes you feel suffocated. It makes me think of my thumb getting caught. It makes me feel sick. It makes my head go round and round, Tricia. So it'd be dangerous. I might fall onto the machine and get my face torn up.'

She ain't chewing, now. Her face is so beautiful. The river sounds like it's laughing in the background. The shop floor noise is still in my ears, though. Machines, Radio 1, people yelling. Click bang click bang click bang click. Wham bang crash.

'What're you looking at me like that for, then?' she says.

'Was I?'

'All funny, Mujeeb.'

Then she sighs. A great blast of it, straight over me, all hot and fruity. I cover my nose with my hands. Then I hold my head to stop it falling off. My thumb's sort of booming. This isn't the joke, by the way.

'I'm sorry, Tricia,' I say. I'm about to explain, I really am, but she's too quick, she clicks too quick.

'So am I bleedin sorry, Mujeeb!' she shouts.

She takes her bubble gum out of her mouth and slaps it onto my zip. Her heels clap away up the street and that's it. All quiet next to the water until the police come about five minutes later, siren going and blue light flashing and all that. It must have been the piano person called 'em. They think I've done her in, done in a white girl, because of that scream. It takes a lot of explaining. I mean, it was me doing the scream, for a start off.

'I couldn't help it,' I says. 'Panic attack.'

They're looking into the river like there's a white girl's face bobbing about. They don't believe me, do they? I spend the rest of the evening down at the station telling them what happened, like I'm telling you. They're practically calling the bloody frogmen out. One of them was at school with my clever brother, up at the grammar. Otherwise I'd have got nicked for doing in a white girl. Click bang click bang click bang.

I punch in late the next morning, of course, just on red. Half an hour docked for a couple of minutes. I never go in with my dad. I just can't. He's always early, and he doesn't even pray or anything in the cloakroom, like old Haz. You have to step over Haz every evening, bum in the air on his little mat between the blue overalls.

Saif's replaced me on the feeder end. He's a tough little bastard, he boxes and that, I can't stand him. He's got this scar on his cheek from a knife fight and is always calling me names. He thinks he's only doing this temporary, but my dad probably thought that about a hundred years ago. When I first come in here they put me on packaging, with the women, and Saif kept yelling at me. There was June next to me on the boxes and she'd say, 'Friend of yours, is

133

he?' Each time, like it was her one joke. Estelle with the bad teeth was next to her and she'd say things like, '*Paki*ging now, is it?' then scream with laughter. I didn't even tell her where to put it. And I'd go home stinking of stale perfume. The whole of the packaging side stinks of it, of stale Avon. All the women in packaging are white and they all splash it on in the morning like they're off on a date and then it goes stale by lunchtime but they don't know it.

After that, they put me on Number Two's feeder, until the accident. Then I went on quality control, which means taking the lit-up bulbs off these electrified clips on a sort of big vertical belt, fifty a minute, chucking them in the right boxes. Your gloves shred after about five seconds and you get shocks and burns. Shitty.

The Torture, we call it.

Saif's machine is pretty near to the Torture. So he keeps yelling at me over the din, but does it more than usual the morning I'm talking about, jumping up and down like he's got ants in his pants. I just ignore him. I can't really hear much of what he's yelling but Rubber Scrubber's pretty clear. This was Tricia's nickname at school. Her surname's Gomme which is French for rubber. I think of her as Bubble Gomme, now, though she's Tricia Farnell these days. I look over at Saif. He's got big shoulders and fists but he's short. He's got his thumb in his mouth, he's sucking it, doing stupid things with his eyes, rolling them and that. I chuck a few bits of sweepings at him off of the floor by my seat, filaments and bulbs and that, but he carries on. Then Alan comes round and ticks us off, but he's a nice bloke, he understands the lot, he's a good bloke, he's the only manager with machine grease on his hands and dirty overalls, without him the whole place would collapse. When the buzzer goes I give Saif a wide berth but he comes up to me in the canteen, all shoulders and chest because his blue overalls are one size too small, deliberate.

'Who's a lucky boy then?' he says to me, in English. I'm

sat down with Mike, the trainee engineer then. When something goes wrong with the machines the trainee engineers are supposed to help, but they don't know a thing. They just wander round the machine like it's a dangerous animal and say, 'I'm not touching that.' When Mr Pryce went and put us on five o'clock start, twelve hours, no overtime, day's notice, the machine was out of action right to eight o'clock, when Alan turned up. And I know for a fact it was Saif who put the spanner in, that time.

I tell Saif to fuck off out of it. I can't hit him, because he'd flatten me straight off. I know this from school. Even the skins don't pick fights with him. And anyway, my old dad's watching from the next table, slumped over his mug of tea.

'Rubber Scrubber rubbed you out, did she?' He was whispering, now, but so as Mike could hear.

'Go natter with the ladies,' I say, really cool. The ladies are always one side, nattering, as if really interesting things have happened while they've been on their shift.

He turns to Mike. 'You know what, Mike? Mujeeb here got the pigs out last night.' Saif bursts out laughing, but Mike doesn't go with him because he hates Saif. He just buries his nose in the paper, doing its Spot the Ball. Mike spends all his breaks working out where the ball is, scientifically, but never gets nowhere near. Saif puts his hand on Mike's shoulder.

'Oh yeah, Saif?' says Mike, scratching one of his sideburns. He's got this Presley look, but he's tiny and he's already married.

Arshad comes up and Saif tells him about the police and Arshad thinks it's to do with the scooter at first, which I left on its lamppost until I remembered it just before I come in this morning. I'm stood up and am moving to go off to the toilet or even back to the shop-floor, anywhere away from Saif, but Saif puts his hand on my chest, just stopping me with it, and his hand's like iron. I can feel my heart sort of bashing up against it, like it's a hammer on a gate.

'Mujeeb here doesn't like girls sucking off his thumb. Even Rubber Scrubber.'

'Who's Rubber Scrubber?' says Arshad.

'A white girl on Bryony estate,' says Saif.

Arshad is very political. He goes on about the civil war to come, black and brown against white, white blood in the streets and that. But he's a decent bloke, really, he's all mouth and reads too many stupid books and all this poetry and religious stuff. So he says, in Urdu, 'You aren't going out with a white scrubber, are you, Mujeeb? That isn't why you borrowed my scooter, is it?'

Mike lifts his finger up and says, 'Scooter! I understood scooter!' He thinks we're having a really serious argument and wants to try to break it up. I say to him, 'Saif and Arshad, they're just jealous, Mike. Poor blokes.'

Saif gives a shove on his hand and I fall back against the chair and me and the chair end up on our backs. Nasty of him. It was a nasty shove. It's because he has a bad time with girls, they don't like him, they're scared of him and they find out pretty quick that he's a stupid ignorant bastard. So I get up and I'm mad but scared, too. I pick up the chair and throw it at Saif. It sort of bounces off him. Marjorie behind the counter is yelling at us to stop and Mike's starting to get up. Saif is going for my throat but Arshad stops him and Arshad's glasses fall off onto the floor. Because of the glasses, it all calms down, because no one wants to step on a pair of glasses. Saif's laughing and then the buzzer goes. 'At least we stopped the girls nattering,' Mike says. My dad doesn't say anything, doesn't even move his chin off of his hand. He never does. Sometimes I have to prod him to check he isn't dead.

The rest of the day is all right, except for me thinking about what happened last night so hard that Yusuf, the other side of the Torture, keeps yelling that I'm letting too

many through, they're all going back up again his side and
he's supposed to be putting the new ones on. I'm getting all
these electric shocks and burns but can't hardly feel them.
I'm sort of numb.

When we check out, I find myself walking out the yard
with Mike.

'What was all that about, Mujeeb? You crashed their
scooter, or something?'

I tell him. It's like I've saved it all up all day and I have to
unplug it. It's a bit rainy and dark in the street but because
he's a decent bloke, he listens. I explain about Tricia and it
being my first time out with a white girl and everything and
going to the pub and that, and about the bubble gum and its
stink every time she breathed and then her putting my
thumb in her mouth on the bench and me screaming,
having one of them flashbacks.

He starts to snort. He has quite a good chuckle. It's not
against me or anything, it's not that sort of humour. He just
sees the funny side of it, especially when I mention the
police coming and that.

Then he says, putting his hand up on my shoulder,
'Mujeeb, you know where old man God put the little neon
bulb when He created Eve?' I shrug, a bit pissed off by
now. He points between his legs. 'All we've got to do is
light it up for 'em. That's what the wife says, it's not
coming from me. All we've got to do is light it up for 'em.'

'Supposing it's made by Rayvo?' I say, without really
thinking about it.

He looks at me and then bursts out laughing again but
even louder, holding himself like he's in pain, and I realise
I've made a bloody good joke. And then we have a good
laugh together, all the way down the street. The best joke I
ever made. Mike's told it to everyone.

You've got to see the funny side of life, now and again.

That's it. Thought of it straight off. 'Supposing it's made
by Rayvo?'

She's married now, Tricia is, to the chief supervisor up in the egg-packing place. Three kids. I'm still on quality control, because I'm saving up to buy a taxi. Yusuf went back to Karachi and he says it's all right out there, he's doing well with his taxi.

When Yusuf went, they put my dad on the other side of the belt, clipping the bulbs in. If I miss any because of the burns or the shocks, they go back under and up again his side and he shouts, just like Yusuf did. He shouts in Urdu. Always the same.

'Mujeeb my son, you're a lazy idiot!'

Sometimes I reckon it'd be better to be on night shift, like Saif is now. He has these stories about night shift being a knocking shop, in the toilets and out in the yard and that, all this easy white skirt, but I don't believe him.

Anyway, I can't be taking a girl out these days, can I? Now that my old man's chosen me a wife. I met Nabila, the last time we went out there, in her village. She's a bit bony and shy and I didn't get close enough to check up on her breath, but it'll be all right. Not mixed-fruit bubble gum, anyway. It'll be buffalo curd or fluffed rice or betel, I should think.

Something like that, I should think.

SHIFTS

Thirteen days went past and I still had not been to Lamb's Conduit Street.

My best friends in the hostel were mainly Irishmen who had no need of permits even though they were not British. They had no trouble finding building work. They told me that if I did not go to Lamb's Conduit Street I would be thrown out of the country after three months.

On the fifteenth day I brooded and bit my thumb all morning in the café on the corner. I could not work out how to prove a 'secure means of support'. After a salt-beef sandwich and Tizer for lunch I made my way by foot towards St Pancras, passing from seedy to smart as a fish sails into a net. I hurried through the City feeling very self-conscious among the pin-stripe suits and bowler-hats and bleached faces. Several times I had to step quickly out of the path of thin bespectacled men scurrying along with pinched expressions. They clutched thick brown parcels and papers done up with string and I reckoned they must be messengers carrying the paper wealth of the old Empire, their backs bowed under its weight. I went wrong several times (even in the next street from Lamb's Conduit Street) so that I only reached the Aliens Registration Office with fifteen minutes to spare, my feet aching.

I had imagined a Dickensian house full of dust and papers and clerks with green eye-shades. Instead I confronted a huge modern tower-block, with *Aliens Registration Office* in big black letters on a slab of concrete. The entrance was up some steps, a row of glass doors set deeply into the building as if under a beetling brow. There were no people crowding outside, only an Asian fellow in a suit smoking a cigarette. He ignored me. The door was heavy to push, as if reluctant to let me in. There was a further row of glass doors leading into a very large open area full of desks and typewriters and with an unusually low ceiling. The people bustling about were white; the others (not numerous) stood or sat with concentrated expressions on their faces. The hubbub sounded hollow and even faint to my ears. My heart sank.

I stood for at least ten minutes by the receptionist's desk not knowing whether I should attract her attention by interrupting her – she was always on the telephone or talking to a busy typist behind her. I was invisible. She had a big silk bow just below her shoulder and a plump necklace of imitation pearl. There was a brightly-spotted poster about tropical diseases and a framed list of regulations on the wall next to me. The long neon strip above my head hung on chains and made a noise like a mosquito. It gave me a headache. My face was swaddled in traffic fumes from my long walk and the roar of the outside world was inside my head. I considered whether I might not exist. As Fanon writes in 'The Wretched of the Earth': *In reality, who am I?*

I cleared my throat and the receptionist glanced up for a second while scratching her carmine lip with a sharp fingernail as green as the antiseptic my mother would put on cuts.

'Good morning, madam,' I said. 'How are you?'

She tutted and rolled her eyes up.

'Have you an appointment? We're closing in a couple of minutes.'

I explained my situation. She pointed to an area marked *Wait Here* as if telling me to get out. I tore a number from a machine and sat on a plastic chair next to a screaming baby and an Indian woman whose red spot on her forehead somehow harmonised with my own marks. European faces were mostly blank, like the milk puddings we were given at school.

Are YOU Vaccinated?

The Indian woman and her baby were called. The hubbub slowly died and people went out of the glass doors in twos and threes. Some of the neon lights flickered out. A woman appeared with sharp spectacles dangling on a cord, clutching a file. She told me that the office was closed.

'Closed?'

'You shouldn't have been let in,' she said.

I spread my hands and protested that I was made to wait a long time at the reception desk, that it was the fifteenth day. I showed her my number, which I had absent-mindedly crumpled up. She seemed not to understand and I started my story from the beginning but all this time she was shaking her head. I realised that in all of that vast building we were almost alone.

I should not have come at the last minute. I could write a letter putting my case if I so wished but she could not spend any more time arguing.

As I was leaving I remarked, 'Does the parrot know what it is saying?' (An expression of my friend Kwesi's which I have never really understood.)

'Could you repeat that, please?'

The receptionist's desk was empty, the typewriter covered in a plastic case. I walked out of the place feeling hurt and crestfallen. I had not dared to speak up. I had not pushed myself forward.

I cried for my father that night. The hostel was full of mad shouts and moans and hyena laughs. I needed my father's advice but it was not only this that made the tears fall. I was weeping for his modest life that began in a smoky hut in the north. I was weeping for his handful of poems and his stubborn belief that building ever more schools would solve Ghana's problems.

The next morning I felt a curious sense of clarity while strolling about the East End. I was pleased that I had not had to tell an untruth and convinced with a youth's conviction that the next two and a half months would yield a solution to my problem. I would meet somebody important and with influence who was concerned by the state of Africa and who would recognise my ambition and my brilliance. I was above the run of ordinary men and stood for the future. It would not be all smooth sailing but the times were with me. At school I had acted in a version of a play by Aristophanes called *The Archanians*. 'Everybody's down in the market square gossiping – if they're not dodging the painted rope that'll brand them red.' That was the only line I could remember with its politically dangerous air and now it seemed thoroughly appropriate. On the balconies of the big council estates near the hostel there were saris flapping in the wind like flags. They were much the same as our women's pagne and I missed home very much then.

It was on that day that I first purchased the *Sunday Citizen* and the *Morning Star*. The *Sunday Citizen* incorporated *Reynolds News* which was the paper my father had always read. These papers cost me 10d. a week because I could not find a local library that took them and no one shared newspapers as they did in Ghana (unless it was left on a seat for strangers to pick up). In one of them I read what Colonel Rainborough of the Commonwealth Army had said when debating the future of England after the defeat of Charles I: 'The poorest he that is in England hath a life to live as the greatest he.' I wrote it out on a slip of paper and kept it in my pocket. It became my inner decree.

Justice, that was all I wished for.

And then immediately I would think of our Independence Arch on Black Star Square with its well-known slogan carved in stone. How a passer-by in its shadow would smile and rub index finger against thumb and murmur, 'Freedom and Just This'. How does one bring the slogan and the reality together so they are as indistinguishable as a man and his silhouette?

The chilliness and damp did not lessen. I sucked Vick Cough Drops and bought a woolly scarf from a second-hand clothes shop. I suffered from cold sores and purchased a cream called Facsil which the chemist said was pronounced 'fay-sil'. When I rubbed it on, it left a bright pink smear over my face which would not wash off easily and made me look like a warrior at a funeral. I read the packet again: 'Facsil is subtly flesh-tinted, which conceals as it heals'.

I started to make contact with my fellow countrymen but I had to be careful because some of them were spies, lackeys of the new regime. I spent a lot of time tramping the streets and trying to see the naked shivering body beneath the imperial cloak. I read Dickens and Richard Hoggart and bought Mao Tse-tung's *Little Red Book* second-hand for a bob. It was published by New Era Books and I thought to myself how that would be a good name for a political party. The New Era Party of Ghana. NEPG. I saw it fluttering on flags in every village like the CPP flags when I was a boy before self-government was achieved. I spent many hours in Lyon's Corner Houses or in public libraries next to the radiator, playing with the initials on a pad of paper and designing a slogan. 'Forward into the New Era!'

I had £19 2s. and a threepenny bit left.

I joined the Young Socialists and Co-operative Party whose members held vegetarian lunches and wore sandals even in the rain and cold. None of the members seemed in any way influential or important. They showed me little condescension and no discrimination and talked enthusiastic nonsense about the African revolution. I was never volunteered to do any leafleting. I am certain there were no racial factors involved in this decision. Sometimes I wondered if my identity was real for when people stare at you it does not define what you are, it makes holes in you like a sieve.

Then one night down a street in Whitechapel I was jostled by three teddy boys. I kicked out and they booted me black and blue. In falling I broke a front tooth on the curb. I was foolish enough to go to the police station – even in Accra before the coup I would not necessarily have done that. I was put in a room and left alone for three hours without any medical aid. Eventually two policemen in plain clothes came in and asked me why I was there. I said that I had been told to stay there – I was very nervous and cold and must have looked frightened because one of them sat on the edge of the table and said, 'Now you can't come over here and start getting our English lads into trouble.'

I protested that I had done nothing whatsoever to deserve the attack and he then leant forward with his hands clasped together in his groin. He spoke to me as if he was doing me a favour in telling me such things. His breath smelt of mint.

'Listen sonny. Those lads are proud of this country. When they see one of your coloured mates walking through this green and pleasant land as if he owns it and sponging off the welfare state you can't blame them for feeling a little narked, can you?' The hands in his groin were writhing in and out of each other's grip. The other policeman standing by the door agreed with a grunt.

'Can you sonny?'

He was provoking me into making an aggressive reply. My friends in the hostel had warned me to give any 'tit-head' a wide berth but that was because some of the inmates were involved in drug dealing. They had also told me not to involve myself in any demonstrations such as those outside the South African Embassy – the 'filth' had pieces of brick wrapped in paper which they planted on you in the station. I felt more breathless with fear than with anger. I shrugged. All I wanted was to extract myself without adding to my bruises or worse.

The policeman glanced at his colleague and then folded his arms.

'You'll be wanting to see a dentist next. That's what our taxes go on. New sets of white dentures for —'

He then used a strong racial term. After a few moments of silence the other one opened the door and I was free to go. As I stepped out into the corridor the first policeman called after me to 'hang on a sec'. He came out and offered me a Polo mint. This was some sort of joke. Nevertheless I took it with a thank you.

'The hole's the best,' he said. 'I always go for the hole. Sorry we have no bananas.'

There was a burst of laughter from inside the room followed by the whistling of a tune of some relevance to this last remark. They had taken my money and a pen and notebook from me and I only now remembered this, though the money was less than ten shillings and the notebook contained only minor memoranda. Having the Polo mint rolling about in my mouth somehow prevented me from demanding back what they had taken from me. There were crude drawings with cartoon bubbles of a racial nature on the walls of the corridor and I decided the best course was to leave as quickly as possible.

Despite my trembling legs I managed to arrive home. I felt so humiliated that I did not even tell my friends in the hostel about this incident.

As a matter of fact the loss of part of a front tooth was a great drawback, as only old men or tramps had missing front teeth in Britain. It was a very lonely few weeks. However I was young enough to treat each day as a fresh chance. My grandfather would say that the trees on the coast are stronger than those in the forest because the wind blows on them off the sea: bowing under such a pressure strengthens the green wood. Most of all I recalled something Mr

Oduntun told us when we were studying the Romans:
'Listen gentlemen. A ship is wrecked off Whitby and
driftwood floats down to the sea-bed and the driftwood
turns into coal and the coal turns into jet and the jet is
fashioned into a gleaming black brooch and this beautiful
black brooch lies on the neck of a mother whose child is
frozen with the cold and there is no more wood. What does
she do? Listen again gentlemen. She tears her precious
brooch from her neck and throws it on the embers. It burns
all through the night until the sun breaks through. Her
child is saved.'

We all knew this was a parable. Now it helped me
strengthen the roof of my spirit through this difficult period.
I repeated to myself my mother's dictums: 'Never put your
hands on the table; never leave your spoon in the teacup.'
Each day I sallied forth feeling the flame in my fortitude
grow. I went to *Goldfinger* and *The Sound of Music* but my
money was running out faster than millet grain through a
chicken's throat. I didn't eat much except fried eggs and
bacon and I drank from the tap. There were election posters
pasted next to advertisements for Omo and Brylcreem: I
remember 'Action not Words' and 'Time for Decision.'
Both these slogans appeared to mock me personally. With
or without a work permit, no one seemed to wish to
employ me and as for a room I could not help noticing the
frequency of that well-known qualification 'No Irish, No
Blacks, No Dogs' – in what I imagine was a hierarchical
order of exclusion. A man chain-smoking Kensitas with a
face like a bloodhound had made offensive remarks in a hut
on a storage site where I had applied to be a night
watchman. The next day a white chap in the hostel got the
job. From that point on I all but gave up looking for
vacancies.

I bought presents for the family. My sisters each received
a snowstorm featuring a famous London site along with a
large sachet of 'Hint of a Tint' colour shampoo. I chose the

shade with care to suit the recipient: gold for Mary, silver for Ama, chestnut for Dede, copper for Elizabeth-Jane, honey for little Fui. My mother received a Carnaby Street paisley scarf and my uncle a wide polka-dotted tie in bri-nylon.

One day I was standing in front of an electric appliance shop watching the football on the banks of televisions with several other people (including a business type in a bowler). I noticed that one of the spectators was black and that he was wrapped about the neck with an Ipswich scarf.

I went over and shook his hand and told him that I had supported Ipswich when Alf Ramsey was the manager. Neither of us had known back then where the blazes Ipswich was. In my case it was chosen because the first *Sunday Citizen* I ever read had carried a report on a match between Ipswich and Peterborough by the commentator Gerry Loftus with a picture of some Ipswich players. This was around the time self-government happened in 1957 but my father was never fanatical like my uncle (who was sorry Hitler had not destroyed the British). My father liked the fact that I supported a British football team as well as my local team and knew that the future lay in co-operation even though he read the *Accra Evening News* from cover to cover and thought Nkrumah was the Gold Coast's Churchill.

The man's name was Chukufidu. He said he had chosen Ipswich because the name sounded Nigerian, like Ibadan or Ife. We both agreed that we might have chosen better but that we were still loyal, having always crouched to the wireless for the English football results.

'Ipswich one, Peterborough five,' Chukufidu intoned in a plummy BBC accent.

We laughed at this. I regretted that Stanley Matthews was no longer playing in the League and Chukufidu agreed. He was an inch or two taller than me but of the same slight build. He had delicate fingers and slightly bulging eyes that made him look surprised at the world around him. There was no gentler man. I was happy to see the flecks of scarification on his cheek-bones, if cut a little shallower than mine. I told him that I had Ashanti blood in me from my mother which explained my restless ambition. He laughed and said that for him ambition is merely keeping alive from one day to the next.

'And I do not like kings and warriors,' he added.

'I am both of them,' I joked.

We went to a milk-bar on the Tottenham Court Road to talk some more. He had left Nigeria after the military had taken power in January.

I shook his hand and said, 'Snap, for Ghana.'

'Now the Hausa are in charge,' he said. His mother was an Ibo from the east of Nigeria and his father a Fulani which explained his delicate fingers.

I explained about my own father.

'They killed our prime minister,' he said, 'they do not care about the small fry.'

He did not seem to react to my personal grief and it was only later that I learnt he had lost three members of his family during the rioting as well as his home. At some point he told me about a basement flat that was vacant. The word 'vacant' was becoming horrible to me. It was associated with slamming doors or suspicious faces looking at me from head to toe.

'There's no landlord,' he said. 'There's no big white chief or General Ironsides. This filth tastes like fish.'

We were sipping our Tizer through long straws and pretending it was palm-wine, pretending the roof was corrugated iron and the light was kerosene clouded by flies and that the thin spotty girl behind the zinc counter was a fat mammy wrapped tight in a pagne, making ourselves laugh with the contradiction. The room would cost me two shillings a week to be paid into a common fund. I could not admit to not knowing where Great Titchfield Street was in case it was famous. I agreed on the spot.

Great Titchfield Street lay only a few minutes' walk away in the shadow of the Post Office Tower. It was broad and long and my first impression was of anonymity and dirtiness. There were some Victorian pubs with wooden fronts that reminded me of the sideboard in the Supreme Court's waiting room, and several cafés (or 'caffs') advertising 'Fresh-Brewed Tea'.

We stood together for a moment in front of the 'squat', as Chukufidu called it. Its brick was black with grime and soot but the front door had bright monsters and flowers painted on it while the main window had a hand-printed poster saying, in blood-red letters, 'I set my heel on the throat of my own song'. Another shiny poster had a large tick with the words 'Count the sheep, go to sleep' printed underneath. Chukufidu told me that he had made the first poster on a silk-screen kit and that it was a line from Mayakovsky. The second poster was put up by the resident anarchist whose efforts at persuasion had been in vain, as Labour had won the General Election for the second time running a few days earlier!

The weekly rent was four pennies less than the bottle of Scentol disinfectant I purchased the next day in order to make my room habitable.

The other 'squatters' were a Cuban guitarist, an Irish bricklayer, an Hungarian-Jewish actor, an Indian painter and the anarchist who hailed from Tasmania. Chukufidu was a poet as well as a journalist. There were tramps from various parts of the Commonwealth who would occupy the basement flat and after one of them had hurled an electric fire at the elderly Hungarian, provoking a small blaze that blackened the walls, the room was put out of bounds until this moment.

It took two days to scrub the blackness off the walls. I swabbed the bare floor free of faeces and chip-grease and

149

soot. There was no bed, only a putrid heap of blankets. I had never seen such filth until I came to London. I white-washed the walls and found a mattress on a tip which I set up on old yellow bricks, made a table from planks and a chair from packing cases and so forth. The smell of cats remained as a disagreeable presence despite all my efforts.

I was proud of my room even with the smell, the lack of proper daylight and the fizzling sockets. I wandered about the area and noticed other squats like ours, cheek-by-jowl with cleaned-up houses bearing brass plaques in which tapping typewriters could sometimes be heard. The little caffs, full of steam and smoke, enabled me to read a book all morning for a few pennies of warmth.

Looking up at the new Post Office Tower made me as giddy as Big Ben's sooty finger had done. So I went up to the top where I watched schoolboys throw paper darts from the viewing balcony. Down and down they glided for a long time over the grey rooves, each dwindling into a white spot like that on a television screen before it blended with the city's panorama spread before us like a feast.

Time was slipping through my hands and the red rope was closing in, ready to brand me. I had been in Britain for over two months. Maybe memories were short enough back in Ghana to leave me alone there and I could go to Achimota as planned and not try for a British university, given the practical difficulties. My mother wrote that my uncle had moved up-country to the Ashanti relatives near Kumasi and become a fisherman again. But London is a beautiful whore with whom you fall in love even though you know it is bad for you. I was simultaneously bewildered and angry and very happy. A scrap of official paper was all that stood between myself and freedom although I knew that, like the signature which granted Ghana her independence, enormous forces lay behind it every bit as tall as the Post Office Tower.

I explained my plight to my new friend. 'If I get hold of a work permit, I will have a job, I will have money, I will be allowed to stay and then I will be able to study here. But you can't have a work permit until you have a job. I am in a Catch-22 position.'

Chukufidu said: 'Do as I do. Live for each day. Each day brings revolution nearer.'

He was a sensitive and intelligent man and I nodded at what he had to say while my innermost thoughts were for the future, the present being merely an awkward obstacle. He read me poems by Christopher Okigbo in a high lilting chant, dazzling and strange:

> Silent the footfall
> soft as cat's paw,
> Sandalled in velvet,
>   in fur
>
>   So we must go,
> Wearing evening against the shoulders,
> Trailing sun's dust sawdust of combat,
> With brand burning out at hand-end . . .

And I would read him Senghor in both French and English. 'Listen to this, this is very fine. "I saw once more the ancient dwelling on the hillside, a village with its long lowered eyelashes—"'

'What is fine about that, man?'

I explained the metaphor of the thatched rooves. 'It makes the picture sparkle, like a fish leaping in a lake. For me, that is poetry—'

He shook his head, raising his hand like an elder at a council meeting. 'It is not *pictures* we need, brother! It is not beautiful feathers that make the hawk strong! Anyway, it turns the village into a pretty bashful girl. Ripe to rape.'

'You cannot have claws and nothing else.'

'You start with an earthquake. Then you sharpen your claws,' he said, showing this with his hands.

'Ghana would be very much to your liking, Chukufidu. There is only one geological fault line in the country and what did they do with it?'

'Tell me what they did with it.'

'They built the State House on it.'

He laughed and clapped his hands satirically.

'There was an earthquake at half past eleven in the morning when I was at school,' I continued. 'Our teacher told us to stand under the lintel of the doorway. There were thirty-six of us.'

He laughed some more.

'That is absolutely the prototypical bourgeois reaction!' he cried.

Then he gripped my arm.

'Can I borrow it for a poem?'

'As long as you give it back when you have finished with it,' I replied.

We would talk and argue and laugh like this for many hours in my room where we were warmed by a paraffin heater I had recovered from a bombsite. His own room was out of bounds. I never went in until afterwards, after Chukufidu had gone. We had not noticed he had gone, not for a few days, so caught up were we in our own worlds. The huge Cuban Carlos strumming his bass guitar so the whole house quivered; the Jewish actor Moishe mumbling in Yiddish over porridge at all hours in the kitchen, always in his raincoat; Colum the Irish bricklayer complaining as usual about the broken chain in the toilet (he had the power of hands which earned him the right to be part of the colony); Tim the Tasmanian anarchist spending all day in his room smoking cannabis and boning up on Revolutionary Syndicalism; Safi out at work or painting his gods sedately in the attic. It was Safi who first noticed.

'Have you seen Chukufidu, Marcus?'

I thought about it. 'Not for a bit.'

Safi shook his head.

'I thought so,' he said.

'What did you think?'

'He's gone.'

'He has gone for a trip maybe. A holiday. Or an assignment.'

Safi laughed. We were on the second-floor landing outside Moishe's room. Moishe was thumping about inside reciting lines in a sing-song. He had played in the Yiddish music-hall in Commercial Road until it was converted for bingo and now he was 'resting'. Safi and I went upstairs. Chukufidu's door had an abandoned look. Although it never shut tight, the padlock kept it closed. We knocked out of politeness. I had a sudden feeling that he was dead, the victim of the long arm of the Nigerian military – that we might find his corpse.

The door splintered easily from the padlock. The room was a mess of papers and clothes with the window stuck open as if he had just jumped. A poster of Muhammed Ali was pinned to the wall next to photographs of elegant black nudes torn from magazines, a smiling portrait of Chairman Mao, a newspaper article about Fanon and another about Che Guevara, and a screenprint of Okigbo's profile on brown wrapping paper with a huge signature that may have been Chukufidu's. Blood-red slogans were stencilled straight onto the bare areas of wall – mostly quotes from Okigbo plus one from Fanon. A lamp and a gramophone player were connected to the socket by bare wires stuck straight into the holes around which the bakelite was blackened by burn-marks like the kerosene lamps at home. In the corner was a huge zinc tub full of a honey-coloured and acrid-smelling liquid.

'Piss,' said Safi. 'He could never be bothered to go down to the loo.'

We each gripped a handle and carried the tub up the

stairs between us, careful not to let Chukufidu's piss slop over the edge. Now and again it did and fell all the way down the stairwell to the ground floor far below because we could not stop giggling.

'This is a year's worth of piss,' shouted Safi. 'A good vintage. The lazy bugger.'

We were taking it up to the roof which was accessible only through Safi's room. His window led out onto a flat area between two sloping rooves of sooty tiles. We manoeuvred our burden through the window still laughing and not caring now whether we got wet ourselves, and with a heave emptied out the liquid so that it swept in a foaming wave across the roof and into the gutter. Pigeons flapped away astonished. For some reason I felt full of joy even though Chukufidu's stewed piss was splashed over my trousers.

'What will he say when he comes back? Maybe he was conducting an experiment. A magic potion!'

'He won't be coming back, my friend,' said Safi, suddenly serious. 'Not in this life.'

I looked at him. The sun was almost warm as it beat off the tiles. The smell of urine was mingling with the smell of traffic fumes. London went on forever all around us. I knew that Safi was right. He felt these things. We went back down into the room and found Chukufidu's papers. We placed them carefully in a drawer in the room and left, pulling the door to and securing it with thick string. All that week I asked after my friend in places he frequented but no one had seen him. London had swallowed him up. Someone told me that people were fished out of the Thames every week and that most of them were never identified. Life plays with us like a leopard.

I had eight days left out of my Visitor's allocation of three months. I was depressed, having grown into the house and got accustomed to the street and its smells and noises and having grown fond of the area. I had given up looking for jobs. Even the few African restaurants or music-clubs or the galleries and boutiques selling tropical trash, where I might have been welcomed, had no vacancies owing to the Nigerian coup having preceded the Ghanaian by a month and provoking through its violence a minor flood of refugees.

Then one day in May everything changed. I was having a cup of tea in Safi's room and moaning about my lot. Apart from anything else I was missing Chukufidu. Safi put down his brush and went out of the door. His unfinished god stared at me with several eyes. I felt very tired in the room, filled as it was with the smoke of joss-sticks. A bowl of perfumed bits to nibble lay on the floor and I helped myself. I touched my broken tooth with my thumb and felt useless and bitter, ruminating on the shoddy way in which I had so far been treated here. Cold air would still find my tooth's raw nerve as insults found my pride. He came back with a paper in his hand, dropping it into my lap. It was a work permit with the Home Office stamp on it. The name was not familiar to me: John C. Ewusi. Then I saw the photograph.

Before I had time to react Safi was telling me of a vacancy at Heathrow in the Wash-Up Department of BOAC (with which airline I had flown over). His cousin was going back to Calcutta. I could step into his shoes on Safi's recommendation.

'But I told you, I haven't one of these. Why did you throw this at me?'

'Marcus, I didn't throw it at you. I was giving it to you. You can have it on behalf of our absent friend.'

'But it's Chukufidu's. It is not in my name.'

'So what? Come on, for goodness' sake, to them we are all the same. Even me and you. Certainly you and Chukufidu. To be honest you are two peas in a pod. You even have tattoos on your cheeks.'

'They are not tattoos. That was my grandmother's fault. Beliefs and religion are drugs. Are you serious?'

'Mr Grierson likes me. He's the Head of Personnel. You just go in and say, Hi, I'm John Chukufidu Ewusi.'

'Why does he like you, this Mr Grierson?'

I wanted to know how to make the natives like me.

Safi smiled, picking up his brush and continuing to paint. The background was a deep red and the face of the god a bright green. It reminded me of the receptionist in Lamb's Conduit Street.

'Marcus, you make them like you by saying "Good morning sir" and "Have a nice weekend madam" and rubbish like that. It costs nothing but your pride. And shake their hands firmly. African handshakes are too soft, they think you are weak. Crack the bastards' knuckles.'

'My pride is all I've got, Safi.'

He looked at me with eyes as shiny black as his long straight hair.

'No it isn't. Pride is your illusion. Your soul has no pride and your soul is all that counts. Your soul is a diamond, life after life has pressed its black matter into a diamond. No one can harm it.'

I do not know whether Safi's religion was orthodox but it was to serve him very well in the years to come. His paintings were in the galleries and so-called flower people came to hear him expound his Eastern wisdom in smart houses. There was something special about him. He came from somewhere high up in the mountains on the Tibetan border where the snow glints and the air is thin. But at the time I thought his views were superstitious rubbish. For me, the idea of the soul kept humanity in fear. And as for diamonds – they came out of Ghana like pebbles but their wealth ended up as American cars driven by government ministers and local chiefs. Like my father I hated all beliefs that were not in the simple cause of putting bread in people's mouths and power in their hands. But I could not say this to Safi for he had just got me a job. So instead I nodded vaguely and watched his brush circle the eyes of his god in black rings.

'I would like that job,' I said, flicking the work permit with my thumb. 'I would like any job.'

'It's not hard. You're inside and they don't work you like a dog. There's a canteen and if you stay more than nine months without problems you can get a half-price return ticket to the destination of your choice, as long as BOAC flies there.'

'They fly to Accra – that is how I came,' I said, very excited.

'Do you want to go back already?'

'In nine months, yes. Just to visit my mother and my sisters and my father's grave.'

'You won't get bumped off?'

'Not if I don't make a fuss. Not if I behave myself.'

It hurt me, to think of my native country as a hostile place. A face with uneven teeth and smelling of mint instead of mangoes.

'Supposing they find out that I am not Chukufidu?'

Safi smiled. He would always glide through life like a serpent with the venom removed. He probably came from a rich family – his room under the eaves reeked of Eastern luxury. Yet looking around it one saw almost nothing that he had not made or found or constructed himself. Only the gramophone player and the sitar were 'luxuries'.

'You are Chukufidu,' he said. 'If you want to be. It doesn't matter, in the end. We are all tiny drops in the river. Identity is just a voucher, a scrap of paper.'

I realised that I had to have more than the work permit. We sifted through the personal papers together. There was a photograph of Chukufidu's family dressed for a wedding. Sisters like mine; a tall father like mine; a plump mother like mine. Which ones had been killed in the riots? Or had he meant distant cousins?

His origins were complicated. He was born near the Nigerian border in what was then the Cameroons at the time when that country was controlled by the British from Lagos. His mother was an Ibo but from over the border and his father was a Fulani from northern Nigeria who served as a mechanic in the RAF. They moved to Lagos after the war. So one might say Chukufidu was a Cameroonian. This 'blur' made me feel easier. I wanted to find some clue as to how he had earned his work permit and had received it so swiftly – was it because he fell into the 'professional' category or did he have refugee status? Safi suggested it was because his father had been in the RAF, that such things are very important for the British, especially so soon after Churchill's death.

It appeared that Chukufidu had been in the United Kingdom before. Then on looking closer at the permit I perceived that what I had taken for a smudged '5' was in reality a '2'. It had been issued four years ago. Things were easier then. He must have moved to and fro between London and Lagos. This changed my view of him although it was what journalists did – even those who lived in squalor and wrote poems instead of articles. He told me he had written for several Nigerian papers – all of them Communist. A yellowed copy of one of them, the *Comet*, lay in his room. It was very insulting towards the military and the government officials of Lagos. No wonder he had been unemployed since the coup.

'You shift between the two people,' said Safi, talking as if one of those people was not me, as if I was multi-headed like the gods in his paintings. 'The Home Office have enough problems without your help,' he added. 'Don't worry. As long as you don't agitate about Vietnam or South Africa or the Bomb or whatnot. Just keep your head down. They don't care, really. If you have a work voucher, you are dealt with. All they care about is stopping too many dark people coming in.'

'But when I have to register for my university fees? Who shall I be?'

He narrowed his eyes and looked very cunning.

'You are a West African. You have several types of name. Your mother is Ghanaian and your father is Nigerian. You have lived in both countries. Aren't they next to each other?'

'No,' I said. 'They are two hundred miles apart. There is a country called Dahomey between them, about the size of England. The old kingdom of Benin, an important centre for the slave trade as a matter of fact.'

Safi thought I was hurt by his ignorance and folded his hands together.

'Forgive me,' he said. 'But they won't know it either, you can bet on it. It is a matter of forms and carbon copies and paper-clips and rubber stamps.'

'I must pretend to be so many things,' I sighed.

My grandmother believed in the power of the ancestors, how they sought wrongdoers and took them out of their bodies in their sleep and swapped them for a demon. Some of this old superstition fluttered like a weak bird in my stomach. 'I hate lying. It is only confirming what whites think of us.'

Safi snorted. 'White people are the biggest liars in town,' he said. 'They lied to us all. And now we are still crawling to them on our knees! Asking for this and that! For their bloody approval! Even after they have murdered us and raped us and plundered our nations! Even after they have committed bloody genocide!'

I had never seen him so passionate. Utterly passionate. He had stood up, waving his brush about, and his long hair was falling over his face as he danced from foot to foot – yet I could still see the whites of his eyes rolling in his head. He had changed so swiftly from gentle to ferocious and for some reason this was the perfect reassurance for me.

He then sat down and reminded me that I would have to

learn how to write in Chukufidu's spiky italic hand –
completely the opposite of my rounded hand, which in
those days resembled a line of low hills and was the legacy
of Miss Mills, my first teacher.

I set to immediately in the privacy of my room. It was
more difficult than I had thought. I had to disentangle his
signature like wool in order to work out how it was made.
Mine was timid, his was bold. A loop overarched it like a
warrior's shield or smoke from a train. It was hard to make
this loop look natural. Tim came in with a cup of tea and
we ended up discussing political theory and the future of
the world – Socialism-Co-operation-Trade-Unionism ver-
sus Kropotkin. Tim had aboriginal blood in him and his
mop of curly black hair bounced about as he talked. He had
an anti-Vietnam banner hanging from his window and
smoked cannabis – I tried some for the first time but felt
sick and giddy. We felt we could move the world that
night, and separated with a friendly hug. I heard him
giggling and stumbling all the way up the stairs to Safi's
room. I ruminated on the possibility that Safi and he were
lovers and consequently felt much lonelier.

In the early hours I lay on my bed and wondered why I
had ever worried about my identity! I could be a hundred
people if I wished. I could change persona like my socks, I
could speak my lines in Ga or Pidgin or English as Moishe
spoke his in Hungarian and Yiddish and English. I started to
float gradually off the bed. I dreamt of sunsets over the
Volta estuary and sniffed the fragrance of charcoal. The Fab
Four were playing 'Love Me Do' under our iroko tree
while my mother and sisters were plaiting their hair and not
even noticing.

The wash-up was in Hatton Cross on the edge of the
airport. It took an hour to get there by bus. Safi introduced
me to Mr Grierson. He was a shy and balding man in a
white nylon shirt with the sleeves rolled up who kept his

eyes on his papers most of the time. His office was full of smoke. A model aeroplane was taking off on a stand next to his name. It was a VC10. Naturally that made me think of the happy crowds in Accra stadium and the shout that went up whenever Joe Dahota kicked the ball very high . . . 'VC10! VC10!' There was a photograph of Mr Grierson as a young man in RAF uniform hanging next to a BOAC calendar showing a white beach with palm-trees. The office trembled every time a plane roared over. Homesickness is not a sickness, it is more like vertigo. I had to sit down.

He had my papers in front of him. Chukufidu's serious face stared up at him. It was a younger Chukufidu but he still looked nothing like me. Mr Grierson glanced at the permit, tapping the desk with his nail.

'Been here long lad?'

My face went hot. I had learnt Chukufidu's details by heart.

'If you mean this time, I have been here since January, sir. The coup in Nigeria. I like London a lot even if it bears little resemblance to anything in the work of Mr Dickens, sir.'

He looked at me queerly.

'You want to study over here, do you? In our socialist paradise?'

'Not yet, sir.' Safi had told me that I must not give the impression of being too clever and that I must make light of my plan to study.

'Not yet?'

'In the future, sir. Research, something to do with journalism.' I waved my hand about. Everyone is suspicious of journalists. 'Right now I want to—'

I paused. I had started on the sentence without knowing how it would finish.

'Work like a demon,' I said. 'Spanking clean dishes!'

Mr Grierson was looking at me suspiciously, his cigarette burning away between his fingers. A packet of Kensitas poked from his shirt pocket and brought back unwelcome associations. I was smiling and remembering to look into his eyes – which goes against everything our parents have taught us, of course. I realised suddenly that my broken tooth was showing. 'Spanking clean dishes' was a slogan from my childhood. It advertised washing-up liquid on a huge hoarding in Accra and had popped up out of nowhere.

Mr Grierson appeared to be tired of his job. He made me fill in another form, a BOAC one with a picture of wings. ('Better On A Camel', Safi had joked. 'Or Blast Off And Crash.') My hand was shaking and I had to apologise. I forced my hills into spikes. It did not look convincing. A word was a northern village of pointed thatch. A sentence was a choppy sea.

'Coconuts,' he said when I finally wrote 'West Africa' as my 'place' of birth. 'Geography lesson. Remember it clear as a bell. Coconuts. Had to draw them. The Gold Coast. Still gold out there, is there?'

I told him that the Gold Coast was now called Ghana because Ghana was the legendary place where the gold came out of, long ago, in the time of the Phoenicians. I wondered if I was sounding too knowledgeable. Maybe he had mentioned my country to trap me. He cocked his head and looked dreamy, smoke pluming from his fingers.

'Funny thing, history, isn't it? You never think of Africa as having a history until we came along.'

This was a trap. I made sure I did not enter it.

I was walking on air when we went across the yard to the wash-up building. £12 16s! And only two bob for my rent! I would not begin today, but I could take a peep. Safi greeted his cousin by the swinging rubber doors and we shook hands. Then we went in. I wondered if the cousin knew who I really was. He looked nothing like Safi – he was short and plump with sideburns, a bronze chain-bracelet and a starched collar.

The sharp-nosed foreman frowned at me and muttered

something I didn't hear. He had brown overalls on while the workers wore thin blue jackets and rubber gloves. It was very noisy within and more humid than Accra. The rubber doors behind us thudded open and trolleys with several tiers began to be wheeled in at great speed by burly white men in white caps.

Safi shouted in my ear, 'The loaders. They get all the pickings. Don't have nothing to do with them.' His cousin nodded and grinned, buttoning his jacket.

The trolleys braked by a long belt with a gulley of water the colour of the Thames running alongside it. A woman with a tall beehive, a smiling bespectacled Asian chap, a boy in a Tony Curtis haircut and a man in his twenties with a skew-whiff nose and open mouth sat behind the belt and its gulley on swivel chairs. The meals and drinks off the aircraft travelled along the belt to be scooped and tipped respectively into the gulley. The dirty plates and cutlery and glasses were placed in separate crates like those used for milk bottles with one person responsible for each. Some of the plates were smart china with a pattern of wings and the rest melamine. The loaded crates were whisked into the dish-washing machines that ran at right-angles off the last part of the belt. This was where Safi and his cousin worked in a fog of steam. They had to work fast because the remains of meals never stopped coming – especially first thing in the morning after the transatlantic night flights.

Safi handled the scalding plates with big sweeps of his arms and bantered and even yelled with the others. So must I change, I thought. Once long ago I scratched my white on a twig in the bush and saw double through that eye for a few days – everything had its twin slightly to the left of it. So must I play the double role. I could hear my teacher, Mr Henry Oduntun, recite the lines of Shakespeare we had to learn by heart: 'And one man in his time plays many parts, His acts being seven ages.' I have had recourse to that description many times since. Yet is there not an essential identity? We are born in the body of Africa; our viviparity is cultural and geographical as much as biological. Wars merely crack the unity that is our natural inheritance and the central pillar of the roof.

The worst job was to empty the leftover food and drink into the brown stream of the gulley right under one's nose. The Asian chap seemed to be enjoying it. If a glass half full of wine appeared in front of him he would tip it down his throat. Suddenly he called out in a way that reminded me of Safi singing his ragas: '*I – love – you – Riii – taaa!*'

He had chosen a moment when the crashing had stopped. It was like something sung in a temple. Rita was apparently the white woman in the beehive, about fifty-five with a double chin. She smiled good-humouredly as if used to it. It was to occur several times a day and always in the same high clear sing-song. And when the trays were piling up he would call out, '*Too much! Too much!*' Never anything else. His name was Aziz and he had been a bank official in Calcutta.

An elderly man with unruly white hair was hunched over a big steel tub on the counter nearby. It was full of a liquid that reminded me of Chukufidu's piss. It was in fact something that brightened up silver. The man was dipping in tarnished forks and knives and spoons then laying them out on a cloth, sheened anew.

'First Class cutlery,' Safi said, coming over to me. 'High flyers.'

The elderly man smiled at me and I caught a whiff of incontinence over the silver bath's stink. 'Good morning to you,' he said in a middle-class accent.

A very tall Sikh in a red turban was washing this cutlery by hand without rubber gloves then drying it until it shone like a mirror. Showing me how to check a fork was bright and spotless enough, he held it up to the light by the handle to check the tines then held it by the tines to check the handle. Sometimes he would breathe on the cutlery before polishing it. This made me smile but the Sikh never smiled, it was not a deliberate thing.

'You must see yourself in it,' was all he would say.

Beyond this space through further rubber doors was another even larger space where the food was prepared. It was full of white women in white tunics. We were not allowed in there without permission – hygiene regulations, Safi said. And theft. He pointed to a box near us that was full of tins of caviar. 'Don't get involved in any shady deals,' he murmured in my ear.

I had no idea what he meant. A foreman as short and plump as Safi's cousin, with a bulbous red nose like a monkey's behind, came up and greeted me. He was holding a clipboard. 'That is Alf,' Safi said after the man had wandered away. 'A nice chap but totally lazy.' He nodded his head over at the sharp-nosed foreman now talking with Alf. 'That is Terry. A nasty chap but totally efficient. Don't upset him. Tell him you are a pigeon-fancier. Now don't hang around,' he added. 'It gives the wrong impression. See you back at the house.'

The rubber doors swung shut behind me and I breathed the outside air – cold after that steamy place in spite of the sunny day. As I walked towards the gates the loaders were hauling trolleys out of the big white van, 'BOAC Catering' painted on its side. One of them offered me an empty champagne bottle but I walked on steadily, my hands in my pockets, ignoring their condescending remarks and bursts of silly laughter. I had a job. I had slipped in unnoticed and would grow and grow until I was very tall. Then I would return to my country and sort out the mess. Avenge my father. Bear the sharp sword of justice.

Just this.

Perhaps my spring became a swagger down the wide road that ran alongside the runway, but I let it. The thunder of the planes stole nothing from mine, for my thunder was silent.

★

What if Chukufidu were to come back one day?

His friends dropped by over the following weeks and we told them that he had disappeared. I became known as Chuku at the wash-up. Sometimes Chukufido. The fore-man Terry called me 'Robinson's' (from the jam) when he was in a bad mood. His secret nickname was 'Bagwash' and Alf's was 'High Speed Gas'. The big white boy with the crooked nose was called Tony. He always looked startled at everything and I soon realised that he was not very bright. He had marriage problems and one day his wife locked him out. He came back with us to the squat and spent the whole evening drinking tea and telling us how all he wanted was to do the right thing by her, to be a good hubby, to give her kids. He droned on in his dull London voice and I thought: I am not surprised she has locked him out. He snored all night on the sofa in my room, filling the air with a stink from his feet.

He pleaded with me the next day to come and talk to her after work.

He lived in Hounslow on the bottom floor of a council block, and I stood next to him as he talked to his wife through the door. There was something like a shoe thrown against the door and then he indicated that I should come and have a go. I did not know what to contribute, but Tony was looking at me so expectantly that I placed my cheek against the peeling wood and asked if she was listening. A muffled voice said something, maybe rude, and then I started to tell her that Tony wanted to do the right thing, to be a good—

'Who are you?' I heard.

'A friend,' I said.

'Fuck off, Tony's friend.' The second 'shoe' hit the door.

I came away. Tony asked me what she had said. 'I'm afraid she didn't want my help,' I reported. An elderly white woman in curlers peered over the sill of her window in the flat above.

'I hope you're not breaking in,' she said, glaring at me.
'He's my mate, Doreen,' Tony called up.

She eyed me suspiciously from top to toe with her jaw
working as if eager to chew me up. Then she tutted with a
toss of her rollers and disappeared from view. Above her the
windows of the block towered and spread out, hundreds of
them, all containing the same unspoken thoughts; the same
jaws working; the same tut and toss of the head. I felt dizzy
and said that I had to get back to my place.

I could see him from the bus-stop. He was a tiny helpless
figure trying to get into his own home – the huge concrete
block punctured by hundreds of windows and this micro-
scopic figure at the bottom. It depressed me because I
thought of Africa and how eagerly we were erecting such
places in our own cities.

I never knew which job I would be on from day to day. I
was peripatetic, as if Terry could not decide where I fitted.
Maybe he did not want me to fit. The worst job was Aziz's,
scooping the leftovers off the plates and into the grey-
brown stream running past your lap like the gutters in Accra
in the rainy season that run past your feet. *I – love – you –
Riii – taaa!* My pink gloves frequently shoved whole
untouched meals into the rippling water – a steak with the
parsley like a bow tie on the top, a clump of caviar, a sole
lying under a sheet of sauce. They had been carried over
the clouds, over the oceans. It was painful for me to see so
much waste. The cold water leaked into my gloves and
down my sleeve as the flood pushed the waste away into
oblivion. I would ruminate on the absurdity of things and
on my futile role, growing momentarily dejected. On other
days I would feel exhilarated simply at the idea of the
gleaming future spread before me. Maybe I was a bit drunk.
There were untouched miniatures of liqueurs such as
Cointreau or Armagnac which we would share out
between us, reserving any Benedictines for Silvo Stan who
would unscrew the little caps and toss the fiery sweetness

back, licking his lips with pleasure. He told me early on that he had a waste bag tied to his stomach after an attack of cancer. When I worked next to him I could smell its hospital smell.

'I love working here,' he said. 'It's company.'

Now and again I would swallow an abandoned glass of champagne from First Class and Aziz would sing 'Happy Birthday' as a joke, the others joining in until it was quite loud. The lads played football in the yard. I was usually with the Asians against the whites. The best player was a teenager from Slough with a Beatles cut whose obsession was the pools, *Tit-bits*, and the Hollies. He told me that I must visit Slough because it was not what people said it was. He was known as 'Haydock' after the bass guitarist for the Hollies. In the canteen Haydock would give me 'perms' for the day's pools coupon or read sensational 'tit-bits' in a robotic voice about Soho's strip-girls and so forth.

'Listen to this, mate. "*It – took – only – one – word – from his – girlfriend and – David Stafford – London's – cheekiest – crook – was – betrayed.*" Never trust a skirt. Have you got a woman, then?'

I shook my head.

'So you won't be needing one of them slot-machines, mate. Listen to this. "*The – silent – salesmen – that – sell – contraceptives – a – searching – investigation – reveals – the – peril – our – teenagers – face.*" I thought they was supposed to stop the peril!'

I was twenty by now. I had not so much as touched a girl since coming out and hardly before. Then one day in late June there was a knock on the house door and a Nigerian girl who knew Chukufidu smiled and said, 'Hello, I want to see Chukufidu.' I had met her with him before but she did not remember me. She was a truly 'slick chick' (to use the slang of those days). I told her the bad news. She shrugged and asked if she could see his room. She had lent him a 'disk'. We went in together.

'What a mess,' she said. 'He needs a woman.'

That she should speak of him in the present startled me. She giggled in a very attractive way. Her skin was glossy, she had red lipstick on and false eyelashes and wore a tight mini-skirt, but this provocative look was typical of many girls at that time and she looked more elegant than the white English variety. We could not find her record. She hung about with folded arms, chatting away to me and smiling. She had very nice white teeth between which her pink tongue would rest while listening to me. When she laughed her hand rested against her mouth, the fingers straight as if she was holding a cigarette, and her body coiled as if the laugh was snaking through to her feet. She told me her name was Molara, the daughter of a high-up official who had made money from selling tracts of forest to European timber companies. She had been brought up in Lagos in a European manner and was known here as 'a Bounty Bar'. When her father had joined her mother in the cemetery she had kissed her brothers and sisters goodbye and come to Britain, just before the tightening up of the race regulations in 1962.

I thought nervously of Chukufidu's history. Had she come over with him? I did not dare ask. I felt like a thief; I felt I had thieved not only his identity but his history; now I was falling for his woman.

I stammered my excuses and left the room.

I heard her go out of the front door, her high heels tapping past my window at the height of my head. I knelt on the bed and squealed into my pillow as I always do when upset and frustrated. It is a kind of grieving song.

The next Saturday she came back. I heard the heels pause and scrape on the front step before the rap on the door. I stuffed the envelope containing Chukufidu's papers under the bed and leapt out of my room to welcome her.

'I'm very thirsty,' she said. 'I take one sugar.'

We got to know each other well, though my strict

upbringing prevented me from acting hastily. She was a
typist in an insurance office and earned enough to enjoy
life, to go out to films and clubs. I went with her several
times but my night-studies tired me out and I couldn't keep
up with her energy. She was 'swinging' and liked to dance
but I preferred to walk with her somewhere romantic like
the bank of the Serpentine. She put her arms around my
neck one misty evening. We kissed. Soon we were under a
bush and wrapped about each other. My hands searched
under her dress and brushed this giant wart – then closed
about the breast like a child's hand around a mango. She
sighed with pleasure. I thought about those slot-machines
that Haydock was reading about, wondering where the
nearest one might be. A chemist in Great Titchfield Street
had an advert for Durex that read on into the sign on the
tobacconist next door – Senior Service Satisfy – and
recalling this made me smile. She felt the smile on my lips
and pulled her mouth away.

'Whassup, now?'

'Nothing. I like this. It could be, well, my first time.'

She gave a short high laugh. 'Well, that is very brave of
you to admit it. You're the first boy I have ever been with
who has admitted it.'

I felt a bit silly.

'Have you been with many?'

She put a finger on my lips. The nail pricked the tip of
my nose. A pair of heels clicked by on the path. The ducks
on the lake quacked in alarm. London moaned and rumbled
and roared. She squirmed on the grass, finding a twig
caught under her bottom.

'Your bed is bound to be more comfortable,' she said.

We walked to Lancaster Gate tube, passing by the statue
of Peter Pan. I told her that I had watched a travelling
theatre troupe from England play *Peter Pan* in Accra just
before self-government. For the shadow they had used a
black dancer who had imitated the movements of the white

actress playing Peter and my father had been very, very angry. When Wendy had sewn the shadow back on he had taken it as a symbol of black dependency. It was not meant like that but those were sensitive times. Molara had never seen the play or read the book so I told her the story, her head resting on my shoulder in front of the statue. I thought of my hands running up and down her naked form.

I also thought of Chukufidu as we walked through that dark park with its looming trees and bushes: was I his shadow, or was he mine? Losing your shadow was like losing your life to an evil spirit who subsequently replaces it with himself and makes you look as if you are still alive. My grandmother told me this and now it came back, all that superstition, in a flood. At work I was Chukufidu; at home I was Marcus. Official and unofficial. Slowly maybe I would lose track of which one I really was. That is what mad people lost, those on the streets of Accra and London who mutter to themselves in a wild frenzy, thinking they are Shakespeare or Trotsky or a hyena or a paw-paw.

I was worried about finding a machine, and as we came up from the tube at Tottenham Court Road I said I had to pop into the toilet.

It stank of sewage. A dirty towel lay in a puddle. The machine was broken and covered in graffiti. One of the scrawls said 'Chuck woz ere' which frightened me. As I was rattling the machine a thin white chap in a crumpled suit and what looked like eye make-up appeared at my elbow and murmured something. I thought he was asking me the time and looked at my watch. 'It'll only take a jiff,' he said. To my thorough astonishment I felt a hand crawling across my buttocks like a spider. I ran out.

We went back to my place and she started undressing. She had on a brand-new trouser suit which to me looked like a pair of pyjamas. I knew it was brand-new because she had told me and it was only just coming into fashion: Molara did a bit of modelling and would inform me as to

what was trendy. It had cost only fifteen guineas, she said – which was more than I was paid a week. She took off the trousers first and danced a bit in the tunic which was no more than a very short mini-skirt. Her thighs gleamed and seemed to continue without end. I sat on the side of the bed not knowing what I should do but unbuttoning my shirt anyway. I felt excited and treacherous and anxious all at the same time. The excitement had something to do with the treachery.

'I have not got any . . . precautions,' I said.

'Eh?'

I was unlacing my shoes, bending down and mumbling.

'You know. Precautions. I have not got any. The machine was out of order.'

Her legs were right in front of my face now. A mature woman, older than me at any rate. She held my head against her belly having lifted up her tunic. My ear was pressed against the little nose of her belly-button while my hands searched upwards like a chap surrendering in a cowboy film. I must not get her into trouble.

'What are you saying?' she whispered, into my hair.

'If we do it, you know.'

I kissed her belly, soft and warm and sweaty from the dancing, with my hands right up fumbling over her breasts. Touching them made her breath quicker, short sharp gusts of breath on my scalp. It was like switching on our old wireless in Accra and hearing the valves warm up. Soon it would be too late. Teenage peril. She was bending right over, her weight forcing me back onto the mattress, her thin but heavy body nestling between my legs and along my stomach and chest so that I could hardly expand my lungs.

'Is it all right?' I mumbled.

My fingers were scrabbling independently of my mind over the lace frills of her knickers, feeling the lumpiness of the crotch under the silk. 'Is it all right? You know, without precautions?'

She tensed suddenly. Then little shivers rippled down her body. She was trying not to laugh. She propped herself up on her arms and told me straight that she had put something inside her called a diaphragm, like the skin of a guavo half. She wouldn't be having babies. Did I think she would be relying on men? She rolled to one side and lifted her tunic over her head. I wondered how many men she had been with. Carlos had told me of a girl called Prunella who paid him to sleep with her when in her case it was usually the other way round. It almost seemed strange to me that there was no cash transaction between Molara and myself and I wondered why I was thinking this when only whores asked for money, whores like the girl Carlos slept with. I had lit a candle and switched off the light on entering the room. The flame now struck copper off Molara's skin, reminding me of a little jewellery box my mother had received as a wedding present carved from ebony with copper clasps and lock. It had its own tiny copper key which she hid somewhere in a place we children never discovered.

'You are a good boy, worrying like that,' she murmured, stroking my head and then slipping her naked body under the covers. I was conscious as I squeezed in with her of how different I must seem from Chukufidu and how it was precisely my innocence and freshness that was attracting her. Freed from my anxiety I lunged at the open box of her body almost too hastily and clumsily. She slowed me down despite her quick breathing, sculpting me with her hands like clay from the river and refashioning me into a man, a strong charm, a power.

I do not know why but it was a bit uncomfortable for me physically when the moment came. I had the key but it would not fit the lock. She seemed to enjoy it, however, which was as important to me. Sitting up against the pillow and smoking, with her nipples brushing the white sheet, she told me not to worry if I had not made it. Normal for the first time. She asked me to guess her age. I said twenty-six, which was Chukufidu's age.

'Twenty-nine,' she said. She did not look it. She said she wanted to be a singer, to do numbers like the Supremes but time was running out. The Supremes had started when they were kids. Maybe it was too late to be Florence Ballard.

'Who is Florence Ballard?'

'Don't you know the Supremes then? "Where Did Our Love Go"? Where have you been in all your life, Marcus?'

I squirmed a bit on the pillow. I had bought a third-hand Dansette for two bob but hadn't yet got it to work. There was a great difference in knowledge between us. I did not even possess a 'tranny'. I had bought the Dansette to play classical and jazz records on. The pop parade was a daily background but not something I wanted to join.

She was singing 'Where Did Our Love Go' now, rocking gently from side to side and making the bed creak while turning in her hands a little figurine I had brought over on the 'plane: an Ashanti charm carved in iroko wood that might have been scooped from her flesh. There were footsteps passing on the pavement and I wondered if I had closed the curtains properly. I felt as if I had passed an exam. My only fear was that the door would suddenly burst open and Chukufidu would find us together. I even imagined him that night in my half-sleep as covered in weed from the river, dripping a foul puddle on the floorboards and smelling of grey death.

Instead, about a week later a letter popped through the letterbox. It was addressed to Chukufidu. I opened it. It was a cheque sent from a bank in Nigeria. £120. No note. The signatory was someone unknown to me with a West African name.

'You know, was Chukufidu rich?' I asked Molara, when we were next out together.

She laughed. 'Rich? What is rich? My father once had two fields of guinea corn and millet and thought he was rich. Then he became truly rich and thought he was poor because he did not own a Rolls-Royce. Chukufidu's father ran a bus company in the north, started with British money when he was still a child. They lived in a proper house. They had a maid and a cook and a gardener and two guards. Then the company was nationalised after self-government and they lost their house and his father died and then his mother of a broken heart. Chukufidu was already a student in Lagos. But he was Communist and so he had to hide this thing about his business family.'

'How did you know?'

'I am his cousin.'

I should not have been so shocked but I was. It was like a slap on the face, something dirty – as if I had been sleeping with my own blood. I had cashed the cheque because I had opened a bank account in his name – I already had one in mine at a different bank. I felt safer depositing my work pay in an account using my work name. It was not theft because he had disappeared and I did not know the address of his family, the money was just sitting there still in his name in case of emergencies. Now I knew that I should have given the money to Molara.

She told me she was only a second cousin through his mother yet she had known him all her life. I closed my eyes, confused and tired after a day's work; the long journey there and back; the roaring of the planes over the bus-stop where I had waited twenty minutes. She had not been sad when I told her he had disappeared without trace. I mentioned this. We were in a pub near Leicester Square. It had red seats which made her shiny green dress stand out. She was turning native heads. My strength and pride had reacted like a snail's feelers to a thumb with this information about her blood-link with Chukufidu. My fingers were raw and dry from the hot cutlery – Terry had put me on the washing-machine next to Safi that day and the steam was tiring even for someone brought up in Accra. Terry had torn a strip off me for dropping a very hot First Class plate. Then the two of us had gone upstairs to clean some dishwasher filters in the sink after the break. He was almost weeping in front of me, saying how once it was only him and the lads and now it was all 'tits and brownies' and he felt ashamed of himself, he could not feel any pride in the job these days and he might as well 'jack it in' and spend all day with his pigeons. I had thought of the mint-smelling policeman with the uneven teeth and spoke as little as I could – like a psychotherapist, Safi commented afterwards. All that had been tiring.

'I don't get sad about things,' Molara replied. 'Anyway, he disappears all the time.'

I felt my stomach contract in an unpleasant manner.

'All the time?'

She was always using expressions that were over the top.

'Twice before, OK? Disappeared into the mist. Then came back again.'

'How long after?'

'A year, two years.'

I could not ask her if he had left all his papers those times in case she sniffed me out. I felt sure this time was different – those other times he had probably gone back to Nigeria on a secret journalistic assignment. I calmed myself down. I had my room; I had my job; I had my girl. Things were going well by any standards.

I hid Chukufidu's papers in his own room, buying a new padlock. This was a good system since it meant I could get hold of them at any time, but in the event of my shadow returning there would be no evidence that I had been tampering. While the bureaucratic problems would be complicated, my youth prevented me from musing that far forward.

In the process of hiding the papers I uncovered a sanza from under a heap of blankets and a torn silkscreen. It was something he must have brought from Nigeria because the wooden resonator and the way the spokes of the bicycle wheel were worked and welded was African. It had an unmistakable resonance of charcoal fires and goat droppings and was slightly warped.

I took it down to my room and began to play. Our school had an orchestra that used local instruments and my father had insisted I play in it. I was not very gifted and was usually given a gourd full of dried beans to shake about but I had tried the sanza a few times. I now played songs my grandmother used to sing to me, soft lulling songs that went on and on with the same words over and over again until you were somewhere different in your head. There was a song called 'Naa-Yanga' about a beloved woman who is far away, very sad. I remembered most of the words and sang it softly, plucking at the sanza to find the melody. Our music teacher was a dreamy white man with furred ears called Mr Holmes who said the sanza must sound like drops of rain on a heavenly gourd. I decided to practise for an hour every evening. Safi heard me from the hallway one day and liked it very much. I went up to his room and he played sitar alongside – a strange mixture but it made its own music. Carlos got wind of this and brought along his Spanish guitar a few evenings later. This was hard because his music had a different 'swing'. Realising this he brought two congas and a shaker the next time, tapping and rustling them behind us like a sea wind through palms. I felt that we were three souls dancing and sometimes pulling each other over. We got drunk on our music, or maybe on the cannabis that Tim puffed into the close air of Safi's room while clapping along on his thighs. Colum came up and played his spoons or blew into a beer bottle or tried to fit 'Danny Boy' to our rhythms, and we made Moishe sing in Yiddish while we improvised behind. Moishe's songs made me cry, they were so sad and passionate. He sang up at the ceiling with his scrawny neck showing and his hand on his heart, his threadbare pullover covered in egg stains, a plaster keeping his spectacles together while I closed my eyes and sang alongside in Ga, words that maybe were about the same things of which he was singing: losing your country and your loved ones, songs of exile and suffering and massacre and old wars and betrayals, making up the words as I went along and threading them into the tissue of my grandmother's songs that she called 'Thinking Songs', weeping as I hummed and sang softly because I was thinking of my father, and how far away my mother and my sisters were, of my home in Accra and my dead grandmother's village many hours up the dirt road, of its dust and its chickens and its big welcome and of the long lowered eyelashes of its thatch.

Nobody had ever made music like this before, I was thinking. I was swallowed up in it – we all were. Even Molara who had begun to sing along at the beginning in a brassy voice that did not mix and had changed it to a hum, and then something like an ululation at a wedding only much quieter and more inside herself, clapping or shaking the shaker and waggling her hips like a mammy at a wedding. But afterwards, after the silence and the shy laughing and grins of our sweaty and tearful faces and feeling the music had floated out through the open window to fall upon the grey rooves of London like the little paper darts I had seen from the top of the Post Office Tower, I heard her say in a high voice: 'That was zany. Absolutely crazy. Give me the Supremes any day, you know?'

I was thinking while breathing in the sweet smoke of the cannabis, choking on its burn at the back of my throat: one day we will take over with this music. Nothing will resist the movement of the oppressed, of the trampled peoples. In China they are smashing the temples and scratching out the bourgeois remnants, starting from zero. Chukufidu had believed this to be the only way forward but I had not agreed, it seemed too unhappy and pure. Now I knew that change would happen anyway, that Africa would rise from its mess, its half-discarded white ways, and along with all the oppressed continents drive the old system before it like a great wave to make a new sea. And over this new sea would float our music plucking and wailing and humming like raindrops on a heavenly gourd, like voices in the bush. And the whites would listen like little children sitting in a yard in obedient rows, with their mouths wide open.

When England won the World Cup at the end of the month we all assembled again and played to drown out the cheering and the rattles and the horns blowing. But it was not the same. For a start we had watched the match through a grey snowstorm on Carlos's old TV and had been swept up in it. Even before it went into extra time we were all on the edge of our seats. We were hypnotised. When the last two English goals were scored it was all we could do not to shoot to our feet and cheer. Our playing that night was a celebration as well as a protest. A thorough muddle.

Molara had told me that Chukufidu played the sanza very well in the old days and so I tried to feel his playing in my fingers. That was a mistake. Something very cold went down my spine and into my hands and I felt them go rigid. Moishe was singing in Yiddish and big Carlos was crooning in accompaniment. My fingers were rigid, they would not play. Chukufidu was blocking me with his anger.

I blinked away my sweat and buried my head in my hands, then got up and stepped out through the window onto the roof. So much noise, hooting and shouting and banging! Here was where we had emptied out Chukufidu's piss as if the piss was his life-spirit. Thinking of how we both supported Ipswich reassured me in some way – that I was not stealing his shadow but continuing his memory! Whatever Molara had implied, I was sure he was dead. But this did not free me from fear. Superstition was deeply rooted in me however much my father had tried to eradicate it in the name of reason and sense. I walked to the

179

edge of the roof: if I jumped, would my shadow fly up like a dark pigeon to save itself as I plunged?

'Marcus?'

The music had stopped. Molara was behind me. She was being careful not to let her slacks get dirtied.

'It's all right,' I said. 'I was too hot.'

'Too *hot?* Hey, have you become an Englishman with ice for blood?'

Far below us the street stretched either side to eternity. There were so many streets and people and so many holes to fall into! So many traps! The black gutter was full of cats' droppings. I had not noticed that before. Its heavy iron trough had been fixed in place in the time of Victoria when iron flowed like rivers through the Empire, seizing it in a deadly grip. Great Titchfield Street was very far down, heads floating upon it like coconut shells. Oxford Street was not visible from here but was marked by a long noise, like the Odaw at full flood. Molara was holding my shoulders and pulling me away a little. I needed my father to guide me. I had no right to be here, I was the shadow of a silhouette. We could play our music until we dropped but the nations were deaf.

'Let us go down into the street,' Molara whispered. She was desperate to join in the fun.

'It is too dangerous,' I said. 'There are a lot of drunkards. That's when they bite.'

She snorted. She hated it when I brought up these factors. (Once she did come crying but it was a couple of Jamaican girls in a club who had teased her for being African, asking her if she had gone around naked as a kid with a bone through her nose, imitating a tom-tom on the table. I told her that it had happened to me with some Caribbean lads and how soon they'll be envious, their tin-pot islands will seem puny in comparison to our ancient lands with their history and culture. She did not agree. That was when she started discarding anything African in her wardrobe – even the malachite earrings that I loved, the bronze bangles that shone bright against her skin, the necklaces of seeds and shells that reminded me of the coast and its long dark sands, the white breakers and the palms. She sold them all and with the money bought a tartan trouser suit in wool for over thirty-five guineas, complete with a jaunty sailor's cap – very fashionable.)

We went out into the street trailing the others, Carlos banging on his congas. The atmosphere was friendly and Carlos started a conga with a lot of strangers down Oxford Street. There was ticker-tape and confetti and klaxons and some American hippies with flowers, like a carnival, but it was still a bit shy and English except for the drunk ones who were very boisterous. One of these was singing and waving a huge Union Jack on a pole in front of Boots'. He must have pinched the flag from a building. Beer bottles were rolling everywhere. Molara and I left the conga when it got to Regent Street, making our way towards Piccadilly Circus. Faces veered towards us ablaze under their caps with the fire of victory, mouths grinning absurdly or huge from yelling and chanting. I was wishing Ghana had won. Or Nigeria, or Cameroun, or even Dahomey. It would help Africa feel proud. By Kingly Street Molara shouted that she wanted to go down Carnaby Street but it was hard to cross the road, to weave between the crowds. Then a familiar face was coming towards me. If I had spotted it earlier I would have dived off, pulling Molara after me – but I seemed to be sucked towards it by my own helplessness and shock as they say you are drawn towards a crocodile's yawning mouth.

It was Tony. He was drunk.

'Hey it's Chuku!' he shouted. 'My friend Chuku! England rules the waves, Chuku! Champions of the Wo-orld! We're going to land on the fucking mo-on!'

I tried to pull away but he had his hands tight on my

shoulders, shaking me. The drink had made his face look less stupid or maybe everyone else now resembled him.

'Come on Chuku! It's bloody well marvellous, innit? Bob-by! Bob-by! Hurst, Hurst, Hurst! Champ-i-ons of—'

'I will see you, Tony. I have to go—'

He was noticing Molara, who looked more confused than suspicious. Tony's head lunged towards her with its big yellow teeth.

'Who's this, Chukufido? What have you been hiding from me all this time, bad boy? Your lovely scrubber, is it? Scrubber of First Class dishes? Dishy dishes?'

Tony had never made a joke before in my hearing. He hardly realised now he was playing with words – it was a type of drunken inspiration. The crowd jostled us. Everyone else was moving, moving. He stared wide-eyed at Molara, licking his red lips. 'A mighty fine dish, Chuku—'

'He's not Chuku!' Molara shouted. She was angry because she hated whites thinking we all looked the same. I writhed under Tony's grip tightening on my shoulders. I felt panic enter me by the mouth as if out of the air.

'That's right! I'm not Chuku!' I cried out.

I wished I had pretended not to know Tony – he was stupid enough to think he had made a mistake but it was too late for those games. He looked at both of us with a drooping mouth hot with beer fumes. The noise swirled around us, rattles and horns blurring my thoughts and my eyes... Tony blinked and thrust his bent nose at me, a little unsure. Then he was laughing and yelling again.

'Not Chuku? Not me mate Chuku? You're fucking Chiko – Chiki – Chikifuckingfoodoo all right, mate. Don't have me on. You're me mate. You saved my marriage. That's right. Chuckofido saved my marriage,' he repeated to Molara, swaying towards her while using me as his prop. 'Saved my marriage he did. We're gonna have kids. My missus and me. I work with him, he's my work-mate, I fucking *love* the bastard—'

Now he had an arm around me and was squeezing me to him. I must have looked lost and fearful because Molara was staring at me intently – I could see that terrible thoughts could be passing through her mind. Tony smelt as if he had not washed in weeks – the heat and the excitement. She let go of my hand which she had been gripping tightly and disappeared into the river of happy people.

I elbowed Tony in the stomach and he relaxed his grip. It was not a hard jab but I yelled an apology as I struggled out from under his arm and dived after Molara. She had not got far on her high heels and I spotted her easily. I plunged through the crowd, caught her by the wrist and pulled us away. We found a quiet side-street to the right and dived down it and stood there, panting.

'Why did he call you Chukufidu?' she said, looking at me through the veil of her false lashes. The whites glimmered like ivory set in iroko wood, like a devil mask.

'An idiot,' was all I could say. 'He was always confusing us. He cannot even pronounce my – his name.'

She stared at me a moment longer and I lowered my eyes. She was picking up white habits. I saw her as covered in invisible grease, smearing herself with white ways. I saw the whole of Africa covered in this grease. The slabs of the pavement were shining in the street-light as if it was sweating this grease. Her heels shifted and clicked as she walked away. I caught up with her.

'What are you angry about?'

'You are lying. I can feel it. I hope you did not kill my cousin! People have killed for such things!'

'What things?'

'A job, papers, all that rubbish!'

She carried on walking away from the noise and the people. I was jabbering by now, denying everything. We found ourselves in Savile Row, full of gentlemen's tailors displaying top hats and frock coats in the windows with names like Huntsman and Hawkes in glass or gold lettering above polished wood, each window like a precious framed painting of history and power. 'One day,' my father used to say, 'the African will buy his Savile Row suit, and burn it in the square. Then we will be free.' There were a few men and women in evening dress strolling down the street, mostly older than those in the crowd and leaving a trail of brandy fumes and perfume behind them. All of them stared at us as they passed as if we were a curious species.

We must indeed have looked curious: Molara ticking fast on her high heels and myself shuffling after her in an attempt to talk, my hand continually shaken off by her arm. We passed a silver-haired group in furs and velvet jackets and I heard a racial term in a voice like the Queen's, followed by a ripple of laughter. It made me stop in a kind of despair. The sanza had worn my fingers raw and its music was still in my head, but these people would never understand me and neither would Molara. They were moving away from me in opposite directions and I felt lost in the middle – lost even to myself.

There was a shop behind me selling smart shiny shoes: 'Fitting can be Arranged' said a sign in the window, written in the type of curling script my father disapproved of on his school inspections. Everything can be arranged if you only know how.

I pressed my face to the glass and let Molara go. It was easier that way. Explaining, I could only lie. Maybe tomorrow I could tell her the truth while we walked beside the Serpentine or hired a boat. Chukufidu himself had said that any means justifies the end if the end is sacred. The shiny expensive shoes were dead men's shoes. I have fallen in love with her. *I – love – you – Molaaa – raaa!* Hearing Aziz's song in my head ridiculed my feelings.

Then I knew what I would say. It was the truth.

I fled Ghana, Molara. My father had ended up in a fisherman's net, murdered by those criminals who unseated Nkrumah and I had all but sniffed them out. I used

Chukufidu's identity only to save my life, to prevent myself from being forced to go back, thrown onto a plane bound for Accra and certain death. The British recognised the new regime almost immediately – I have no friends in high places over here, Molara.

She would understand this, even if it was exaggerated. Surely, I reflected, she would not demand the papers or give me away like a lamb to the Ministry of Labour or the Home Office or the police or even Mr Grierson in his smoky office if she knew that I too might finish my days floating head down in the Volta estuary, my smashed skull bumping against the rafts of logs, iroko and mahogany and ebony! My poor face like a worm-eaten mask, no longer my own. No longer anything at all.

There was singing down Piccadilly. I would get very drunk tonight. Dive in and get drunk and not worry so much. My father had always said that life was a ladder and that after a certain moment you must not look down.

BODYWORK

They discovered him hanging in his bodyshop one morning. Wife and three kids. What I wanted to know is why. My brother. Never one to get under about nothing. Never a shaky one. Yet there he was, dangling from the main beam in the bodyshop, a half-restored Morris Minor in moorland green dinting the main door with its brakes off, a couple of planks laid at an incline, and a couple of legs hanging in mid-air. It took *me* to realise, coming along that evening (belting down the M6 and M5 as fast as driving rain and bloody awful traffic permitted), what the planks were for; there was a trolley jack between them, but at lowest lock. He'd jacked up the Morris onto the planks, put a chock in front of the nearside wheel, let the handbrake off, scrambled onto the roof, put his neck in the noose –

And then what? How was it chocks away, with him up there and the chock down here?

And why hadn't he just jumped off?

You don't know my brother. That wouldn't have been his style. It had to be a motor, and it had to be original. Anyway, you try jumping off a car roof with a rope around your neck. You'd swing back against the trim, knees knocking the glasswork, and nine times out of ten you'd hoist yourself back on again before anything vital snapped or got blocked. The way he did it, he had no second chances. Once the Morris started rolling, he'd bought it. But how did he get it rolling?

The chock was there, innocent-looking, no strings

attached. The police were sure it was suicide, but all I could see was a boot kicking that block of wood away and then its owner scarpering. I watch too much telly, I suppose. And Sandra, once she'd been put on tranquillisers and the kids packed off to her sister in Droitwich, told me that I was a lump of shit thinking such thoughts: our Gavin had no enemies, he never mixed with dodgers. She assumed I was thinking it was a business thing, when I might not have been. It might have been a psychopath, there are plenty of them. I looked through the books, just to see who'd been in and out, what motors he'd been dolling up in the past few months. There was a Jensen Interceptor, a Jag Mk2, and an MGB Roadster, but everything else was run-of-the-mill.

I was surprised he'd gone out on a Morris Minor, even if it was an early Series II from the fifties – he had a soft spot for cuddly little fifties saloons (he drove about in one of those podgy Vauxhall Crestas for years). But Gavin was always a bit of a boy racer, even in his middle age, and the Jensen or the Jag would've been a touch classier. But maybe he wasn't in trouble when he was dolling them up. Maybe the trouble suddenly came upon him, like a puncture. Worse than a puncture. The head gasket going. A fire in the wiring.

Sandra said he'd been OK, business tootling along nicely and weekends under the Austin Healey or playing footers with the boys. Breaks my heart, to think of the boys. I opened up the garage and there was all his gear as messy as ever, with a drive-socket set open and the racket wrench tossed onto a dirty rag next to the '53 Healey up on its blocks, waiting for its master. All happy and expectant, like the 100/4 models always look, with that daft rad. It always amazed me, that Gavin would spend all day in the bodyshop and then come home and spend his free time with his own motor.

I can understand the attraction: if I had the spare time I

can think of worse things to be doing than banging away at the underside of an Austin Healey 100/4, ice-blue metallic, doeskin seats, wire wheels to spend all your waking life keeping clean – the lot. 'Worth more than twenty grand when I've finished with it,' he told me, not a year before he topped himself. Sandra hasn't touched it since, and that's three years now. Rotting away quietly in the garage, cobwebs from dash to gearstick, those spots of rust spreading like gangrene through the doors he'd just re-skinned. Breaks my heart. Maybe she sits in it from time to time, thinking about him. Maybe the boys sit in it and go vroom. No, they're too old for that now. Eleven and thirteen and Gareth must be *fifteen*. Jesus. We hardly see each other since the firm moved north, and my circuit never takes me south of Solihull.

The trouble is (before you get tut-tutting), spending all week pointing the bonnet at a moving car-park does not endear one to the idea of in-law visiting, not when they're at the awkward end of the country. I have to spend weekends restyling my back, for a start off. Driving an F-reg Rover 241 ST might be a lot of people's idea of a good time, but when it's for six hours a day five days a week with the exception of high days and holidays you begin to go a little numb in the hindquarters. Getting in touch with my bum again, that's what I call Time Off. So I've taken up a bit of jogging around the estate, am considering some form of martial art conducive to my advanced years and weight, and mostly lean on the bar to watch the telly. The wife grumbles about it. Maybe if I had a Lamborghini Miura throbbing gently in the driveway, and a shapely blonde at the wheel to squeeze in with – but I don't. The biggest shopping centre in the world can wait, my sweetheart. It's an hour and a half away, for God's sake.

Gavin always said he'd take me for a spin in the Healey, before selling it. Now that would have been a lark. Like the old days. His first motor was a '55 Hillman Minx, same colour as my Dinky. Mud brown. I helped him polish up the chromework, but that was about it. Part-exchanged for the charred shell of a Lagonda Drophead Coupé with some very scorched burr-walnut internals and an early and very tatty Triumph Herald which he bare-metal resprayed in Carmen red and then went and crumpled into something not even Gavin Restoration Inc. could make good. It would have turned the driver to scrap too if Triumph hadn't had the foresight to install one of the first collapsible steering columns on the Herald.

Cars never interested me, as such. Gavin could never stomach the way I let a scratch go, or didn't splat wax on the paintwork every week. Let alone my non-relationship with spanners of whatever size. I didn't even have a pair of overalls. The truth is, I did not like to get my hands dirty, greasy, or oily. I still don't. In my line, a blot of Little Chef's curry special on your best suit is a leg-up to your competitor. These things matter. People notice the details, it's all in the details, the details say what kind of a person you are, what kind of a product you're promoting. There was a very bright rep with the g-of-the-g called Barry Simpson who drove in his jacket and wondered why he never got many orders. A nice grey Austin Reed number, but it looked like Mother Teresa's cheeks on a bad day. I always lay my own coat on the back seat, I never let it swing about on its hanger from the rear hook, I'm not that sort of rep, am I? You don't want to go advertising to the world at large that you're a rep. That's how it is. The world at large does not think a great deal of reps.

Gavin was never happier than when squirting himself with engine oil, the dirtier the better. Our dad had a pre-war Riley for his veg deliveries and Gavin's idea of heaven was to de-coke the cylinder heads and grease the suspension. You could just about see his eyes by the end. We had to share a bedroom for years and I admit I found it painful. No, difficult. OK then, *challenging*, as we're required to say these days. It was very *challenging*. Mum spent an absolute fortune on carpet cleaner. I'd clean it myself, once a week. Then I rigged up this sort of dividing wall out of plastic sheets, until Gavin ripped it down. Dad and Mum weren't exactly sympathetic to my plight; they reckoned Gavin would be a rocket scientist or something, he mended everything in the house and fixed up its electrics, so a bit of grease here and there didn't bother them too much. Anyway, they weren't the world's cleanest or tidiest. Dad had his vegetable patch and Mum took in washing: I had to put up with neighbours' dirty smalls near where we were eating. Even clean, they'd put me off. Old ladies' bloomers and brassières. Mr Vaughan's underpants. No lesson to Gavin, who'd leave his underpants dirty on the floor just where I walked. Skid-marks showing and all. When he deigned to change them, that is. He'd go to bed in the same pair, most days, no top. I'd hook mine on the lower rung of my chair so nothing was showing and get into my pyjamas. There's nothing much pleasanter in life than pulling on a pair of freshly laundered pyjamas. I insist on this pleasure once a week. I don't insist on much. I'm not a man of great appetites.

One of these bloomer-sporting neighbours told Dad that kids who didn't like rolling about in mud or dangling off trees might have homo leanings later on, and Dad got all worried about me, kept asking me whether I didn't find Doris Day or whoever 'attractive'. I was about thirteen. Gavin by this time (he was three years older than me) was snogging with Samantha Davies down the road. The thought of snogging with Samantha Davies made me feel physically sick. She had lanky hair that hadn't seen shampoo in months and cheeks covered in pustules. But I couldn't say this to Dad, could I? Or to Gavin, whose hair was also lanky and quite long by this time. You could see the effect on his pillow in the morning. He'd started to smell like a bloke, all armpits and socks, and it was sheer nasal torture for me to share that room. But I still thought he was top of the pops.

We weren't rivals, like a lot of brothers are. One time, we did Bob-a-Job Week separately to see who would earn the most and of course I did, because I'd worked out my time-efficiency ratios and kept the cost-base down with one part Fairy Liquid to God knows how much water (we were washing cars), and Gavin had done a complete valet service practically, an hour spent on each vehicle, finishing with a wax massage. You could spot where he'd alighted straight off – his vehicles stood out like Belisha beacons and you had to long-jump the suds. He'd done next door's and Mr Vaughan came out and looked at his Cortina with a pair of sunglasses on, as a joke. I made about ten times as much as Gavin did, for Scouts, but he got so many repeat orders in the weeks following that he charged two and six a throw and employed me to fill the bucket and hand him the sponge. Not my favourite job, but it paid for a new set of points on my third-hand Hornby.

It was through that valet service wheeze that he started down the bodywork track. He'd say to the owner, 'You've got some nasty bubbles on the wing there,' or 'Your exterior trim's a bit doggy,' or 'That Mazak door handle's got serious acne,' or 'You know your out-riggers are a bit flaky?' And he'd be given a few bob more – or a pound or two if it was serious – to do a cosmetic. I don't even know where he learnt the trade. But he got better and better. I'd watch him for hours, so I should know. Cutting out, filling and sanding and filling and sanding and filling and sanding until an oblique check down the section showed nothing but perfect smoothness, then polishing, painting, waxing. He even mended a dint in an Alvis TD 21 rad belonging to the local bigwig, who was loaded but very mean. By the time he apprenticed himself over at Laine's Bodyshop in the truckyard, he'd done everything but serious welding.

That's the only reason I know a little bit about cars,

especially cars from the fifties and sixties. I'd hang around my big brother for hours, I must have been a bit of a pain. I didn't have any neighbourhood pals, really. All the boys were a bit scabby, a bit grotty and rough, to my mind, and I hated football except when Gavin was knocking a ball about. I liked being on my own, too. I *liked* being on my own. That's why I'm a rep. I drive thousands of miles a week in a little room all on my own, with built-in radio, CD player, phone, laptop, the works. The scenery's always changing. If they downgrade the car to a Fiesta or whatever, even a Fiesta XR2i, I'll either shoot myself or quit. I'd rather sweep the streets than put up with that sort of humiliation. Imagine what the wife would have to say about it. Imagine being passed by some geezer in a Vauxhall Astra with his jacket swinging around in the back and not being able to floor the throttle and give him a bit of exhaust to think about. Imagine rolling up at a client's in a Fiesta and clearing your throat for the gab to a load of interior giggles. I'd rather ponce around in a manky old Ford Anglia with rope to keep the bonnet down.

First car I ever owned, a Ford Anglia. Only four years old and not a lot of mileage but it had had a knock and the wishbones were a bit wonky. Gavin did it over for me and I handed him the spanners. My big mistake was buying Virginia's dad's Alfasud to butter up father and daughter and because the price was bloody good. Or so I thought. About a month later I drove it over to Gavin's, who was married to Sandra by now, and he almost had a heart attack. I can hear him now.

'Who paid you to tow away that lump of tinworm then, Colin?'

'They're bloody good machines, reliable, handles super-bly –'

'Alfasuds? Colin, you've been had. You'll drop through the floor in about three months. The bird shit'll come in through the spots in the roof. The rot'll start in the seams, the sills, the subframe and the middle of the doors. All at the same time. A bit of salt on the roads this winter and you won't hear yourself nattering to your sweetheart for the munching in the bulkhead. I hope you paid the bastard who sold you this in blunt nails.'

I didn't dare tell him that it was Virginia's old man. He slid himself under on a piece of manky cardboard and banged away a bit and came up laughing, brushing flakes of rust out of his eyebrows.

'More corrosion than the *Titanic*, my lad.'

'Before or after it was sunk?'

'After, Colin.' He was no longer laughing. He didn't like me to cap his jokes.

I couldn't go back to Ginny's dad, could I? I was so daft on the woman that when he kept asking me how I found her (meaning the car), I pretended it was a dream. Anyone would have thought we were talking about an MGB, the way we went on. Meanwhile she (meaning the car) was gently rotting down faster than my dad's compost heap. Then the electrics went outside Granada (Spain, not the service station) on our honeymoon and I part-exchanged her then and there for an ex-pat widow's stationary 1964 Sunbeam Alpine which only needed the battery changing. I'm afraid to say (it's a complicated story), I ripped off the widow something dreadful. I feel very manky about it now, but she was a drunk and liked her late hubby's Alpine about as much as she'd liked her hubby and cars don't rust in Spain, I'm sure of it. When we got to Dover, I phoned Gavin from the first coin-box to tell him, but he was disappointed; he'd been going to restore the Alfasud as a wedding present. The personal challenge of a lifetime. 'It would have been like raising the *Titanic* and getting it to sail again, dance band and all, but I *like* that sort of thing, Colin.'

I was touched. He added that Ginny's dad was dead, heart attack the week before, funeral tomorrow. Blimey.

She saw some link between her dad's collapse and the selling of the Alfasud, of course. This is the same woman who said, when I told her about Gavin topping himself, 'It's genetic.' Gavin and I had this older brother, ten years older than either of us, who got tangled in a hand-towel at school, the unhygienic washable type of hand-towel that does the rounds on a wooden roller. He was ten or eleven. Must have been ten, because Gavin wasn't even born. Small enough, anyway, for his feet not to touch the ground when the towel was around his neck.

'Bruce's wasn't necessarily suicide,' I said. 'It might have been an accident.'

'I was thinking of your uncle.'

Uncle Denholm had definitely topped himself, but he'd been in the trenches. He used to pay weekend visits and Gavin and I would turn purple trying not to giggle. Mum reckoned he was better out of doors.

'Uncle Denholm didn't hang himself,' I replied, 'he put his head in the oven. And he was already nuts. He used to wink before turning his head. Gavin reckoned Uncle Denholm thought his eyes were courtesy lights. Gavin was not nuts. He wasn't even dodgy.'

'Maybe he was tired,' said the wife, meaningfully, with a knowing sigh. You can fall in love with a car as you can fall in love with a woman: for their looks. Then you find you've got a dud. But at least a car stays pretty. In fact, it gets prettier with time. The older the better. Even our dad's clapped-out Vulcan van would look pretty now. He replaced the Riley when I was nine, and I physically cried. That's because Gavin had put so much of his childhood into keeping her ticking over. TLC, he called it: Tender Loving Care. Cars respond to that like nothing else does, Gavin always said. I've tried a lot of TLC on Virginia over the years, and I tend to agree with Gavin. One thing you can't do with wives is strip them down for a full respray. What you get with the champagne is the original, and no amount of tarting up can hide the fact that the original is all you've got. And they're very rot-prone, are wives.

Gavin pulled the girls like nobody's business in the old days but he always looked such a mess, that's the funny thing. He never restyled his hair from the age of about fifteen, when he lost his sideburns and let it grow. I don't know how he saw through it to do all his fiddling and fussing, to be honest. And he had no idea about safety, not at all. He'd spend all day spraying in the paintshop without a mask, and the fan wasn't up to much. He'd come out looking like a walking rainbow, so God knows what he'd breathed in. I pointed this out to him once, at the paintshop door, practically suffocating in a cloud of BMW red, and he shouted back that he liked having multi-coloured lungs and would I close the door because the draught was screwing up the finish. He came out a bit later and said he was going to have to sand out all the tears, thanks to me. Funny thing this, but I've gone all watery in the eyes now. What a coincidence. 'They're murder to sand out, too,' he added, prodding my belly with his luminous finger. You could've arrested him on the prints left on my nice clean and very white Van Heusen. Looked like I'd been machine-gunned. Silly bugger.

He wasn't really annoyed with me, of course. It was a professional observation. Prodding my clean shirt with a finger coated in wet paint was carelessness, not vengeance. He didn't even wear goggles when welding new sections in or gloves when beating panels out. Even as a kid, he'd do things I wouldn't do. I'd always say to myself: it's because he's older. Then I'd get to where he'd been three years ago and realise that I still couldn't do the things he did at the same stage: riding the bike downhill without hands, shinning up trees, that sort of thing. Mum worried because of our sister.

I haven't told you about Carol, have I? I've told you about Bruce, our big brother, but not about Carol. Carol was my baby sister. I thought she was a pain, covered in jam or snot the whole time, messing up my half of the bedroom, interfering with my layouts, but Gavin adored her. Then don't ask me how but at the age of five she fell out of the van. It was out of the Vulcan she fell; Dad wasn't even going fast, apparently, he was just pulling up outside the baker's on the corner when the passenger door swung open and she fell out holding a box of eggs. I wasn't there, so I don't know more than that. I don't even know what finished her, but she must have fallen on her head and Dad had told her to be careful with the eggs, so maybe she didn't use her hands to break the fall, maybe she just hung on to the eggs in her lap in case they broke. Dad's hair went white, Mum went hysterical and then religious, and Gavin didn't talk to anybody at all for a week. I never saw him cry, though. I reckon he didn't sleep for a week, either, because when I woke up in the morning he was staring at the ceiling in exactly the same position as when I'd dropped off. There was some little history about the door handle having needed a new spring for a long time, but I don't believe for a moment that Gavin could have felt responsible. Niggly stuff like door handle springs weren't Gavin's thing, anyway. He'd do them, but not in a hurry. What he liked was making something doggy and tired look nice and swanky, but it would be nice and swanky right to the heart. He was no bodger.

In fact, he was a bit obsessed, was our Gavin. That's what the clients went for. That's why there was a Jensen Interceptor, a Jag Mk2, and an MGB Roadster on his books the month before he died. He was getting the collectors, the serious boys, the ones who'd spot a dodgy restoration job with their eyes closed. You know the type. Running their little fingers over the re-skin, prodding away at the underside like they're Customs looking for the hard stuff – the sort that know what a diagonal crack across a front sill's paintwork on a Jag Mk2 means (big trouble), but are too busy making money to have a swipe at it themselves. The type who paid mortgage money for poor old Dad's old Vulcan, after Gavin had finished with it, even a decade back.

They all knew how obsessed Gavin was, these classics bods. But what they didn't know is that it wasn't panting after the nice thick glossy look or all that tight-arsed authentic stuff that drove him to work on some bloke's scruffy Mazda long into Friday night. It was something else. It was the rats. It was the thought of all those invisible little rats eating away from the inside out. It was the idea that a tiny little rat left behind in a rear bulkhead or a floorpan might be tucking in as he's shining up the third coat of Hammerite. That's what obsessed our Gavin. That's what made him so bloody good. Before he set up on his own, he worked for some top-notch Rolls-Royce and Bentley dealer in Putney, turning the shabby into the immaculate. That's when the rats thing started. Gavin was dyslexic, could hardly get his own name right. He had to write up a makeover estimate for a Silver Cloud some tosspot of an earl had wet-stored in his barn and the poncy type that ran the place thought he'd written 'rats' for 'rust', believed there were several families of rats nesting on the floorpans. Seriously – it had been known. From then on, Gavin couldn't get this rats thing out of his mind. He claimed he could hear rust nibbling and squeaking. A sort of sixth sense for it, I suppose. This got to him much more than the exterior threat – all that grit and tar and salt and sunlight, acid rain and dirty winds, you name it. Everything that lurks outside a dustcover, I suppose. Bird shit. Yobs with sharp fingernails and an Amstrad for a brain. We went out for a pub crawl not so long ago, for his forty-fifth, and I parked the Rover under a lime tree and he didn't say a word, although he knew exactly what I'd find through my hangover. Good business practice, I suppose.

The firm supplies me with a new model every year, so

my little number never has a chance to go grotty and the wife doesn't drive. Gavin was a funny old sod: he'd get at me in a nice brotherly way for this and that, but one thing we were clear on was doing the job properly. His job, my job. When I first got into shelves – into Tideaway Shelving Products UK, to be precise – he laughed like a drain. 'Had shares in them when we were kids, didn't you, Colin?' Pure chance Tideaway turned up, actually, when I was sick of the shit I was getting at Barratts – but if I've made a bloody good something of it over the last twenty-one years, then that's because I share with Gavin a concern to get it right all the way down to the bottom. Being a rep is much more than polishing your teeth and purring sweetly, you know. Much more. If my weekly fuel consumption makes Concorde's bill look thrifty, then that's because I bother. The only little bone of contention I have now with Gavin is that he never purchased so much as a yard of shelving off me. Nothing. Not even from our select garage range – not so much as a rollcab on swivel castors, in mimosa, burgundy or chocolate brown. I could have done him a very decent deal at all-but-warehouse prices, but he never bit. I'm afraid I took that as a snub each time it came up.

'Don't Delve – Shelve!' That was our motto, when I arrived. But Gavin liked delving, I realise that now. He once lost his butane blow-lamp and it turned up under this heap of old Standard nose panels. I could have sorted him in the time it takes to fill out an order form, but Gavin always shrugged me off, or laughed. I felt sick about it, sometimes. A leopard doesn't change its spots, does it? Me picking my way over his gear in our bedroom. Unpleasant smells. Grease on the pillow.

When Mum got her cancer, last year, I couldn't help thinking of Gavin's rats. I was visiting a few weeks ago and she kept on as if we were all still going – even Bruce. She had what Gavin used to call, in the old days, 'gearbox chatter' (my Herald had it, worn bearings I suppose), and whenever she'd start on at one of us he'd tell her to check her bearings, but she never got it. Anyway, when she finally conked out and dropped off that day in the hospital, I looked at her and physically cried. It doesn't matter how many shelving units I sell this year or whether I'm burning through more fresh deals than my Embassy cigs. Gavin's gone. Mum's almost gone. I'll be the only one.

Sandra was feeling nice all of a sudden, a few weeks back – probably found a new boyfriend; anyway, she sent me Gavin's old scrapbook, full of snipped-out magazine pictures of cars and Basil Cardew cuttings from Dad's *Daily Express*. Gavin sounded a lot like Basil Cardew when he talked about cars, in the old days – I realise that now. He'd snip around the pictures with Mum's nail scissors, following the curves. When he came to a wing mirror or a Rolls flying lady, his tongue would stick out but he'd never lose the detail. I've looked at it quite a few times, searching for clues. But there aren't any, like there weren't any in the bodyshop or at the house. Life just preys on you. Doesn't it? Watching Gavin work on this corrugated Volvo Amazon, one time, I thought there was nothing he couldn't restore. But perhaps there was. 'You can't up-rate a dud or respray a hole,' as he used to put it to some client wanting a job on the cheap.

'You can't put shelves up till you've got something to fill them' is how I'd put it.

This is what happens when you spend a lot of time on your own on the same circuit, with nothing to do but whistle and pick your nose and point the bonnet forward: you think too much. I sometimes find myself only surfacing when I'm driving up the exit ramp – and it's never not the right exit.

I still can't work out how he did it, because of course he did do it. All that business with the chock under the Morris, no strings attached. Requires a touch of lateral thinking, I suppose. But Gavin always was ahead of me. He always got there first, with me trotting up behind a few years later.

I did have a go at impressing him once or twice, though. I had this jet-black Triumph 2000 for a bit a while back, and he noticed some stone-chips on its paintwork around the nearside wing. I said to him that I'd have a go at it myself, with one of those retouching pencils. I reckoned even I could manage that without getting dirt under my nails. He looked at me as if I'd said I was about to make good a bullet-riddled Aston Martin DB5 or replate the chrome on a Bentley Continental.

'Do you know how many grades of black there are in the trade, Colin?'

I took a wild guess. It was obviously a lot. 'Thirty', I said.

He was very cheesed off because there are, in fact, sixteen. He didn't ever like to be capped by his kid brother. Sixteen grades of black: that still surprised me. But he didn't let me show my surprise, that was the trouble. Not that time. By Monday morning, I found he'd done it. Immaculate job. Without saying a word.

GLASS

I said to her: Look, Marie-Cecile, we'll have a holiday. She said: Oh, with what? I showed her the paper, front page. That's not right, she said. What isn't right, my love? It isn't right, paying us to do nothing, Jean-Luc. It's in lieu of, I replied: in lieu of what we've given 'em with our sweat and our muscle. It's owed.

She kept quiet for a bit, chewing on her coffee, nose in the article even with her spectacles on. To be honest, I was a bit uncomfortable with it myself. To be paid to take a break! It went against the grain.

They'll all be out there, she said. They'll all be out there jamming up the roads. You won't see the river for tents and folk we don't normally hob-nob with, half naked.

Her face was all sour. More and more she looks like her mum, with her hair rolled up like that, and the parting. You can see her bare skin in the parting. Like it's been engraved. Like her head is smoked glass and I've taken a sand-engraver to it. Or brushed a line of my hot glue mixture, ripping it off when it's hard. Like those nice effects I did for the butcher's window a few years back, in Le Cateau. Or like I'd got my thickest quill and done as I did on that chemist's in Guise in '25, my first big engraving job. 'Beauty Through Health Not Artifice', that was it, across the left-hand window. Hydrochloric acid, zinc chloride, and a touch of pompeian red. A week's work, with all the tucks and frills. Lucky if you can get it, these days.

Steady hand. I learnt my lesson early, but I've never

forgiven myself. Let me put it like this: my one slip-up, the one time I made a hash of it, is up there for eternity. Or at least until some cock-eyed idiot decides to have another war. Reckon it could be tomorrow, the way Herr Hitler's going on.

The first time I let it out, this thing about my one cock-up, was then. I mean, this holiday I'm talking about, three years back, '36. Miracle year. First paid holiday in history. Taking it for granted already, are you? Marie-Cecile was right about the jams. Dust, dust everywhere, and the banks of the Somme like it was in the war, only instead of soldiers stripping off it was people like us, rolling up their trousers and knotting their skirts. And all the sweet young charmers in the packaging department were somewhere else. Along with their oily headed boyfriends, the type who whistle at each other in the cutting-shop, as if there isn't enough damn noise in there. Glass shrieking like it's being hurt.

It was quiet, at least, by the river. We'd put up this tent, if you can call it a tent. Awning, more like, propped up by a couple of bamboo sticks and pegged into the grass to say: this is ours. This is our bit of the Republic on paid holiday. About three square metres of the banks of the Somme, willows and water and bloody peace. And me lying back and thinking: I'm being paid to do this. I'm being paid to do nothing at all.

That was the difficult bit. You never don't do something, do you? I put my cap on my face to keep the sun off and tried to forget the glassworks, the engraving workshop, the stink of ammonium and burnt alcohol, turps, sodium fluoride, potassium salts, Monsieur Thellier's whine, the sand-blowers, grit in your eye. All that. We don't get out much – I mean, from the workshop. It's the younger ones now who get the on-the-spot jobs. They think my frills and tucks are old-fashioned. No one wants Persian flower-motifs or Chinese blossom on their letters any more. It's all clean and straight, these days. They can keep it.

She'd hung her shoes up. The wife, I mean. Marie-Cecile had hung her best cream-leather shoes up, on the tent. One right next to my face, by the laces, the other off the cross-piece. Don't ask me why she couldn't have done like everyone else did, and laid them in the grass. The ants, probably. Well, no ant would have got within a mile of those shoes because, to be frank, they smelt like the glassworks' engraving department. The Somme smells sweet and green and fresh, even in high summer, but Marie-Cecile had to hang her stinking shoes next to my face.

I sat up and protested, of course, but when I lay back down again she was under me. I mean, her legs were. Her knees and lap, to be precise. She was staring down at me and giggling. We'd had a litre of good red between us – and what made me want to go to sleep, made her giggly. Go and paddle, I said to her. You know I can't swim, she said. I didn't say anything. I had this terrible thought: I thought of the river and of her sinking into it. The sun was flashing on the water and I kept thinking of the molten glass in the works, the ovens going white-hot, the men with their gloves and their eye-shields, sweating all over, working the glass, pressing it flat under steel. And into this river of molten glass I could see Marie-Cecile sinking forever. It must have been the wine, or not being at home for a few days. I couldn't fiddle about. There was nothing to do. It was hard doing nothing. Also, I'd got the wrong socks. They were black. The sun was burning through them. But I couldn't take them off. Northern skin, I've got. The sun etches it. Pure hydrofluoric acid on peachblow.

Wake up, she whispered. I'm not asleep, I said. Your knees are digging into my neck. Folk will think we're lovers. She giggled. Fat chance, she said. I noticed her old checked dress was only kept decent by one button. Mind you, she had a black undie on. But you've never seen Marie-Cecile, have you? She still had her rollers in, she's shaped like a *brioche*. Her naked shins and feet were bright red. She looks more and more like her mum, flat-faced and doughy. I can't understand how I ever fancied her, but I did. My eyes were smoked in youth, I couldn't see properly. Someone had taken a burin to them when I was about fourteen and written LOVE on each one. She was the pastry-maker's daughter; covered in flour, giggling behind the counter, plump but shapely, she was as sweet as a cream *chou* and she was my *chou-chou*. Well, we did it together before we were married, in the back of the shop, tipping over a tray of éclairs. She didn't even wipe the flour off her hands. I had crystal sugar on my *zi-zi*. It was like one of those dirty postcards Raoul used to pass round in the trenches, before I stopped the bit of shell in my shoulder.

Now all I could feel was a bony knee in it. In my shoulder, I mean. No cream left, no sugar. But there she was, pretending life was covered in flour again. When really it was covered in glass-powder. You can kill someone with glass-powder. Put it in their drink. Blow it up their nostrils. Fancy thinking that on holiday! Paid to lie on your drunken wife's legs on a river-bank and think horrible thoughts! What's the country coming to?

Then I felt a drop on my cheek. Her spectacles were off. The sky was clear blue, with a few birds in it. They have to piss somewhere, I thought. Then another fell on my mouth. It was salty. The wife was crying. Just sitting there, crying. The old folks – older than us, I mean – were too busy with their fishing further up to notice. Blow your nose, I said. I haven't got anything, she mumbled. It's the kids. It hurts her, sometimes, that we've never had kids. Nothing. Not a jot. I told her that there was a handkerchief just behind her. A giant-sized one. I meant the tent but she didn't get it. Instead she used my cap, holding it to her face. I was so shocked I couldn't say anything.

Then she said: The worst thing I ever did was marry you. I know, I said. I thought: I'm not going to go on about the cap now. She stared at me over it and gave a big sniff. But

she wasn't hating me. It was like she was blaming herself.
There was none of that hardness in her eyes, like there
usually is. This time it was all soft and flowing because we
were on a paid holiday, we were being paid to lark about,
to lie full of wine and lunch on a river-bank with the river
chuckling past, willows and poplars and grass and all that.
Sunlight. Head full of bits of sunlight.

That's when I thought of it. Or saw it. Saw it in shards in
my head, just as it was. The worst moment. So I said, The
worst thing I've ever done wasn't marrying you. Oh, she
said, that's nice. I knew I had to tell her. I was looking up at
the big blue sky. It goes on and on, deeper and deeper, the
sky. Infinity. A window without glass is the basic unit of
luminosity. When God judges me He'll have red hands.
Cathedral glass, fifty units out of a hundred at two metres
distance. I have all the figures. For prismatic green,
vermiculated, ribbed, fine-frosted. The lowest is luxfer.
Lucifer, I call it. Fourteen units from a metre. Kind they put
in brothels.

I heard, from a long way off, but in my head, that nasty
smash a stone makes when it's sent through a window.
Only this was different. This was glass coming to the stone.
It was someone throwing stones into the river, but we'll let
that pass. It was a sort of sign, anyway. So I told her. I took
a glazier's diamond to the sky and scrolled it out up there,
for God and his blessed angels and for the wife. That's what
it felt like, anyway.

It was in the war, I said. 1916. My shoulder still ached
where they'd left some of the shell-case, but it was shells
that gave me work. Boom, smash and tinkle. Then we were
given the biggest job yet. And it wasn't putting glass in, it
was taking it out. What's the biggest building in Amiens?
The cathedral, she said. Her lap wobbled. I closed my eyes
and thought of pastry and cream and flour and crystals of
sugar. God, you choose what you choose. I'm no picture
myself. Wouldn't be worth the glass, let alone the frame.

Anyway, we had to take the whole lot out. All of it. Precautionary measures. She was sandbagged up to her nostrils, or at least up to Hell on the Last Judgement, but a few shells in the cathedral square and poof! – you'd be wading knee-high through colour. Colour like no one can make these days. Forgotten recipes. Forgotten ways.

I was inside, getting the scaffolding up for the west window, the big rose. I looked at it and I thought: it's like the kaleidoscope I had as a kid, holding it up to the light. God turned this kaleidoscope until its crystals fell into exactly the right pattern and since then He's kept it there, very still. One jolt and the whole lot will shuffle into rubbish. We were going to climb up into this giant kaleidoscope and remove its crystals one by one. Then after the war we were going to put them all back again. There were these blokes with their easels, painting it in watercolours, for when we had to put them back again.

Then we went up and we all looked like clowns, not angels. All multi-coloured. They'd tried criss-crossing the glass with strips of paper, but it was a joke. Well, the old solder broke easily, it wasn't too difficult. We wrapped each bit of glass in brown paper and put it in the bucket to be lowered down. My hands had Latin on them. Some journalist said we looked like worms, poking our heads out. Tiny worms. Each time you removed a bit, the sunlight blinded you. That's why I dropped it. This red chunk, right from the middle of the rose.

My hands red, like in the war. Then a bang of sunlight. It was that. The big bang of sunlight, taking this bit of glass out. One hundred per cent luminosity, all of a sudden. Deep, jugular red jumping out of my gloves and bouncing on the planks and then spattering way below on the stone floor. Echoes. The blood spattered like I was looking down at my own death. Like I was a soul going up and up, leaving my flesh, my filth. But this was the other way round, Marie-Cecile. This was me staying, and the lovely piece of light gone. Because that's all glass is. A piece of light taken out of the sky.

She'd nodded off. Just as well, maybe. One day, I'll take her to Amiens and stand in the square and point up at the big rose window and say: There's my sin. Not the same red, see? Well, I can see it, at any rate. There until Doomsday. Bang in the middle. It hurts. It still hurts. Maybe it won't now, now I've told it to you. And I didn't even mean to tell you. It was the paid holiday I was on about. Our first paid holiday. And we've had another two since, but we've preferred to stay at home. Too much to do. It's not right, doing nothing, letting it all go, staring into the sky like that.

DEBAUCHERY

When I first came to Paris, in 1956, I felt like a refugee. My family were rich and stifling, part of a great Boston clan, something out of Henry James with the addition of electric gadgets and tupperware bowls, television and Saran Wrap. These things didn't sit well with their cut-glass accents, but I didn't like the accent either. I didn't even like the Oldsmobile 98s in the garage. I wanted something else, but I wasn't sure what that was. I stood there on the Pont du Carrouse and looked down into the still grey water that first morning in Paris and thought to myself: I want to be wicked, *poetically* wicked. Only I didn't know how.

My coat was all wrong. It was smart and wool with a wide collar, it looked expensive because it *was* expensive. There was a cold wind blowing with some light rain but I took the coat off and dangled it for a moment over the edge. It was a Sunday, there were very few people around. In those days there was so little traffic you could wash a car on the lower *quais*, stroll among the pigeons, savour the low hum that was almost a silence, hear the bells coming from far away. Now the sides of the river are like freeways apparently. There's no room for anyone.

I left the coat on the parapet, rolled up neatly. I was too decent a guy to drop it into the river. Hemingway would have done that. But the rain was dampening my hair and darkening my suit – it was a beginning. I wanted to go downhill a little, unbutton myself and look disarrayed, but honest to God – don't laugh – I didn't even know where the damn hill was, let alone how to go down it. I'd always been high up on this kind of plateau. My birthright. I was intelligent, I tested well, I was smothered in Ivy League values like a young sapling planted in the wrong place. I had a year free in front of me before I took the legal track, straight towards the heavy oak doors of the family law firm. Once they'd shut behind me, there'd be no going back. My parents were paying for this year. I don't know now whether they knew what Paris stood for, what might happen to a callow youth let loose there. The best way to improve your French, my uncle told me on my departure, was to translate Racine. But I could translate Racine in Boston, I replied. A flicker of some subdued panic passed behind his eyes. He'd been in the last war, in Normandy. He'd seen France after the Liberation. Perhaps he'd gotten unbuttoned too, for a time.

I made it to the end of the bridge and then I glanced back at my coat. It looked so neat and well behaved there, I felt disgusted at myself. I ran back and cast it with a pitcher's toss down into the river, where it kind of curled up slowly and sank with its arms spread out. There were two lovers in their Sunday best standing on the path below but they never looked up.

I made straight for the Latin Quarter. The tugboats were hooting and the cobbles were wet and slippery, the light mist made everything almost industrial. It was a weird moment. There were ragged humps with bottles lying in the lee of the *quai*, mumbling or snorting, and a few guys fishing off the bank down below. There was someone getting their poodle to swim, but it didn't like it. The first leaves were dropping. Smart women walked by with their dogs, both species with their noses in the air. The women were muffled in furs but still elegant on high heels, clicking past me one after the other as I advanced with a beating heart toward what I could only think of as my destiny.

The cold and wet of Paris was soaking in. I mussed my

hair, but it was too short to muss properly. As I crossed the place Saint-Michel I vowed to grow it long. Then I had to consult my tourist map. It was given to me at the hotel, where I was staying until I found suitable lodgings. My hotel was on the quai d'Orsay. In those days suitable rooms could be rented cheap even on the quai d'Orsay. As I struggled with my map in the wind off the river, trying to figure out exactly where the Latin Quarter started in case I missed it, I pictured this garret and me inside it, painting or writing poetry. I was stained with oil paints, ink, the juices of the streets and boulevards, you name it. I was *living*.

Not clean living but *dirty* living. Europe was old and dirty, we all knew that. That's why my fellow Americans were such notorious tenants: they left their apartments looking dirty and broken because that's what they thought Europe expected. No one else could figure this out, but I could. A cream-and-blue bus, open at the back, flicked its tyres over the wet cobbles, *flicker-flacker-flicker-flacker-flicker-flacker-flick* – one of those crazy Parisian mating calls of the old days. I responded. The map crumpled in my hands. I knew where the Latin Quarter was: it was in my heart.

I was feeling really mushy by now, so I stopped at the first café I came across, near Saint-Severin, and ordered a coffee and a pastry. The place was almost empty, but it was warm. I was so green that I tipped the waiter. We Americans still think that money buys smiles, but all it does is spoil the fruit of the soul. Then I explored, looking around for this hill, the garret, some tight buttons to fumble at inside my head. I liked the little dead-end alleys most of all. Paris was darker in those days, blacker, it had a deep smell of drains, there was undifferentiated poverty, a shabby genteel joy that had drawn itself out like a greasy greatcoat's thread all the way from the nineteenth century. Everyone old back then in the fifties was not of our world, they were born elsewhere, in some other time, before technology and American ease and the glide of cars. This guy with the white hair, he might have passed Mallarmé or Baudelaire. That old dame with the moustache, she might have slept with Auguste Rodin. Rimbaud or Verlaine or both at once might have heard this legless guy blowing his flute through his nose.

I remember that legless guy, he was there most days that year, I got used to him like I've got used to wealthy nuts in a thousand divorce cases since. But he'd jerk his head like a maniac and I couldn't stand the sound that first time, the guy looked like a grub, he was completely bald, all you could see was the top of his glistening head. They were washing the street and the soapy water sailed past his stumps, making a stream between us. There was the damp, soapy smell of a Sunday morning in Paris, with grey-black buildings and somebody singing high up and this jerky head with a flute stuck in one nostril, wailing and whistling over alien shouts down the street. There was me, fumbling for foreign coins, feeling so young and American and excited and lonely and disgusted all at the same time. Frightened, even. Frightened by the prospect of so much life in front of me, this strange land I would have to negotiate in strange tongues. Shivering without my coat.

I scurried back to the hotel and ordered up my first pernod ever. To go.

Then I fell asleep in that heavy, linen-scented room, on that big double bed, and tipped my drink over. A lonely American from Boston, still suffering *decalage d'heure* or maybe just too much champagne and turbulence in the downstairs bar of the Pan American Stratocruiser, President class. Paris rumbled and snored outside through the afternoon, dropping fall leaves into the sweet mush. I dreamed I was a plane tree along a flicketty-flacketty boulevard, growing up through my ironwork doily, its spokes trapping cigarette-ends and gum and torn pages of newspapers. I had one last leaf and I wasn't letting it go, not even when my father and mother hugged my trunk and shook it. The leaf turned into a bird and flew off over the grey shining roofs and towers. I tried to join it, but the metal doily wouldn't budge. Then I changed into a curvy *pissoir* and nearly wet myself. When I woke up properly I felt like death. I would go do it with a prostitute, I decided. In one fell swoop I would gut my moral well-being.

A small excursion into the Mouffetard that night yielded no more than a fellow American, drinking a secretive absinthe through a sugar lump. It was outlawed, absinthe, but he knew the right places, the under-the-counter places. I tried it (it was not to my taste) while enduring the guy's drone. He came from Missouri, was here as a clerk in the war, had never gone back. He and the *patron* talked about the war, about power cuts and painted stockings, how the rich got by and the poor got cold and hungry, how even tobacco was so short the *patrons* would collect up the butt-ends at the evening's end. I started to feel good, heady with the absinthe; the place smelt of musky baskets, like the pantry at home. My fellow countryman, who was about sixty and bald with wet eyes from his cheroot, started checking out my knee. I looked down and there was this hand sliding onto my crotch. I fled, stumbling on the step. Laughter in my wake. I didn't even recognise the hill when I was standing on it, I was so green.

I explored some more, after a day or two hiking through the galleries and museums. I checked out the Folies-Bergère; these slim beauties with glitter on their nipples dangled on floats in front of me, but I felt like a kid. There were deeper places of pleasure with steep steps but I was too chicken, and I didn't even figure for a while that the women on the sidewalk with tight skirts and cardigans and black gloves were whores. I hadn't pictured cardigans. Mom wore woollen cardigans, but these cardigans were kind of sharp and thrusting. The bright-red mouths did not look easy to kiss, they had this sardonic curve and kept opening up to yawn. Sometimes they whistled at me, jeered in some language I couldn't identify. Then I realised they were calling out to me in English. They were as awesome as the giant cut-out of Marilyn Monroe in her flowery underthings, the height of three storeys. It towered over this sober queue of men and women in hats waiting for the evening movie, all looking over at me as if I was to blame for something. STRIP-TEASE STRIP-TEASE flashed in neon down the next street, straight off some lousy dive back home. Then a student sitting next to me in a jazz concert told me that Paris had been raped not by Germans but by Americans. He was a Red with thick spectacles and I hated myself for feeling hurt.

I found a room to rent in a side-street off the place Maubert. Too bad that a greasy slate roof hid the view of Notre-Dame's spire. It wasn't a real garret, more a dirty top-floor hole out of Dostoevsky, but it was cheap. I was reading *Crime and Punishment* and Raskolnikov's student cupboard was my model. It meant I had plenty of extra money: I wanted to slide in style. What I liked about Raskolnikov was his total existentialism. I had already studied Sartre and Camus back home and had now bought myself a black polo-neck sweater and black trousers and black brothel-creepers. My new coat was what the English call a 'duffel'. My hair was growing out and I wasn't washing it every day. I had the uniform, but I lacked the confidence to volunteer. Debauchery meant tearing buttons off your best shirt. Buttons sewn on by your mom. I liked my shirt too much, if not my mom.

The room was not free until the end of the month. Every day I received a letter from my folks, with news of everything I wanted to forget back home and a reminder to write and to bathe daily. I should have torn them up but even Raskolnikov read his mom's letters. Then one arrived telling me about Cousin Ingeborg's apartment. Cousin Ingeborg was extremely rich and a bit nuts, and had shacked up with some count in this palace near Seville. She

had an apartment on the rue Bonaparte in Saint-Germain-des-Prés. She wanted me to 'sit it' for her until the end of the summer – around when I was going back home. This apartment was unbelievable, stacked with Louis XV furniture and even older tapestries and works by the School of Fragonard and a Boucher sketch and all that stuff. It smelt of floorwax and expensive scent. There were two maids and a cook on tap. It was all mine in return for keeping it warm and watering her ferns.

This was terrible. It was a terrible decision to have to make. I balanced the Raskolnikov hole with its bad drains and the swell suite with its marble sweep of stairs and came down on the swell one day and the hole the next. But the most debauched guy in *Crime and Punishment* is the one who shoots himself at the gates of St Petersburg. He had land, an estate, horses. I could be Byronic about my debauchery. Raskolnikov was a miserable, murderous runt, anyway. I could be lavish in my slide, I could be existential with gold-plated taps and rebellious with silk pillows. I mean, I could become *notorious*. I was standing under a copper-green cherub on the Pont Alexander and I felt myself smile evilly.

It was right at that moment that I saw him.

He was walking very slowly and kind of dazedly toward me over the bridge. He was a tramp. There were thousands of them in those days, they had their own little empires along the river. He had a beard and a cap and this stick which he didn't use to walk, and a long coat I knew very well. It was my coat. It was like watching myself walking toward me – myself in twenty, thirty, fifty years' time. It was my own phantom come to haunt me out of the future. I was frightened again, I wanted to run. Then he stopped and stabbed the ground with his stick and lifted it and took something off the end. It reminded me of the park attendants back home, harpooning fallen leaves off the lawns. He opened his – my – coat and put away whatever his stick had picked up. There was great deliberation in his actions. I know that deliberation. A lawyer has it, a business executive, an engineer, a surgeon. It's the mark of a professional engaged in his life's task. I didn't have that yet, not then. I was still one hundred per cent amateur.

I let him pass. There was a big bottle in his pocket. He had fished my coat from the water or maybe it had snagged on a fisherman's rod – whichever, he had salvaged my coat and taken it over, including the pockets. I'd worn this coat right through Yale, it was a birthday gift from my grandparents. Now there was a bottle stopped up with paper bulging out its pocket. Had I emptied the coat completely before dumping it in the river? Maybe there'd been some old loose change in there, a few cents or a dime, a dirty handkerchief, sticks of gum, a ticket-stub for a game. I caught the smell of spirits and body odour as he passed – and something else, something muskier, almost sweet. Off of his back hung one of those little accordions they call a *musette*.

I followed him. It wasn't easy, he kept stopping and stabbing at the ground with his stick. I remember the glistening fish-scale cobbles, the slabs, the uneven stones, and this stick with a long pin tied on the end, harpooning butt-ends. He only picked up butt-ends. He picked one up off an Eiffel Tower chalked in yellow on the sidewalk and the artist thanked him. He did it all with such deliberation that I became hypnotised, Paris fell away around me into something else, something totally outside of us both. He was wearing my coat. I had this strange, unpleasant sensation of familiarity with him, and also a kind of resentment, as if my coat had been stolen. Each time he came to a bench he would crouch and do some more stabbing underneath. Women would shift their legs, as if they knew him, as if this was an ancient custom. Old men would growl but shift their legs too. He was filling a bag of patched cloth underneath the coat. The sweet smell he'd had was of tobacco. His stick kind of flickered – so deft, so tried and tested was this action. But the closer I got, the more I saw how old he was. He shuffled and was dazed more with age than drink. Nobody drunk could have been so deft.

The only time he showed interest in anything other than his pickings was when he stopped by a movie poster near the Odéon. The poster showed a grinning and big-mouthed variety dancer with long curly locks baring her thigh under her flounced skirts. *Les Nuits de Montmartre*, it said, showing in Eastmancolor. In the background was this mean-looking fellow in a raincoat, wielding a pistol. I blushed with shame as I loitered in a doorway on the other side of the street, waiting for the old man to move. I thought of myself as the mean-looking fellow, desperate for action, for some Paris thigh. I'd been dreaming these dreams and this ugly movie poster mocked them, showed them for what they were. *Eastmancolor. Cinepanoramic.* And the old tramp in my coat was telling me this. Why otherwise had he stopped? I thought: this guy has been sent, like an angel or a devil, to teach me about myself.

The door behind me opened and a fat woman in a flowery skirt emptied her suds on the step as if she hadn't seen me. I hopped off and she laughed and the laughter echoed off the stone buildings. This woke the old tramp out of his dream. He shot a glance at me and then he carried on walking. It was evening by now, my feet were tired, but this guy took me along the café terraces of all the main streets and boulevards of the Latin Quarter. The night was warm for early October, warm enough to sit outside. He threaded his way between the tables like a shadow, stooping, stabbing from side to side, while I hovered like the shadow of a shadow out of the lights. Now and again a mean-eyed *garçon* would shoo him away or give him a squirt out of a soda syphon. Most of the time he was tolerated, greeted with a name – even an occasional bite to eat, which he instantly pocketed. I only realised it was his name because it was repeated so many times. It was le Père la Pêche. Or maybe it was one word and didn't mean anything. Just the name he was born with.

I stumbled through that night like a madman in a stupor. I had this idea, this *idée fixe*, that if I lost sight of him I would lose my soul. I was hungry, but I didn't eat. At about three o'clock we were in the slums of Les Halles. He squatted on a pile of rubble and rubbish and worked his way through the morsels given to him by the cafés and restaurants. His bag lolled, fat as a pregnant woman's belly, through my coat. No – *his* coat! Occasionally he'd glance up but his face was in shadow and I was huddled in my duffel further along the alley, by an overflowing dustbin that attracted cats and stank of piss and rotten vegetables. Cries came from nowhere, echoing and dying on the night air. Metal shutters slammed shut and there were high-pitched rows, or maybe they weren't rows. A woman, probably a whore, clapped by briskly on high heels. Her black bag was like our doctor's medical bag back home, only much smaller. She kept her head down and clapped by us like she didn't want to know, like she was afraid. She'd have reckoned I was a tramp, a *clochard*, a *pochard*. I ran these French words through my head as we ran through other words in the first classes I'd attended that week in the language school. If Mom could see me now! I didn't smoke, it hurt my throat, but I was wishing I'd gotten into the habit. Cousin Ingeborg's apartment was burning in my head, the swell pictures and furniture were engulfed in flames, the tapestries were charring and falling off the walls, the whole damn place was blazing. I was cold, but the fire was burning in my head. Meanwhile my familiar was chewing slowly, scrabbling about in his pockets. Then his sack became his bed and he slept right there, snoring and mumbling and coughing.

I was very angry about this. It wasn't safe for me to sleep

here. It was a slum. I couldn't sleep. I could work my way
back to the hotel, it wasn't very far, I could wake up the
hotel porter and sink into my bed, my cotton sheets. I could
be warm (the night had turned chill, now we'd stopped).
But if I did this, I would lose him. It was a test, sticking it
out, sticking to him. For once I had an aim, a challenge. If
this beat me, then my whole life would beat me. My father
and my uncle had been in the war, I remembered them
being away and Mom crying quietly a lot of the time. They
had both been lightly injured but they could have been
killed, hundreds and thousands of Americans had been
killed. There was a Red in our town, he ran the hardware
store; before he was arrested he told me that very few
Americans had been killed compared to the millions of our
comrades in the Soviet Union and elsewhere. We had not
been bombed, he said, we had not been bombed out of our
sleep or lined up against a wall and shot, our women had
not been raped and our kids had not been slaughtered in
front of our eyes, our villages and towns had not been put
to the torch. All this had happened in Europe. Sitting there
in the slum alley, where there were gaps like the bombsites
I'd seen in my stopover in London, I was suddenly afraid of
Europe. Afraid of its hot women and cold nights, its strange
tongues, its old dazed knowingness. I wanted the clean
reliability of home. The fixtures that held me in a groove.
And as soon as I wanted it, I knew I'd lost it. Because this
man had led me to a place where I could want it as if it was
outside of me.

When dawn came we both woke up. There was a
trickling sound everywhere, as if it was raining. It was dry
and clear. He shuffled off without looking at me and I
followed him. He made straight for the river. The trickling
sound was the streets being washed, the water sluiced along
the gutters like the beginnings of a flood. Every day in this
city started clean, I realised. It was a forgiving city. My
limbs were half frozen but movement warmed them, the

fresh peeks of light through the mist excited me. I had never known the strange pleasure of a night passed outside without shelter, the triumph of passing it through your body and surviving, as if your skin has soaked up the juices of being alive as it's soaked up the juices of the city; the raw exhilaration of survival, of not ceding to the night's throat. The intense little victory that another day drums inside you – you who have previously taken the days as given, barely noting them as they meld into weeks and months and years until you're old and grey and it's too late.

He stopped by the river, near the Pont Neuf, down on the quai de l'Horloge where in those days you could hear the ticking of a bicycle or the plop of fishbait even when the rest of Paris was bustling and tooting. I leaned against the stone column of the bridge and watched from just a few yards away. It was only then, as he was cutting open his harvest, his catch, gutting them like tiny fish, husking them like barley, that he addressed me.

'*Je sais ce que tu veux*,' he said. 'You've heard about me.'

He wasn't looking up but it had to be me he was talking to, there was no one else. I came over and squatted on my heels and denied having heard anything about him. My voice came out like a little boy's. A name-tab was peeking out from under his lapel, above the inside pocket. It was mine. Mom had stitched it in. *James Sherman King, Jr.*

'English?'

'American.'

He grunted. He was reaching into the bag and pulling out each butt-end, cigar or cigarette, and slicing it open with the smallest Opinel in the range. The *musette* lay next to him. Its keys were like old yellow teeth, grinning at me. Some of the cigars were huge, slices of best American cured tobacco. The mist was rising off the river, the light was pearl. For some time we said nothing. I just watched him. It was very fine watching him. I felt I knew him better than anyone else in the world. It was the dawn of my new life, I

thought to myself. But what exactly did he know I wanted?
What *did* I want? Not my coat, certainly not that. I didn't
even want to tell him about the coat: he would think I'd
want it back, which I sure as hell did not. I wanted
something deep and different and here it was, it was
happening. He was making two piles on some sheets of
newspaper. He pulled out small lumps of pipe tobacco like
my father's dottle – they must have been dottle, knocked
out against shoes as the smokers chatted and laughed on the
terraces. This and the cigars' innards made one pile. The
cigarette tobacco lay by itself in the second pile. There was
care and industry in what he was doing.

'Americans, I know the Americans,' he said. His voice
was so hoarse and deep everything emerged on a growl, I
wasn't certain of his tone. His fingers were busy. The piles
grew. A breeze lifted the edges of the newspaper around the
stones that were holding them in place, the tobacco stirring
like the fur of something alive. 'They always want things
easy. But you are all lost. You are like le Fou.'

'Le Fou?'

He looked at me. He smiled for the first time. He had
about five teeth.

'Le Fou', he said again. 'How could you not know him?'

'I don't know anyone in Paris, not in the whole city.'

This was amazing to him. It was especially amazing to
him that I didn't know le Fou, the nut, the most famous nut
of the Latin Quarter. He had rat skins and mole skins
stitched on his rags, his wand was topped with dead mice,
he had hens' feet for feathers on his cap and a little tortoise
shell bouncing on his belly. It was just as amazing I didn't
know Sidi, Sidi with his obscene tattoos, mostly of his
mistresses. Or Eugene le Foetus stinking of alcohol, selling
his decaying foetuses out of a sack to painters and scribblers
who liked the bones. Or Sapeck the practical joker with his
ape's face and tiny dog or the poet Georges Caubel de la
Ville-Hingat treating the ladies for venereal disorders or

Coulet with his crazy monologues and dirty prints. It's amazing I could be alive and not know these people. Not know le Marquis de Soudin hawking his pencil portraits around the tables for fifty centimes or the blind seller of paper windmills in the Jardin de Luxembourg or the anarchist cobbler le Père la Purge or the would-be poets shuffling around like ghosts smelling of hashish and ether or Pharaoh with his glistening black locks selling his miraculous hair restorer or Amedée Cloux the pasticheur or Victor Sainbault hawking his verse in the crowds under the electric lights or the huge nymphomaniac at the Château-Rouge shouting, *Qu'est-ce que vous voulez, moi, quand j'tronche pas j'suis malade!*

'I haven't seen any of these people,' I said.

Amazed that I'd never heard Fifi l'Absinthe and Gaston Trois-Pattes singing and strumming in the Père Lunette with its crazy murals or had never picked my way through the rag-and-bone market of the rue Saint-Medard between the chipped vases, the deformed corsets, the *risqué* novels and the rusty tools, brushing with my shoulder the firmness of laughing girls in their tight calico. Never never never. Amazing. I roamed the Latin Quarter looking for these people in the morning and listened to him in the afternoon. For about a week I did this. I saw only drunks and sidewalk artists and beggars and shabby street musicians. I didn't want to tell him that I hadn't seen them. I began to feel personally afflicted, I started to feel screwed up. Then he happened to mention the whores in their long skirts. Long skirts? Not cardigans? In their loose frilly blouses. Frilly blouses? Their corsets with pink ribbons. Corsets? Had he seen *The Nights of Montmartre* after all?

No, this was not a movie.

Maybe it was a litany, maybe he gave the spiel to everyone like a guide does to a coach party, but I didn't care and I still don't. It was taken up again whenever I visited, which was nearly every day that first month. He growled it out like a tune on an accordion, a tune from sixty years before, from the last century, from the golden age. I didn't mind that all these people were long gone, long dead. Their echoes stayed. One time, walking back to the hotel through the place Saint-Michel, I passed a blind man standing by a table on which a small gramophone player was playing a scratchy tune. Progress! But the old man's growl was like that record; it just needed me around to place the needle. The tobacco was damp with saliva and the night: I'd watch the piles of it grow, I'd watch him spread it out to dry in the sun when it was sunny, I'd watch him crouch on the steps and ease his boots off and wash his socks and shirt in the river, I'd watch him eat the cakes I'd bought – I'd watch him do all these things as if I was waiting for something beyond the lost world he was summoning back. It was like he was working toward something. Three weeks in, I sensed a change of tone, an alertness, an urgency. This was that something.

First of all, he became aggressive. Then he became personal. He included himself. I already knew, watching him and listening, how things had faded in his life, that when he said that once there had been thirty or forty in his line, how his *métier* had once been a proud one, he wasn't boasting. It was the truth. I even believed him when he said that he was the last *ramasseur de mégots* in Paris, that the *clochards* who picked up butt-ends and smoked them didn't count. He told me how the tobacco market had hung on in the place Maubert until the last war when even butt-ends became scarce (and I remembered what that guy had told me over his absinthe, about the *patrons* gleaning the butt-ends for themselves, and felt the pieces come together and knowledge grow). Now the old man's stall was a couple of upturned crates on the quai de l'Horloge, and his buyers clutched their fiddles or their perambulators full of old clothes and bargained him down.

I guess he was legendary, and I was privileged. He would

set out his stall at four o'clock in the afternoon and play his *musette* behind it. Tourists took snapshots, but tourists were fewer in those days. Some of them were American. I kept my mouth shut in case they'd realise I wasn't a guy born in the juices of Paris, with its bitumen and dust in my veins. I'd sit against the wire fence where the trees were and watch the boats go by, the tugboats and barges and the *bateaux mouches* winking their glass in the sunlight. It was a fine autumn. Or maybe I'm just remembering it that way. I'd buy us coffee and croissants. I'd buy enough tobacco from him for a couple of cigarettes and roll my own, trying not to think about the spittle dried on the shag's threads, wondering how polio and syphilis were caught and then coughing and laughing at myself – loving this, loving le Père la Pêche, loving Paris, loving our lost world from the last century I could wander through with just a word, a nudge, a question.

I was a couple of days away from the final decision on the room. That's when his tone changed. It was after breakfast and a sunny morning, the water flickering and the leaves ablaze. I had a letter from Mom in my pocket. It wondered why I hadn't written, fretting about Cousin Ingeborg in Spain, who needed to know. I was pulling on a cigarette plump with cigar tobacco. A pretty girl passed and smiled at me. Le Père la Pêche had drunk too much of his sour liquor the previous night and his old eyes were very red, his movements were slow. I'd been working out how old he was: eighty, he must be eighty, because he remembered the brothels in the 1880s like he wasn't a kid then, he remembered the pungent powdered whores and their fixed-rate kisses like he'd actually picked their *fleurs du mal*! I was smiling after the pretty girl and feeling good and grown up and quoting Baudelaire to myself when le Père la Pêche came over from shredding his wares and held my elbow in a mittened grip that was almost painful. My reverie was broken. I choked, inhaling too swiftly. There was madness in his eyes.

'*Mon p'tit Indien –*' (that's what he called me, I liked it), 'I cannot stand it any longer. You are breaking me. You are here to steal.'

I was so taken aback, I couldn't find the French.

'You are watching me all the time, I know why you are watching me all the time. Don't you think I know these tricks? You've heard in your country of le Père la Pêche, of what he –'

Here the old man looked about him, let go my arm. But his eyes were still wild under his matted fringe. Then he brought his face very close to mine. The liquor was still hot on his breath. He never smoked. This was the first time I realised that he never smoked, because there was nothing on his breath but liquor. His voice was a hiss.

'– of what he has for the *right man!*'

My look of total perplexity, a hint of tears even (the aggression was that sudden), must have persuaded him of my ignorance. He was old and knew how faces work. As I stammered some kind of reply, his suspicion relaxed into a distant smile.

'What *do* you have?' I asked finally, like a kid.

He took out a small tin from the inner pocket of the coat. (Not ever mentioning the coat gave me a secret feeling of intimacy with him.)

'This', he said.

His hand was trembling. It had never trembled before, despite his age and drinking habit. Now it trembled so much he nearly dropped the tin. It was dented and pocked with rust, and the style of the smoker's clothes on the faded label dated it to the era he had opened up for me. And now he was opening the tin.

'*Voilà*,' he whispered, like a magician.

Inside was a cigar, three-quarter smoked. Something about it made me think that it had not been picked up yesterday, despite the musty aroma of tobacco. It looked almost fossilised, had the blank dead look of something in a museum case. I made to pick it out but he snapped the lid shut, almost on my fingers.

'Bibi la Purée', he said, sitting on the slabs next to me. 'I must begin with Bibi.'

We watched the river. He told me that Bibi was the weirdest, the king of the weirdos. High gleaming forehead, piles of hair, no beard, a cadaverous face that should have been seen over footlights. He dressed like an old rake, a dandy – except when he was playing at being a blind beggar in front of Saint-Sulpice, when he'd don a frock. You'd see him sitting at a café table under his top hat, winking at everybody – then he'd suddenly leap up with a shoecare set in his hand and start waxing a lady customer's boots, planting a kiss on her stockinged ankle as a preliminary, her big skirts falling around his ears. *Ah, cher Bibi!* No one knew where he slept, but for eight days in the year he would pour all his savings into a hired suite of rooms, keeping open house, girl students drifting in and out like concubines.

Le Père la Pêche gave a great sigh. Amazing that I didn't know Bibi! Then he gripped the tin tighter in his stained hands. It was some kind of talisman, drawing him closer to whatever had lain beyond everything we had shared these last weeks.

He explained how Bibi would hang around some of the big guys of the *quartier*, the important poets and painters and thinkers, doing odd jobs and running messages. One of these big guys was Paul Verlaine. (I nodded: Verlaine's poems lost me but I knew he was extremely renowned.) The week after Verlaine's death in the winter of '96, Bibi set up a stall selling some articles belonging to the great man: his silk handkerchief, his calling card, his tin of shoe wax, a curl of his beard off the barber-shop floor, and the cane he wobbled around on towards the end, wracked by syphilis. Bibi did good business, and each day there were more of these treasures. But when the sixth tin of Verlaine's shoe wax appeared, fervour snapped to suspicion and Bibi packed up for want of custom. Le Père la Pêche raised the tin in his hand. The morning sun gleamed on its dull grey metal.

'I never told him, not then,' he said. 'His prices were too low.'

'What did you not tell him?'

'I told him afterwards, when the whole charade was long finished. But he didn't believe me. He laughed, *mon p'tit Indien!* Laughed in my face! He was guarding bicycles outside some café or other on the Boul' San' Mich', I forget which one. Got up in a bolero, tartan stockings, spurs on his heels, chauffer's cap on his head. Ridiculous!'

'No one dresses like that any more,' I said. I felt the weight of seriousness in my dark, existentialist clothes like I was in water and needed to struggle free.

'Laughed in my face! The d'Harcourt, that was it, always full of women, it was a woman's café and the men were there to oblige them. With *sous*, my friend! I told him what I had seen.'

There was a pause. He was looking older and tireder than he was when I first knew him, and that was only three weeks ago. He was kind of bundled up on the slabs next to me, staring down.

'What did you see?' I said, gently.

'Verlaine was staggering up the rue Racine smoking his cigar. I knew his face, this strange face with its Chinese eyes and bulging forehead and sharp whiskers – a bit like Comrade Lenin, now I think of it. I knew all their faces, of course, *mon p'tit agneau Americain*, all the great scribblers and daubers. But he was alone. He took a last puff and dropped his cigar, coughing like a sick child. He disappeared around the corner, tap-tap-tap with his cane, shivering all over. He was a sick man, sick with the clap, like most of them. Dead within the week. The whole *quartier* mourned. Never read a word of him, mind. But I fished his butt-end like any other, that evening in the rue Racine, just like any other. It was only when I came to gutting my catch that I thought to myself: here, this is Verlaine's smoke, I'll hang on to that, there are strange folk about who like souvenirs of great men. So I found a little tin for it and then he was dead and then there was Bibi doing a roaring trade in fakes. This American soldier – the first cock-up I'm talking about, back in '18 – he loved poetry, he offered me a hundred francs for this if I could prove it was Monsieur Verlaine's. Prove it – I ask you! Who did he think I was? Bibi la Purée?'

He spat and growled an obscenity I hadn't covered in class. He stroked the tin with his dirty hand. The sweet cud of his body-smell enveloped me. I told him that I would buy it from him without proof because I knew him and trusted him. He looked at me with a suspicious grin, his teeth as yellow as his little accordion's. Perhaps he had engineered this whole moment, but I didn't care. In an instant I had decided what I must do, the one time in my life that true inspiration has ever come to me, whole, like a heavy gem. He gave me a price that was very high – I blush to quote it now. OK, it was a month's expenditure. I realised immediately that he wanted to keep it, that he expected me to balk, to back off. But I think now he was working in an old tradition: the rag-and-bone men of the rue Saint-Medard would always sell at a third of the asking price, in the old times.

I didn't even beat him down. I came with the cash the next day, a fat bundle of notes. He was dealing with a shabby customer who had nothing but an old Vichy franc on him. I asked to see it, and bounced the thing in my hand – it was as light as play money. Dated 1942, when I was still a little kid. *Travail, Famille, Patrie,* and a sprig of oak leaves. Exactly the values my own folks expounded. They didn't seem tall any more. Le Père la Pêche took the coin from me and spat on it and threw it over his shoulder. Tainted, I guess. The shabby customer plodded off without a word. I produced the notes and he stared at them in astonishment.

'For Verlaine's *mégot*', I said. Verlaine's butt, in the version I make people laugh with.

'*C'est pas possible, mon p'tit —*'

'*B'en ouai, c'est possible.*'

He looked at me and laughed. Then he coughed. Blood dribbled out onto his beard. He wiped it off as if it was spittle. The last one of his kind. The last dodo. Where would he die? Right here. By the great river where he stretches out on the warm stone on nice afternoons and dreams with his beard pointing towards the sky, still, in my own dreams. He's done it now for over a century, and will do so until the parapet crumbles under him along with the rest, into rubble and weeds.

We did the deal. He didn't count the notes, just stuffed them into the coat. I took the tin, checked its contents, and said I would be back after the weekend. He clapped my hand as they used to do in the markets, carried on laughing and waving on the *quai* until I lost him to sight.

I walked out to the rue Racine and waited there until dark, sipping a big milk coffee and then a few pernods in a corner café where this black guy was playing some doleful sax. I walked up and down a bit, tipsy, thinking of everything le Père la Pêche had told me. At some point a gaggle of students bumped me as they were running past and the tin was knocked into the gutter, but it didn't open.

It was after midnight. The sax had stopped. A whore stood at the corner, scowling out of her heavy mascara. She was smoking. As I came up to her she kind of wiggled, with the usual stupid little bag in her hand. She was clothed too light, in a one-piece woollen dress buckled high with a thick black belt; her high heels clicked on the cobbles and she even smelt high above the scent. The wiggling was like some terrible dance, which had been spectacular once and

228

was now faded to something so small it was grotesque. I asked her for a light, prising the tin open. I held Verlaine's cigar up to her silver lighter and drew on the butt. The flavour of the Latin Quarter of all those years ago, the whole *belle époque* of it, sank down my throat and filled my mouth and nose. Every drag drew me closer. It was Verlaine's breath in mine. I was more intimate than anyone could ever be with the past. Time was my whore.

I walked away from the woman as she began to talk dirty and sat on a stoop at the far end of the street, pulling on the butt with my eyes closed. The sweetness of all those lost names and places smoked in my head: true debauchery destroys as it pleasures and the butt was crackling down to plain nothing. I saw Verlaine and this young guy with a stick a little way behind him, they passed me and I was so very scared, crouching into my dark doorway. I thought: I will not tell le Père la Pêche what I've done. I smoked it down so far there wasn't anything to toss away, nothing to pick up. I burnt my fingers on the last breath.

I went to the quai de l'Horloge after the weekend but he wasn't there. I asked around and the sidewalk artist told me that he'd fallen into the river, Saturday night, and been fished out with a hook, Sunday. He'd drunk too much. The sidewalk artist was chalking out the spires of Notre-Dame. The old man had gotten rich somehow and blown it all in every café on the San' Mich', then toppled into the drink. Nice way to go, the guy added, but we should be so lucky, *hein*?

I threw the tin into the water and watched it float. His old newspapers blew away and the stones were kicked and the crates were sat on by fishermen flicking butts that stayed there. I'd like to go back one day, to that place, smell him on the wind, catch him out of the corner of my eye, standing like a shadow in my coat. I've been all over, on legal business, but never back to Paris.

You'll be wanting to know which room I took: Cousin

Ingeborg's or the bohemian one. Does that really matter, now? Does anything matter, in the end, but what you dare yourself to do just once in your life? Just once? As if that's enough?

RIGGING

When the wind blows seaward it's smoke. Otherwise it's
fish. High as a bloody kite. Glutinous, all innards. You get
used to it. Only rarely do the great rollers rinse it all out.
The great rollers of the Atlantic bloody ocean. Too far out
and lofty for this peevish little bay, was how he'd put it,
holding a spanker steady while the Uhu set. The great
rollers of the Atlantic. The foaming rollers. Peevish little
goitre of a bay. Fucking little glass-fibre dinky dinghies
bobbing and bobbing. Little runts.

I'm quoting.

Holding the spanker steady with a finger. That's how I
see him, in my best moments. Me there with my
Bournville, the chipped mauve mug, at the door, and he
holding the spanker steady as a match to a candle, or an oil-
lamp, or whatever, in a Force Tenner like in the films, and
mumbling. Swearing his heart out, bless him. Railing.
Railing ever so quietly, because if not quietly the spanker'd
never set. It helped him, railing. Crouched there under that
dirty neon in that little tin-pot shed holding the spanker. Or
rather, to be strictly proper, the spanker's spar. Between
friends. Or boom. Booms swing, don't they? Out over the
choppy ocean, some poor bugger reefing it up like a
monkey, clinging to the aft-boom. In all the films.

Him blinking away the smoke from his Benson &
Hedges. In those days. Before that it was roll-ups, funnily
enough. Navy Cut. In flat tins that clip shut from old Mr

Fletcher by the harbour wall. Old Mr Fletcher from St Albans, originally. They all come down.

That's how I see him. That tin-pot shed. Fish landward, smoke seaward. In the winter months. In the summer you'd get no end of grockles strolling in because they'd have seen the big clipper in the window, never mind the grime and cobwebs and the STRICTLY BLOODY PRIVATE in red on the corrugations, as he'd call them. The sides of his tin-pot shed. The corrugations of iron. Never corrugated. He'd lean his head there in his less lucid moments. Swear the wind had driven them deeper. The corrugations. Lean his head on the shed like a bull and swear they were troughed deeper. I'd tell him it was the sunlight. Shadows. Filth all over his cheek.

They peered in, those grockles, with their ice-creams plopping all over the rush-mat and he'd tell them no end of stories. Tall tales. Holding a finger on the mizzen-mast until the glue had done its bit. Or coating on the linseed while he spun them a yarn. They loved it.

In the old days, anyway. Then it was all truculence. Scowls. The English understood and hopped it but never the Yanks. Not that we had many. I'll come to that. The truculence.

They loved it in the old tale-telling days, though. Especially the Yanks. He was a picture, wasn't he? The old cap, the roll-top, the clutter, the drawl. Fag-smoke. Paraffin stove and that bloody kettle. Fish-nets. Wrack. The works. Digestives sprawled on the work-bench. Swan Vestas. That tin bloody mug of his from the navy days. And there she was, in all that muck, rising out of all that junk, beautiful and clean and sprightly, as he'd put it: a gleaming three-foot hull with a shower of rigging. His fingers in there. Those bent fingers. Fiddling, carving, fixing, steadying, coating. Lavishing, lavishing, lavishing.

He only did one for a film the once, though. And that went down. It was meant to. He watched her break up on the rocks and said never again. Terrible film. All swinging lanterns and Cornish corn. Yelling under tricornered hats into fog. The smuggling lark. Wreckers. Ten seconds flat it took to smash her up and you could tell the waves were spuming all wrong. Slow-motion and all that. Wrong kind of spume. We had to walk out. It had taken him six months to get her right. Ten seconds flat and she was driftwood.

Yes, in my best moments. Sipping my Bournville. I used to bring him the tea but then he stopped. It was all bottle. Desperate gin bouts. But what I'd not gathered was the secrecy. I'd thought it was the linseed or the paraffin. Old sailors never stop. If they don't drown in one they drown in the other. I don't really blame myself. The worse it got the more he had the worse it got, if you see what I mean. I'll come to that in a minute. It's pathetic watching him now. It's cruel. When you consider it.

The grockles got various versions but this is the most authentic. About as authentic as you can bloody get, anyway. And I slept with him. I'd have sailed to Zanzibar for him, in the old days, if you can sail to Zanzibar. Algiers, then. Rains less at any road. Than this pot-hole. And his fingers were still a mess when I met him on one of those geological lectures. Touring the cliffs of a Sunday with the luminous anorak lot and all strata and faults and fossils. He was the only one who wasn't jolly. Not jolly at all, in fact. Very depressed. I thought he was a divorcee. Or a widower. Who'd got his hands caught in a car-door, probably. Then we bumped into each other at the Frigate's Rest (the Frigger's Retch, he'd call it) when I was doing the meals there and he had a complaint about the chili con carne. We got talking geology but it was obvious neither of us cared a bitch for strata and it was something in his eyes that had me flushing. A far-away sadness. The far-away sadness of the great rollers he was always on about. The great rollers you sometimes see flashing out there, not the mean buggers that sud the High Street from time to time.

233

That you watch on the telly after unless you want to do a Jason Rickards and get swept off, poor sod.

The great rollers.

The grockles loved it. He was on this submarine cruising about in the Minch, I think it was, and they came up to the surface, as is their wont, submarines, and he pottered about a bit on top then went over to the hatch to yell something down it, rocking on his heels by the big black hole when the hull's given a helluva kick and in he goes head-first, big dive, hands out, crunch. Flat calm it was, too. The mind boggles. They've seen things out there, the fishermen, you wouldn't credit. Something big enough to jolt a submarine, anyway. Perhaps it wasn't the Minch, given wherever it was was flat calm. Every finger so much matchwood. Steel deck. Fifteen-foot drop, probably. You'd be surprised. Wheeeeee.

Might have been off the Maldives, come to think of it. A bit shaky on names.

Anyway, the surgeons did about twenty ops and inserted little rods and by the time I met him he could grasp, but there wasn't the strength. Given he was a submariner turning big pump-wheels and whatnot, with shoulders like an ox, all sweaty singlet and gleaming skin like in the films, there wasn't a lot of future. Down in the dumps time, wasn't it? I reckon the boozing proper started then. He wanted to be a surgeon, went on and on about his fingers. He'd show us with matches and pins between the beer-mats. Look, he said, you'd never believe what it takes to make a knuckle. I'd feel a bit sick, watching him reconstruct. Then he'd lay his hands ever so gently on the matches and pins and say, it's all in there. I'm a walking bloody miracle of surgical precision. And he'd lift his hands up off the table and flex. Flex his finger-joints. You wouldn't believe the clicks and squeaks and we all groaned. He liked that. The groaning. We could imagine it all, all the stuff inside. He liked that. Drowning his chaser and chuckling, after.

It was Godfrey said, how about doing my yacht to scale. I think it was Godfrey. Godfrey had the nice old peeling one that had been in Dunkirk or something, anyway. Your yacht? My yacht. Okeydokey, if you'll get me another. A joke, really, but he stuck at it. Then it was galleons for the Armada thing and then little fellers in bottles for the grockles and finally clippers. With the odd frigate. The odd frigate. But mainly the schooners. The clippers. Three-foot-six from spanker to jib. Jib o' jibs. Wet varnish. Crease your eyes up and you could see them clipping a heavy sea. He put Earl Grey in the hold once. Crates the width of your thumb-nail. That was for a Yank. The 'Taitsing' if I remember rightly. Broke the gaff in transit, bloody oafs.

Bloody oafs.

Then it was that one day, that awful bloody morning it was. First I've got to say this: he'd have made a very fine surgeon. It's all in the fingers, isn't it? He'd spend a week just on the bowsprit. Him and his Stanley. He wouldn't read the paper in the morning, he'd read the blue-prints. Rustle rustle. Then there they were smoothed out on the work-bench with a bloody forest of balsa on them before you could say crossjack. I'd tell him, at night, between the sheets sort of thing, that he surprised me. Because he was a bit of a prude, when it came to getting me going. I'd say come on I'm spread up to me royals. Out to me stuns'ls. Drive me.

No elegance, when it came to that. A bit of a bloody dinghy, truly. Yet watch him for ten minutes crouched over some little bowsprit or other, or reefing up a main-mast or whatever and you'd hold your breath. Fingers played those ships. Bent fingers, that much metal in them they could dangle a magnet. Took three years before the last splint came off but it gave him the fascination. The patience. You couldn't see him sometimes for sails and rigging. And he'd always do me on the prow. Topless. His little joke. Blonde. The last lick was always the nipples on the figure-head. A bit bloody cold I'd say. A bit bloody cold and wet stuck out topless over the cutwater, spume all over me lovely locks. I wore it loose then.

One time I bared myself. When he was dipping and dabbing at some nice slim tonnage, as he'd put it. Just set the Bournville down and raised my cardie and slip and stood there. And they weren't unnoticeable exactly when they were out, as you can well imagine. Famed, they were. Then. Bloody hack-saw. Saved me, though. Touch wood. One can't complain.

Just stood there. Ten minutes. Goose-pimples. Then I burst out laughing. He looked up with his little pink tongue stuck out the corner of his mouth as it always was when he was hard at it and he railed. Gold on black and you made me jolt. Stupid cow. Doing the name, would you believe. 'Ariel', probably. One of the big tea clippers, anyway. Gold on bloody black. I felt a right fool. A bit of turps I said. But I knew it smeared. He'd do each bloody nail in Airfix copper. Then I burst out crying. A real weep. Him standing with a brush in the air and a little paint-pot. Stupid cow he said again, but quieter. That bloody great ship with about thirty bloody sails full set next to him all done bar the fancy gold name and me on the prow. A bloody good weep, neon flickering, big bloody ship and him just ogling because I'd still got my top deck showing. The cardie and slip rolled up and stuck up here, they were that big.

They were that bloody big. They had to do both, didn't they? It had got right into both, or something. Though I only felt one. Anyway, ballast. Ballast would have been all wrong. I'd have been rolling over. All styrofoam and rubber or something, these days. Forget it. Too old.

I said you'd better get that neon fixed. Blowing my nose. Bad for your eyesight. That's when I first noticed it. His tremble. Holding that paint-brush out in the air. You couldn't help noticing. Not with the paint-brush emphasis-ing it, as you might say. Then he sat and got on with it. With that 'Ariel' name. He managed. Did me with the biggest top deck ever. And crying. I said you would be bloody crying wouldn't you if you were stuck out in front cutting the high seas at a clip. Afterwards, in bed. Between the business. He even did a few tears. Sky-blue they were. You'd have to get right up and peer. Lobby of the Hong Kong Hilton, if you're interested. They didn't complain.

That's when I first noticed.

But the worst bloody morning, the real one, that was almost a year later and I knew all about it by then. Gin bouts but also the secrecy bit. He never took a drop of tea all day. Even the paraffin and whatnot couldn't drown it out. He'd always smell of linseed himself and so on but it mostly showed in bed. Up close. It was coming off the skin. And the business. He could never finish. He'd get all excited and drove himself until he was red in the gills but he couldn't ever spume, as I called it. Believe it or not it was the American muck. I can only stand it with Coke. Go down his gullet like tap-water. Alone in that bloody tin-pot shed with his needle, stitching up canvas. Those tiny bloody reef-points I couldn't even see on his bench with my reading glasses. All that nylon rigging. Like a bloody cobweb. No wonder he helped himself along a bit. The worse he got the more he had, because he knew. And the more he had the worse it got. Get out of that one in a hurry. And his fingers. They never stopped telling him what an idiot he was. Taking a dive through the hatch. He'd moan in his sleep and I'd watch them grasp. Pushing on the Stanley to get the hull curved was agony he said. He couldn't hold a shopping bag if it was tins. Which it mostly was, in this dump. He suffered silently, that was the trouble. And his railing got worse. Scowls.

Then that bloody awful morning with the Yank. The Yank's son, really. I came in with the Bournville and there was this big Yank and his son between me and him. Staring. They were crew-cut, practically to the bone, so I knew they were Yanks straight off. Sort of indecent, all that knobbly stuff. He'd joke about sandpaper, to their faces, but they'd never click. I only came in with the Bournville now for a chat. He was working on the 'Cutty Sark' for Brooke Bond's, I think it was. Conference room or something. I thought he hasn't scowled them out at least. I said good morning and the Yank said hi I suppose. Then we both watched, and the son. The fingers were fiddling and he was sticking his tongue out and he winked at the boy. So I thought something was off, straight away. He was on the main topgallant staysail. I'll always remember that to my dying minute. The main topgallant staysail. He told the boy. He held it up and said this is the main topgallant staysail and here we go. Let her blow. Then he started whistling. He had one end of the line and he took it up to the mast, almost to the top, to fix it on. A tiny little hook. Whistling. Those bent fingers. That tiny little hook. Then it was silence, except for the kid chewing. Horrible habit. All of us watching. He couldn't get it on. He couldn't get the bloody thing on. Like threading a needle only worse. It was his hand. It wasn't his fingers. Oh no. His hand. Shaking like a bloody leaf. Shaking and shaking like a bloody leaf. I'd thought actually he'd been taking his time on this one. The 'Cutty Sark'. He'd done her before, though. Went all the way up to Greenwich to smell her, as he put it. Thought he'd been taking his time. But he'd been clever with his hands in his pockets or something and that was when my little trouble had started so I wasn't paying attention.

Then the kid, horrible little kid really, piped up. Hey mister, you're never gonna get that. *You're never gonna get that.*

When the wind blows landward it's fish. High as a bloody kite. Fills your mouth. Seaward it's smoke. I've said that already. That day it was fish. I remember exactly. It was bloody fish.

I remember exactly.

Bloody little Yank!

I held the door open for them and made it obvious. In came the wind and the fish. There was bits of sea on it that day, against your cheeks. Lips. Spindrift they call it, off of the wave-tops. Spindrift. I can feel it now. How I felt it then. Bloody awful morning. By the door of that bloody tin-pot shed. Those Yanks going out, ducking. Spindrift and fish. We were right up close, in those days. Blustery. I can feel it now, exactly how I felt. I'd got my results that week but it wasn't that, surprisingly. We all have our allotted span and I didn't know it would be both or even one right off. They can do miracles these days, so Mrs Grove kept saying. It wasn't that, though I was worried. No. It was that bloody main topgallant staysail. It was that. It was the end of it all. I could hardly look in of course but I did. The door only open for a minute but I felt like I'd been out in it for years. In the wind. That spindrift. Fish. I could hardly go back in but I did. I didn't want to look at him. No I didn't. But I did. Oh I did.

ACKNOWLEDGEMENTS

With grateful thanks to Jan Salas and Bill Garner for their painstaking help and advice on the language of *Stonework* and *Debauchery*; to Jill Waters, Jeremy Mortimer, Shiv Grewal and Nigel Anthony at the BBC for their care and attention; to Monsieur Fuster for showing me how a mattock is made; to Brian Scrivener for inspiring *Sawmill*; to Niek Miedema for certain precious minutiae in *Shifts*; to Robin Robertson and Bill Hamilton for keeping faith with the project over the years; to Jason Arthur for researching awkward details; to all those friends, colleagues, fellow-workers and strangers who have stimulated the first germ (or more) of an idea, and to my wife and children for supporting me at my own shift with suggestions and cups of tea.

My thanks also to the editors of the following publications in which some of these stories first appeared: *New Writing 3, 6* and *7* (Minerva, Vintage), *Obsession* (Serpent's Tail), *Time Out Book of Paris Short Stories* (Time Out/Penguin), and *New Statesman*.

Glass and *Neon* were first commissioned for broadcast on BBC Radio.

GR